Shameless Puckboy

Also by Eden Finley and Saxon James

Puckboys

Egotistical Puckboy
Irresponsible Puckboy
Shameless Puckboy
Foolish Puckboy
Clueless Puckboy
Bromantic Puckboy
Forbidden Puckboy
Possessive Puckboy
Stubborn Puckboy

SHAMELESS PUCKBOY

EDEN FINLEY & SAXON JAMES

First published in the United Kingdom in 2022 by Absolute Books

This edition published in the United Kingdom in 2026 by

Canelo, an imprint of
Canelo Digital Publishing Limited,
20 Vauxhall Bridge Road,
London SW1V 2SA
United Kingdom

A Penguin Random House Company
The authorised representative in the EEA is Dorling Kindersley Verlag GmbH.
Arnulfstr. 124, 80636 Munich, Germany

Copyright © Eden Finley and Saxon James 2022

The moral right of Eden Finley and Saxon James to be identified as the creator of this work has been asserted in accordance with the Copyright, Designs and Patents Act, 1988.
All rights reserved. No part of this publication may be reproduced or transmitted in any form or by any means, electronic or mechanical, including photocopy, recording, or any information storage and retrieval system, without permission in writing from the publisher.
No part of this book may be used or reproduced in any manner for the purpose of training artificial intelligence technologies or systems. In accordance with Article 4(3) of the DSM Directive 2019/790, Canelo expressly reserves this work from the text and data mining exception.

A CIP catalogue record for this book is available from the British Library.

ISBN 9 781 83598 487 1

This book is a work of fiction. Names, characters, businesses, organizations, places and events are either the product of the author's imagination or are used fictitiously. Any resemblance to actual persons, living or dead, events or locales is entirely coincidental.

Printed and bound in Great Britain by Clays Ltd, Elcograf S.p.A.

Look for more great books at
www.canelo.co | www.dk.com

This series is about the PR Nightmares of the NHL. These characters are flawed on purpose. Please don't expect perfection because it does not exist here. They're hockey players. The only guarantee is missing teeth.

The use of the NHL and any of its teams is a work of fiction. It in no way reflects the policies or opinions of the actual organization.

Names, characters, businesses, places, events, and incidents are either the products of the authors' imaginations or used in a fictitious manner. Any resemblance to actual persons, living or dead, or actual events is purely coincidental

Chapter One

Lane

I stare at my screen, watching the CCTV footage that's gone viral. The back door of a club opens and spits Oskar Voyjik and two others into the alley. They're a tangle of groping limbs, hot mouths, and clear intent.

The PR manager in me is fucking pissed this has happened *again*, but the red-blooded gay man in me is struggling to pull my eyes away. If this was a random clip online instead of our star player, it'd be perfect jerk-off material.

Which probably explains why it's the center of most news stories this morning.

"I'm sorry," Keerson says, burying his face in his hands. "He's out of control."

Well, I can't disagree there, but this isn't a simple *oopsie* that we can talk our way out of. Oskar's becoming a real problem for San Jose, which means he's a real problem for me.

"You had one job," I remind Keerson. "And I'm sure I was clear in my expectations."

"What was I supposed to do? Chain him to me? I've been available at his beck and call, and the things he's been calling me with ..." Keerson stops to take a level breath. "I'm sorry. I'm out of ideas. I dropped him off at his place at nine so I could go home to bed, and he said he was going to do the same. I remember specifically because he said, 'You can tell your boss I'm being a good little hockey player.' What else could I do? Short of sleepovers, I just …" He mouths wordlessly, and even though I try not to be softhearted when it comes to work, I do feel for him. He has a family he's barely seen for the last month, thanks to being solely assigned to Oskar.

The PR department is supposed to look after the entire team, but it's true what they say about twenty percent of the people taking up eighty percent of the time. In this case, Oskar is the complete twenty percent all to himself.

I'd thought giving him a direct PR liaison would help him make better choices, but Keerson is the third person I've assigned to him, and the third person to completely fail at keeping up. At this rate, San Jose is going to fire my ass and find someone better equipped to deal with the situation.

Oskar should be the one getting fired, but he's too damn good at what he does. Team management has made it clear that it's our job to put an end to the scandals. It's kind of hard to do that when he has threesomes in seedy alleys.

I rub my jaw, gaze straying back to the screen and where Oskar has his hand down one of the guys' pants while the other drops to his knees. It might be my imagination, but I swear Oskar's eyes keep flicking to the surveillance camera, and if that bastard knew it was there, he won't need to worry about being fired—I'll kill him myself.

"This is my fault," I say, finally tapping my keyboard to pause the video. "I've put too much on the rest of you when you have lives outside of work. Unluckily for Oskar

Voyjik, that won't be a problem for me. I'm a thirty-nine-year-old, single workaholic who will do anything for this team."

Keerson cracks a smile. "Are you ... do you mean ..."

"It's my turn. If I can't sort him out, they might as well fire me now."

He cringes because we both know that while my words are light, it's a very real possibility. "He's, ah, waiting in the hall."

Oskar Voyjik showing patience? I wouldn't have guessed that.

"Good. At least he can follow *some* directions." Still, I need a minute before I can face him. A minute to gather my weak professionalism and remind myself that his flirting is all bullshit. He might be my exact type, but I absolutely cannot look at him that way unless I want to kiss my career goodbye.

"Are you sure you can manage?" Keerson asks. "He's a handful, and you already have a busy schedule."

"I know how to delegate. If this is where my focus needs to be, then so be it." I compulsively straighten my desk. "Send him in on your way out."

Keerson jumps up, clearly relieved to be free, and I watch him all the way to the door, refusing to let my focus slip back to the monitor beside me. Murmured voices sound from the hall, and it's easy to pick Oskar's low, scratchy tone.

A second later, he walks in and closes the door, and my resolve about being professional flies out the window.

All the air in the room suctions his way, like there's this great gravitational pull toward the man who is literally sex on legs. From his just-been-fucked dark blond hair to the scruff on his jaw, his intense eyes, and those sexy tattoos all over his body, every day is a mission to be good.

Especially when he opens his mouth.

"*Mr.* Pierce." His confidence takes all the air in the room as he stalks closer and takes the seat opposite mine.

I lean back in my chair, holding his gaze and doing everything in my power to show he has no effect on me. He might be hot, but my willpower always holds. "Look at that, you do know how to be respectful."

His lips quirk. "When it gets me what I want, I do."

"Is what you want to continue playing for this team? Because if so, your professionalism could use some work."

I tilt my screen toward him and hit Play, right at the moment things start to heat up. Oskar doesn't react at all to the footage—not that I thought he would.

"Interesting ..." he says.

"Not the first word that comes to my mind."

He sniggers. "It's interesting that you've watched so much of it. Like what you see?"

"Personally, of course, we both know how good-looking you are." And for the first time since he walked in, he looks like I've said something unexpected. I never should have admitted that, but I'm an openly gay man with eyes. He'd know I was lying if I said otherwise. Good-looking might not be an apt description, or enough of one, because when it comes to Oskar Voyjik, I don't think there're enough words in the dictionary to describe how sexy he really is. "Professionally, this makes me want to hit you over the head with a hockey stick."

"You're not the first person to say that to me."

"Not surprising at all."

Oskar threads his hands through his hair and leans back, lifting the front two legs of the chair from the ground, and mimicking my relaxed posture. "You know, if you're into corporal punishment, I hear spanking is more effective."

"I have something better in mind."

He eyes me. "I'm not a fan of paddling, but I suppose I could give it a try."

And damn that asshole, a laugh slips from me. "I'll keep that information in my back pocket. But no. Congratulations, *Mr.* Voyjik, you've been upgraded. You're looking at your new PR minder."

"You?" He doesn't look anywhere near as worried as he should. "Aren't I below your pay grade?"

"If you're calling yourself cheap, I'm not going to argue, but don't worry, I like getting my hands dirty."

"Cheap and dirty. If I didn't know better, I'd say you were coming on to me."

"Do you talk to all your PR managers this way? Because it would explain why you've been through so many in the last few years."

"Only the hot ones." He winks, and he has no right to make it look so smooth. "Cute of you to assume this club revolves around me though."

I don't point out that it basically does. It was a fast lesson I learned when I was first accepted for this position and moved to San Jose. It's why I'm bothering with trying to control him in the first place. The reasons given for the high turnover of my position have been bogus things like *scheduling conflicts* and *culture fits* when I know that the actual reason is sitting right in front of me. If San Jose had any other players with even an ounce of Oskar's talent, I can guarantee he'd be out on his ass already. So the way I see it is I either need to step in and help the coaches find a D-man with Oskar's talent or keep him under the thumb. And if I can pull Oskar Voyjik in line, I'll have teams lining up to work with me.

I give him a benign smile. "Feel free to drop off a key whenever you get a chance."

His calculating eyes narrow. "Key?"

"I know we'll be together a lot of the time, but I'd like to have the freedom to come and go as I please."

His chair *thunks* back to the ground. "Back up. I'm not following."

"You want to act like a child? Fine. We're playing by kindergarten rules now, and from today, the buddy system is officially in place."

"I don't think I like where this is going."

"Probably a good thing since this *is* a punishment." I tuck my hands behind my head this time because while this isn't an official dick-measuring contest, I'm sure as hell going to show Oskar who's in charge. "The buddy system is simple. I know where you are at all times. At *all* times. You won't need to call us to clear if you can go out or not, because when you do, I'll be right there beside you. And the only way for me to monitor you that closely is to move into your spare room."

The worry I'm expecting doesn't come. "Technically, if you want twenty-four seven supervision, you really should share my bed. You know, to be safe."

"We both know sharing a bed would be the furthest thing from safe. And like I said, this is a punishment."

He sneers. "There's no way management is agreeing to that."

"I think you're underestimating how far management is willing to go for these antics"—I point to the screen, where Oskar and his guys are finishing up—"to go away."

"So … what? Sleepovers at home, sharing a room at away games?" He pumps his eyebrows. "I hear Ezra and

Anton made great use of their shared rooms while they were on the road."

"And you will make great use of ours too. By not sneaking out and going right to sleep."

"I don't know whether it's adorable or naive that you think following me around will stop me."

"I don't know whether it's adorable or naive that you think I'm not up to the challenge."

We hold each other's stare for a moment, and I know Oskar is puzzling out how to play this. On one hand, the whole situation isn't ideal—for me as well as him—but on the other, I know that backing down isn't in his nature.

He'll agree, if for no other reason than his need to prove he can outsmart me.

"Fine." The smile he gives me is dangerous. "I've always wanted a roomie."

"Oh, Mr. Voyjik. You should be careful what you wish for."

Chapter Two

Oskar

It's not my fault I was left unsupervised. Or that Lane's guys trusted me to do as I was told. Everyone from the PR department has been really slow to learn their lesson.

But Lane's certainly figured it out. Or figured me out. I'm not sure which it is yet, but living with him is going to be fun. So fun.

Starting now.

When my doorbell rings, I drop my sweats to the floor so I'm completely naked and then run a hand through my hair to make it look messy in that *I've been fucked six ways till Sunday* kind of way.

Yet, when I answer the door, I don't get the reaction I expect. Or want.

There's no exasperation, no large sigh. In fact, Lane's not even looking at me.

He's looking up at the house, which is only a few years old. It's boxy and modern but lacks all the frills of what people expect a professional hockey player to have. I'm only renting because I'm not dumb enough to think my antics will be tolerated forever; I assume San Jose is only a short stop on the ever-changing trades the NHL like to do. I've been with San Jose for almost three years now; before that, I was in Texas, and before that, I was with

Columbus. I get passed around more times than a bottom in a gang bang. And hey, I will never complain about being *that* guy.

I don't want to lay down roots. It's not me. I get antsy if I'm in one place for too long. My talent as a hockey player keeps getting me contracts, but my PR nightmares are what get me traded.

After an insulting amount of time, Lane looks at me, and there's the reaction I wanted: a loud sigh, a set jaw that's unshaven and has speckles of gray filtered through the dark scruff, and his intense brown gaze locked on my face. As if he's picked that one tiny, singular freckle I have on my cheek to stare at so he's not tempted to look anywhere near my junk. Or my full chest of tattoos that's a fucking work of art.

"Your house is unexpected," he says.

"My house or my dick?"

"Definitely the house. The dick is … typical."

I act offended. "Excuse me, there is nothing typical about my dick at all. It's a phenomenal specimen of masculinity and pleasure."

"Uh-huh, sure. Is that why you had to tattoo a phrase that translates to orgasm above it? To remind your partners of what they're supposed to do?"

"I didn't realize you'd taken *that* much notice of my tattoos."

He does the grown-up version of rolling his eyes—directing a derisive, unimpressed look my way, gaze still firmly set on my face. "I'm your PR manager. You don't think I had to approve those naked shots you did at the beginning of the season? We actually had issues finding one that hid that specific tattoo."

"What's wrong with my tattoo? It's advertising what to expect."

Outside, a neighbor walks by and glances up as Lane follows my gaze and turns. His shifting means I'm no longer blocked from view and ends up giving them an eyeful.

I wave. "Hi, Mrs. Huxley!"

"You might want to put some clothes on for once, Oskar. It's a bit cold out here."

My mouth drops, and I ask Lane, "Did she just say my dick is small? She obviously needs glasses. Poor old bat can't see properly."

"I can't believe she didn't even blink at you being naked."

"Oh, they're used to it. There's one rule in my house, and that's no clothes allowed. Welcome." I step aside to let him in. "You may enter once you get rid of that awful sweater and suit pants."

"Not going to happen." Lane pushes past me. "And while I'm here, your rules are void. I make the rules from now on."

"Okay, Daddy."

"Rule number one: no calling me daddy."

"Yes, Daddy."

He already looks like he wants to kill me.

"Okay, fine, I won't call you daddy. But I'm not calling you Mr. Pierce either."

"Lane is fine. If you put some goddamn clothes on."

I pick up my sweats and pull them back on. "Better?"

"Rule number two: clothes consist of pants *and* a shirt."

It's my turn to sigh. "We really are going back to kindergarten rules, aren't we?"

"You act like a child, I will treat you like one."

"If you treat me like one, I'll act like one." I stomp up the staircase like a pissed-off teenager, but I'm already having fun.

I go to pull out a team shirt when I remember I have some mesh tank tops for when I go out. I pull out a black one that has a rip in it from an overeager plaything I hooked up with once and throw it over my head. It's technically a shirt.

When I walk back downstairs, Lane's head is in his phone, so I stand at the bottom and wait for him to take in the view. It doesn't take long. Only this time, he does actually roll his eyes. But there's something else there. Something that says he doesn't want to like my antics but can't help himself.

"It's an improvement, I'll give you that."

"I think you're the first man to ever prefer me in clothes. I'm trying to work out if I should be insulted or flattered."

"Flattered?" Lane asks.

"Well, yeah. The only reason I can think of why you'd want me to cover up is because you're too worried about resisting my charms."

"If being naked is the only charm you have, we won't have a problem."

I chuckle. "Damn. You have willpower of steel."

"Or, you're not as loveable as you think you are."

"*Everyone* loves me."

"Must be nice."

"Being so adored? It is."

"No, I mean living in a world full of delusion. Now, where is my bedroom?"

"Right this way." I turn on my heel and run back upstairs, waiting for him to catch up. "I put you right next to me so you can keep an eye on me and make sure I'm not being a naughty boy."

"Works for me. Shorter distance to walk to kick out random hookups."

"I thought I wasn't allowed to hook up? Ooh, does this mean you'll come to my rescue when they won't leave the next day? Once they've had a taste of me, they never want to stop drinking from the fountain."

Lane blinks at me.

"My dick. They want to always suck my dick."

He lets out a loud breath. "I'm starting to see why you've been through so many PR reps already."

"Aww, you say such sweet things to me. We'll be fucking each other before you know it."

"Sorry to disappoint, but I actually know how to keep a professional distance."

"That sounds like a challenge to me."

"Of course it does. I'm going to settle in and unpack a few things. Why don't you go jerk off or something? You're going to have to get used to having sex with only your hand for a while."

Hmm, that actually sounds like a good idea. I touch my chest. "Moving in. Asking me not to have sex with anyone else. You want to be my boyfriend that badly?"

"Wrong B-word. I'm your *babysitter* because you don't know how to keep it in your pants. If chastity belts were still a thing, I'd be buying you one."

"You know, they have cock cages for that now. Kinky. I like having a boyfriend who's kinky."

Lane starts muttering to himself, but I can't understand what he's saying.

"What are you doing?"

"Reminding myself that I love my job and I can't hurt you because prison isn't fun."

I laugh. "We're right on schedule, then."

"Speaking of schedules, you need to give me yours for All-Stars week coming up, seeing as you're not going."

"I'm flying to Boston to hang out with my boys." Anton and Foster won't be there because they are playing for All-Stars, but the rest of the Queer Collective will be, and I can't wait. I love All-Stars week. Especially when I'm not chosen. It's like I get an extra week to recoup and fuck around while everyone there has to *work*.

Not that hockey is work. Well, it is. It's a lot of hard work, but given the choice to do anything else? Hell no. Hockey is my life. But by this point in the season, we're all ready for a break, and anyone who says otherwise is lying.

"Please tell me '*your boys*' is not a code word for a weeklong orgy with twinks."

I whistle. "Damn, I wish, but no. I'm hanging out with the other queerios from the Collective."

"The Collective? Tell me the truth. Are you in a cult?"

"Yes. We worship dicks, and on Wednesdays, we wear pink. But for real, the other guys in the league who are queer catch up every now and then so we don't feel so alone with all the heteros floating around in hockey."

Lane smiles, but it quickly drops. "It's an orgy with other hockey players, isn't it? Who's involved? I need to get their PR guys onto it too."

"You know, considering you're so adamant we won't have sex, you're certainly picturing me in a lot of different sexual situations."

"You had a threesome on camera, and you have made it my job to make sure that doesn't happen again. I need all the details."

I fold my arms. "Oh. Well, settle in because it's story time. It all started when this guy approached me at the bar and said he wanted me to fuck him and his boyfriend in that little private room out the back. You know how some places have those? Anyway, wasn't public enough for me, so I suggested—"

"I need to know the details of any of your more permanent arrangements. Like with this sex collective you've got going on."

Sex collective. I'm so telling Ezra we need to change the name to that. But then when Lane eyes me expectantly, I realize …

"I don't have any permanent arrangements."

Permanent means serious, and no way in hell am I letting anyone get that close to me.

The guys in the Collective are as close as I'm comfortable with, and even they aren't that close. I'm used to being alone. It's how I survived childhood. It's how I live my life.

The only person who'll ever truly have my back is me.

I accepted that a long time ago.

Chapter Three

Lane

I'm ready to take everything Oskar has to throw at me ... I just didn't realize that would include listening to him every night, giving his hand a pep talk as he rubs one out. If I have to hear, "Oh, yeah, baby, harder. Just like that. Bit more ..." one more time, there's no telling what I might do.

My only comfort is that a jury would undoubtedly be on my side.

"So sorry I couldn't spring for your ticket," Oskar says from his seat across the airport table. "But at least you can enjoy the first-class lounge before you're relegated back to coach. San Jose are cheap bastards, aren't they? Just because this isn't a team-sanctioned trip, that doesn't mean you should have to deal with being squished into the back of a plane like sardines in a can."

We're on our way to visit this orgy collective in Boston for All-Stars week, and as much as Oskar's been insisting he can go alone, I'm not dumb enough to fall for it. My other PR members might have been trusting, but I am not.

It's been a peaceful ten minutes while Oskar stuffed his face with all the food he could find and I got to enjoy my coffee in peace. Now, it seems he's back, and I get to deal with ... *him.*

It's no puzzle to me why all my guys have failed when it comes to Oskar—he's annoying as fuck—but for some reason, I find his wild personality entertaining. I've known a few fuckboys like Oskar in my time, and while those men are people I try not to think about often, they taught me how to deal with entitled hockey players. It probably helps that he hasn't tried to sneak out or throw some wild house party, even though I've been ready for both of those things to happen.

He'll try it at some point—it's only a matter of time.

And I'll be ready for him when he does.

Our flight is called, and Oskar jumps up to board with a smug look thrown my way. I let him go ahead and give him all of five minutes to disappear and enjoy his superiority before I pick up my carry-on and follow.

If I thought he could be trusted around anyone on board this flight, I would have been happy in coach and enjoyed the next five hours of peace. But if the past PR reps have taught me anything, it's that you can't leave Oskar's side. Not even when you're thirty thousand feet in the air. And the look on Oskar's face as I arrive at his row and come to a stop might be worth the next few hours of pain.

I keep eye contact as I shove my bag in the overhead compartment with one hand and wave my company credit card at him with the other. "Like I said, San Jose is prepared to do anything."

And maybe I should be concerned by the calculating look that crosses his face, but he wouldn't be Oskar if he didn't rise to the challenge. I have to make sure I'm a match for him.

Let's face it—at this point, I don't have much to lose.

I take the seat across the aisle from him and watch as he shoves the headphones over his messy hair. Thank God. Guess that means we're back on quiet time.

While he plots, I pull out my laptop, prepared to spend the next few hours catching up on work. Oskar isn't the only guy on our team, and he isn't the only idiot either. For the others though, their headlines usually come down to alcohol, dumbassery, or accidents. Oskar ... well, he doesn't fall into any of those categories, but I'm still trying to figure out *why* he's so blasé about risking his career.

Is it arrogance? Issues with authority? Or does he have some kind of sex addiction that can only be filled in public?

"Hey, boyfriend?" The rumble in Oskar's voice is pure sex, and I can't stop myself from looking over. He's pushed back one of the earpieces on his headphones, and as soon as he has my attention, his grin is automatic. "You answered that time."

"This time, we're in public, and when it's a choice between causing a scene or letting you quietly be ridiculous, I'm paid to do the latter."

"Does that mean we can go back to *Daddy* if I'm quiet?"

I shake my head. "Even San Jose doesn't pay me that well."

He sniggers, and it's a fight to keep my passive expression. I've done well over the last week to act completely closed off, even when I was dying inside to return his flirting. The way I see it, at the office is fine because it's a controlled environment where nothing could happen, but in his house? I might be strong-willed, but even I have my limits.

"Did you want something?" I ask.

"Oh, right. The guys. While Anton is away, Ez gets to play, and Tripp loves to share Dex around. You'll probably get an eyeful while we're there, and it's totally up to you if you choose to join in or watch. Though ... the idea of you watching ..." He pretends to drool, and I pretend to be exasperated, even as that plants tempting images in my head.

"As long as nothing ends up online, your sex collective can do whatever it likes. I'm sure I'll have work to do in the meantime."

"I thought I wasn't allowed to hook up?"

"You're not. But as they're all within the league and I'm in contact with their own PR reps, this is as controlled of an environment as we're going to get. You better make good use of your time because it's the last you'll have in a while."

Oskar rubs his hands together like he's excited, but if I thought for one moment that we were heading to an all-out gang bang within the NHL, there's no way I'd have let him get on the plane.

After he mentioned this collective, I've been looking into the other members, and from what I can tell, Tripp and Dex are more loving and monogamous than any couple I've met, and he can pry Ezra out of Anton's cold dead hands.

I could be wrong, but after talking with Boston's and Las Vegas's PR reps, I highly doubt that I am.

The rest of our flight is spent with Oskar trying to get a rise out of me and me ignoring him in favor of work. The only time I look up is when Oskar's telling the flight attendant what nice arms he has. The poor guy blushes to his hairline, but there's no risk there other than Oskar's wounded pride when he completely strikes out.

We land and I let Oskar go first, but as he passes, he leans in to whisper, "Last chance to join the Mile High Club."

"Way too late. I've been a member for years."

He finds that hilarious, like he thinks I'm lying, and keeps walking, pausing long enough to flirt with the flight attendant again, which gets him a solid shove to the middle of his back from me.

"Seem a bit jealous there, boyfie," Oskar says as we're walking through the terminal.

I scoff. "Jealous of what, exactly?"

"My flirting. But don't worry, there's enough of the ol' Voyjik charm to go around."

"Flirting? Ouch. If that was flirting, I seriously question how you're in the tabloids so often."

"But you don't deny I have charm?" He rubs the scruff on his jaw. "That's interesting."

"I didn't deny it because it goes without saying."

"That you're falling in love with me? I agree, but *whoa*, slow down there, Hoss. I only want you for your body."

Even with how hard I'm trying, an exasperated breath leaves me. *Do not engage, do not engage.*

The mantra repeats through my mind as we take a car from the airport and Oskar directs the driver the long way to the hotel he's made a reservation at.

"It's *Oskar's sex in this city* tour," he says. "It's going to be a ton of fun, and the best part is, we get to take it every time we travel. Okay, so *right there* was the time when ..."

If I'd thought getting away for a few days would quell my urge for murder, I was wrong.

When we finally arrive, we barely have enough time to drop off our bags before we leave again. Our hotel is close to where Ezra Palaszczuk lives, and on the walk there, finally, Oskar is silent.

Which would be a good thing if it wasn't for the way his lips keep twitching like he wants to smile. The whole change in attitude is putting me on high alert.

The doorman doesn't question us as we walk in and take the elevator to Ezra's floor.

"How often do you come here?" I ask.

"We try to make our orgies a twice-yearly thing, at least."

I don't respond because I don't need to call him out on the lie when the next five minutes will do it for me.

Only when Oskar raps his knuckles on the door, and it's thrown open to reveal Palaszczuk himself, I'm suddenly scared I've gotten this completely wrong.

Ezra locks eyes with Oskar, running a hand down his shirtless chest. "Thank fuck. I've been ready for you all morning." His teeth sink into his bottom lip, and my gaze flies to Oskar's face, where I find him eyeing Ezra hungrily.

Oskar steps forward and grabs a handful of Ezra's ass, hauling him close. When he replies, his voice is even deeper than usual. "I'll make it up to you, baby." He bites his ear. "I know what you like."

What the hell have I gotten myself into?

Chapter Four

Oskar

I try to hold back my laugh as Ezra looks over my shoulder at Lane and says, "Did you convince him to join us yet?"

A strained noise comes from behind me, and I can't help it. The laugh bursts from me.

Ezra steps away from me. "Well, that lasted all of two minutes."

"That's what Anton said. Oh, snap."

Ezra slaps the back of my head. I think it's supposed to be playful, but he might have overshot it.

"Ouch." I rub the tender spot.

"Come on in."

I walk past him, and as Lane goes to enter, Ezra says, "Hi, Lane. I've been told *so* much about you."

"Mm, I bet. That show just for me, then, was it?"

"Yep. If Anton knew Oskar's hands were on my ass, he'd fly home from All-Stars and cut them off, and then San Jose would lose their best defenseman."

I turn to Ezra, put my fingers in a love heart against my chest, and mouth, "I love you too."

"There are more players on the team than Oskar," Lane says.

"None that show up to play like him," Ezra points out, and I love him even more.

We make our way inside Ezra's apartment, where I find Ollie Strömberg and Caleb Sorensen already with drinks in hand and talking between themselves.

When they see me, they stand and give me a hug, and the second Ezra and Lane are close, I say, "Sorry, we can't have those orgies anymore. I have a boyfriend now."

Both Ollie and Caleb look at me like I've grown two heads, but then Lane has to open his big mouth.

"You pronounced babysitter wrong again."

"Is that why Ezra took off his shirt to answer the door?" Ollie asks. "To mess with your …" He glances at Lane and decides to take his side. The traitor. "Babysitter?"

I throw up my hands. "It's not my fault that CCTV caught me having sex."

"Actually, it's exactly your fault," Lane points out.

"What's that, boo? I can't hear you."

Ollie offers his hand to Lane. "I do not envy you."

Caleb agrees. "We thought we gave our PR reps nightmares back when we were the only ones out."

Lane smiles politely. "If only you'd known back then what can of worms you were opening."

"Hey, I'm not doing anything straight guys aren't doing," I protest.

"Except for, you know, having sex with women," Ezra says.

"And no one in the league has been caught having sex with two women in an alley," Lane adds.

"Is everyone against me in this place? When is Tripp going to be here? He'll have my back."

And I'm excited to see him too. He's probably the guy I'm closest to in the league, and since this past summer, where he was the one involved in scandals with his best friend turned husband, Dex, I haven't seen much of him.

Which is mainly my fault. I was trying to protect him from Dex breaking his heart, but just like when it comes to my own love life, I was way off base. Dex was in love with Tripp as much as Tripp was in love with him.

Turns out I have trouble seeing the best in people. Go figure.

It only goes to prove that I might know hockey. I might know sex. But actual emotions? Letting people see the real you? Why do people put themselves through that when they can get satisfaction from having their brains fucked out by random people?

When Tripp and Dex do arrive, I tease Lane some more about being my boyfriend, throw in some sexual innuendo, and then we settle in to watch the first night of skills, but I keep locking eyes with Tripp.

As if having a silent conversation, he stands and nods for me to follow him to Ezra's kitchen, where there's a fully stocked fridge.

Tripp grabs out two beers and hands me one. "Out with it."

"Out with what?" I ask innocently.

"Tell me how Dex is still going to break my heart, how it's unhealthy to be in a relationship where you love the other person more than they love you, and how you're mad I've been avoiding you because I've known this lecture is coming."

Wow. Okay, maybe I was too hard on him, but before he and Dex were together, Tripp was a wreck of inner turmoil thanks to unrequited love. Why anyone would put themselves through that is beyond me, but like I told him over the summer, if he's not going to fight for his own heart, then why should I?

"Okay, first, if Dex breaks your heart, I'll break his face, but I'm not worried about that happening. When I see the way Dex looks at you …" I turn to where, yep, there's Dex staring at Tripp like he hung the goddamn moon. "I see it now. That he really loves you and has all along. We were all too oblivious to notice. Well, except Anton, but I'll never tell him that. Secondly, relationships are unhealthy. Period. Monogamy is so not natural. And thirdly, you can stop avoiding my calls and me in general because there is no lecture and I miss my friend."

"Y-you do?"

"I'm even happy for you." I mock gasp. "What? That's crazy."

"It is not. I know Oskar Voyjik has a heart deep down. Somewhere."

"Hmm, nope. Just black sludge."

"What's the real deal with you and Lane over there?" He points his beer in Lane's direction, so I step closer and lower my voice.

"He's a pain in my ass and not the way I want him to be, but shh. It's a secret."

Tripp's gaze darts to Lane and back again. "I don't think it's too much of a secret. He looks like he wants to murder you."

"Oh, no. I'm a pain in his ass, that's no secret. But I'm not letting him see that he gets to me."

"Gets to you how?"

"I have all these rules, and they suck. Can team management really police who I have sex with? I'm not even allowed to hook up in the privacy of my own home anymore. All because of one little sex tape."

Tripp flattens his lips as if trying to hold in his amusement.

"Okay, fine. The leaked footage was a bad idea, but it was so fun it almost makes it worth it. Not worth having my own personal parole officer though."

"Hmm," Tripp says and sips his drink.

"Hmm, what?"

"Nothing. I've just never seen you so rattled over a guy before. It's refreshing."

"I'm not rattled. I'm frustrated." I point at him. "But that is a secret you have to take to your grave. I can't let Lane think this isn't fun for me."

And I have to admit, messing with him is fun, but there's also a point where even I know it's getting old.

"God forbid anyone outside of me and the Collective find out you're human," Tripp says.

"You take that back."

Tripp throws his arms around me for a hug. "I really hope Lane knocks you on your ass."

"I hope he does something else to my ass."

"Not happening," Lane sings on his way to the bathroom.

"I can't even have a private conversation anymore?" I yell after him.

He laughs.

"Do you see? Do you see what I'm putting up with?" I exclaim.

We head back into the living room to join the others, where all eyes set on me.

"What?" I ask.

"We like him," Ollie says.

"Probably more than we like you," Ezra adds.

"Well, aren't you the best friends a guy could ask for."

"Why don't you be nice to him?" Soren says. "He's only trying to do his job."

"Did you really open the door naked when he moved in?" Ezra asks.

"I always walk around my place naked."

"Ten bucks says they're fucking by the end of the regular season," Tripp says.

"Another ten when Oskar becomes the last single guy in the Collective to fall head over heels for someone," Ollie says.

That's the most hilarious thing I've ever heard. "I'll take that last bet definitely. Because if there's one thing I'm sure of, I will never fall."

Ever. I don't think it's even possible. I'm never in one place long enough to catch real feelings. I don't even know what *real feelings* are. I swear it's all a conspiracy. The whole love of your life thing.

"We need some new blood around here if I'm the only single one left," I say. Preferably someone to take the heat off me.

Lane gets back and takes the seat next to me. "Good. You didn't sneak out while I was in the bathroom."

"Don't give him ideas," Ezra warns.

I try to suppress a smile because I had actually contemplated an escape, but I'm not at that level of desperation. Yet. I'm close, but I'll wait for a more opportune moment to make my move. Tonight, I want to hang out with my friends.

Babysitter or no babysitter.

But all too soon, the skills challenges wrap up, and that's it for the night until tomorrow for the actual All-Star games.

Ezra stands. "Okay, everyone out. My boyfriend is going to be calling any minute to tuck me in and fuck my brains out over video call."

I almost ask if I can stay and watch because I'm itching for some action, any action, but I already know the answer will be no.

Monogamy is contagious anyway, so I wouldn't want to witness it. It might rub off on me.

"Where are you guys staying?" I ask the others as we all file out into Ezra's hall and hit the call button for the elevator.

All four of them are staying in the opposite direction to us, so we say our goodbyes in the lobby and go our separate ways.

It doesn't take long for Lane's smug voice to let me have it. "Tonight was fun."

I sense a trap.

"I couldn't help notice the lack of orgies though. You talked all this big talk and didn't deliver. I'm disappointed." He's so not disappointed. Just like I push his buttons, he's trying to do the same.

It won't work. "If you want, we can have an orgy right now."

"Isn't the definition of orgy more than two people?"

"We can bring my current boyfriend along for the ride." I hold up my right hand. "And my side piece." Now my left.

"No, thanks. Street sex really isn't my thing. I know it's yours, but some of us have dignity."

"There's nothing embarrassing about being shameless. It's actually really freeing. You should try it sometime."

"I would, but my pride would get in the way."

"Ah. There's your downfall. Dignity. Pride. They're not worth it when people will strip them away from you anyway. People can't take what you don't have." I tap the side of my head.

Lane searches my face as if trying to work out if I'm being serious or dramatic. "I'd say that's very philosophic of you if it weren't so depressing. Do you really have that little self-worth?"

Now there's a loaded question and a half. One I don't want to look into too deeply. I shrug instead.

The truth is I got rid of my self-worth years ago when I realized people would underestimate me or want to use me because of my outside appearance. No one cared to know the person on the inside, the person under the façade, because they either thought I had nothing worthy to say or because they simply didn't care. Being treated as an afterthought, as someone who isn't worth people's time, really does a number on you if you let it.

Either way, it didn't take me long to realize if people were going to take what they wanted from me, I wasn't just going to sit back and let it happen. I was going to take what I wanted too.

"You okay?" Lane asks.

"I'm horny. How long am I going to be in team-enforced celibate hell?"

"Hmm, maybe about the same amount of time it took us to bury the video of you fucking two guys in an alley."

"How long was that?"

"Oh, my guys are still sending out takedown notices to various websites."

Urgh.

"Sorry. You'll be stuck with your boyfriend and your side piece for a while yet." Now, he holds up his hands.

I stare over at Lane, at how calm he is ... confident. I wonder how confident he'll be later tonight while he's asleep and I'm at a club getting my rocks off.

I'm experienced in sneaking past my PR handlers, though this will be trickier seeing as we're in the same hotel room.

Lane says he's playing by kindergarten rules—well, I've upgraded them to high school rules. How to sneak out of home without anyone knowing.

Chapter Five

Lane

After devouring room service for dinner, we each retreat into our separate bedrooms next to each other in the two-bedroom suite we're staying in. I turn the lights out and wait. Oskar hasn't given me any reason to expect he'll sneak out tonight, but I'm going off a gut feeling. I have a hunch that Oskar isn't going to be able to resist the temptation of being in a new city with endless possibilities.

He's been way too well behaved so far.

Sure enough, just before midnight, I hear the slightest shift. Feet over carpet, the front door cracking open and then softly closing again. There goes my peaceful night.

I grab my wallet and phone, shove them into the pockets of my jeans that I haven't taken off yet, and follow. The elevator doors are sliding closed as I round the corner, so instead of waiting for the next one, I take the stairs. We're only five floors up, and by the time I get down there, Oskar is already out on the street.

He really is behaving like a child. The brazen way he walked out and assumed I wouldn't follow …

Admiring his spunk—and unfortunately, I'm not talking about cum in this instance—probably isn't the right reaction.

I'm beginning to see where my guys were going wrong though.

They let him get to them.

It'll be harder for him to do that with me because I've dealt with narcissists and liars before. Not that Oskar falls into either category, but he pushes the same buttons in me. I'm starting to work out that Oskar is calculated about what he does. I don't know much about him, but I've picked up enough to tell he'll push me until he works out how much I can take. Like his own way of finding out what I'm made of. He's a lot smarter than people give him credit for.

Unluckily for him, I'm ninety percent stubborn grit and ambition.

Oskar doesn't jump into a car, which is helpful because it would be easy to lose him in traffic. I follow at a distance until we're a few streets from the hotel and standing outside a gay bar. The bouncer clearly recognizes him and lets him right in, which unfortunately gives me the first hitch in my plans.

Damn it.

If I wait in line, who knows how much trouble Oskar will get into while I'm out here. But I don't really see another way around it. Maybe if I lurk in the alley, I'll get lucky ...

Oskar's not dumb enough to pull the same move twice.

Well, shit. I guess I'm going low and praying the odds are on my side.

Gathering up my nerves, I approach the beefy bouncer who's not currently letting anyone in—not a great sign—and paste on my most professional smile.

"Good evening." I hold out my hand, which goes ignored. "My name's Lane Pierce. I'm with San Jose's public relations department, and I've been sent to retrieve one of our players who just went inside."

He grunts. Fucking *grunts*.

Resisting the urge to tell this guy he's a walking stereotype, I hitch my smile wider. "Oskar Voyjik. He arrived a couple of minutes ago."

"Haven't seen him," the guy snarls.

I almost laugh. There's no way I'm letting Oskar win this thing because of a guy with a god complex. "Would a Boston jersey signed by Ezra Palaszczuk and Anton Hayes help you remember?"

I have no clue how I'm going to get my hands on one, but San Jose management said *anything*, and if that means shipping some random man a signed jersey, they'll do it.

His face twitches from its grumpy mask. Bingo. "I don't know you," he says.

I have never retrieved my work ID faster. The man squints at it like he's trying to puzzle out whether it's a fake or not, and considering I doubt he's been around a lot of people who work for the San Jose NHL team, I have no idea how he's supposed to figure it out.

"The whole team," he says.

"Pardon?"

"I want a Diedrich jersey signed by the whole team."

Of course he does. "Deal."

"Got a business card?"

I quickly pull one out, and he swaps my ID for it. "My office line, email, and cell is on there. Send me your address, and I'll get it organized." I hope.

He steps aside, and I rush past before he can change his mind.

It's impossible to know whether my life has reached an all-time low as I step into the crowded club and look around. The odds of finding Oskar here aren't in my favor, and it's only my determination not to let him win that has me pushing my way through the throng of people.

As soon as we're back, I'm asking management what the law is around me handcuffing Oskar to my side at all moments except games and practice. Surely if it's consensual, they won't have a problem with it? And if Oskar thinks it'll lead to sex, I don't see him having an objection. Even if there's no way that will happen.

The first places I check are the hallway and some of the back rooms, but either Oskar has already left, or he doesn't work as fast as I gave him credit for.

The VIP areas are upstairs, and even though I talked my way past the lineup outside, I can't see me getting into those. I also get the feeling Oskar wouldn't have gravitated that way anyway. He's here to hook up and get back before I figure out he's left, so if my hunch is right ... My attention returns to the heaving dance floor ... he's in there somewhere.

I love pressing up against half-naked, sweaty men as much as the next gay guy, but not tonight. It seems almost cruel to put myself through it when I'm not allowed to touch, so I turn my back on the dancers and head toward a group of people sharing a bar table.

"Hey," I shout. "Can I jump up on your chair for a minute?"

The guy I've approached shoots his friend a look.

"Only a second. See, Oskar Voyjik is here, and I want to see if I can spot him. If you get my drift."

"Who's Oskar Voy ... Vo ... who's that dude?"

I stifle my laugh, wishing Oskar was here to witness his anonymity.

"Famous hockey player!" the friend shouts.

And there goes my fun. I point his friend's way. "Yup. Him."

"Nice." The guy jumps off his stool and then holds it steady as I climb up to see over the crowd. Which really isn't the smartest move on my behalf because I might not be a hockey player, but I'm still heavy, and I don't trust this thing under my weight.

"See him?" the friend asks.

Maybe if I'd been looking for more than two seconds.

I ignore him and study the dancers, trying to spot that head of stylishly messed-up hair. I've studied it so much professionally—and personally, if I'm honest—that it doesn't take me long to pick him out amongst the dancers. I watch them for a second before Oskar leans in to whisper something, and he and the guy he's with start to head in the opposite direction to me.

"Found him." I jump down, thank the guys, and leave before they can send any more questions my way.

The direction Oskar was heading in leads toward the back of the club where the private rooms are, and I trail along behind them, pausing at the top of the hall to watch which room they walk into.

I chuckle as the door clicks closed and pick up my pace because while I want to toy with him and make him think he's won, I also don't want to walk into any compromising positions when that's the thing I'm actively trying to avoid.

When I reach their door, I whip out my credit card, slot it into the safety latch, and turn until I hear the lock disengage. Then, because I like the idea of making an entrance, I kick the door open and stride on in.

"Gentlemen." I stuff my hands casually in my pockets. "This looks like …"

Well, I was going to say *fun*, but ... I'd been expecting kissing or groping, and apparently, I'd been completely wrong.

Oskar's sitting on a couch, arm running along the back of it, nursing a scotch. He's completely composed compared to the guy beside him, who looks like he's about to piss himself over my entrance. They're both completely clothed.

I rock back on my heels. "I'm not sure you know how hookups work."

Oskar tilts his head. "I was playing the odds. I figured there was a chance you'd followed me and a chance you hadn't. I was waiting to see which it was."

That clever shit. I should be mad. Or frustrated. Or ... well, literally anything other than amused. I'm smiling in spite of myself. "Now you have your answer. If you want to sneak out, you're going to have to work harder than that."

"If you think I didn't close that front door loudly on purpose, you haven't worked me out at all."

I eye him, trying to decide if he's full of it or not. He wanted to hook up tonight, but I also know he wanted to play with me. Which of those urges would have been stronger?

"Ah, hey," his trick says. "If this is going to turn into some group thing, I'm out. So not my style."

"You're out anyway." I nod toward the door.

He ignores me and turns back to Oskar, who barely spares a glance his way.

Oskar waves a hand. "What he said."

The guy scowls and leaves.

"Really?" I ask Oskar. "Dragging some poor innocent *horny* man into this?"

"Technically, it's your fault he's leaving disappointed. If you hadn't walked in, I'd have had him on his knees already."

And I *don't* let my mind go there because the thought of Oskar's pants open, head thrown back, hand buried in that guy's hair is a hot one, and I'm determined to hold on to the one scrap of professionalism I have left: not getting hard in front of him.

"This room is oddly private for you," I say.

He takes a sip of his drink. "Maybe I've learned my lesson."

"No chance."

"Then maybe I'm just trying to be a good boy for you."

"If you hadn't already made it clear how much you love a spanking, I might believe you."

He chuckles and takes another drink.

I'm trying to stay detached from his shit, but I can't help asking the question that's been circulating through my mind for a while now. "Why do you do it?"

"Have sex? Because it feels good."

"Make yourself a target," I clarify. "You play dumb and carefree, but you're not. You have to know that as good of a player as you are that they'll trade you eventually if this keeps up."

There's something in his expression that's just out of reach. Similar to how he looked when we first got back to the hotel earlier. "They'll trade me anyway. It's part of the game. Good, bad, whatever. We're all at the whims of people who want to make more money."

That's the second time in one night that he's surprised me with his answer. It makes him more ... human. I don't like it. "I've decided Boston makes you depressing."

He stands, closing the distance between us. "And Boston makes you fun."

"I'm always fun."

His piercing eyes meet mine. "Not fun enough to get on your knees though, are you?"

"For anyone but you, Mr. Voyjik."

And hey, if I screw up this entire thing and end up being fired anyway, I can always take him up on his offer then.

Guys like Oskar are a dime a dozen.

And I refuse to risk my job for a quick fuck.

Even if it's guaranteed to be a really, really good one.

Chapter Six

Oskar

The week after All-Stars starts with an eight-day road trip. Normally, I don't mind away games because we go out afterward as a team, whereas at home, the married guys are quick to run home to their families. On the road, we're a unit. We play together, stay together, and eat meals together. Other than being with the Collective, it's the only real sense of belonging I get.

It feels more permanent, even though it's not with the constant rotating roster of players on any given team. I guess it's that hockey and everything that goes with it is more stable than my sex life, and that's why I push myself so hard to be the best.

This road trip though, I'll be lucky if I'm even allowed out with the team. And if I am, Lane's going to stay glued to my side the whole time. As much as I like teasing him, I do know where the line is, and undermining him in front of the team is something I wouldn't do.

In front of the Collective? Sure. But I only want to mess with the guy. I don't actually want to do serious damage to his career. Or his reputation.

As I get on the team bus taking us to the airport to fly to Detroit, I take a seat next to Aleksander Emerson. I've roomed with him a couple of times, and he's the perfect roommate. He's laid-back and doesn't get involved in drama. He's happy for me to do my thing, and he doesn't pester me with questions or lecture me. He never goes out because he has a wife at home, and I like that he's just ... there. He has a calming presence about him.

At least, he usually does.

I stare at his dark and messy hair that's normally styled neatly, his overgrown beard that's generally trimmed to show off his amazing bone structure. His green eyes are dull, and the bags under them belong in the undercarriage of the bus with the rest of our luggage.

"Rough night?"

He lacks his usual happiness. "Rough month, really."

Where has my head been? Oh, right. Up my own ass. I wait for him to elaborate, and he must feel my gaze burning into him because he meets my eyes and sighs.

"Rebecca and I are getting a divorce."

In the aisle, Lane is passing us and practically trips over his own feet. Then he narrows his eyes at me. "What did you do, Voyjik?"

"Why do you think I did anything?"

He shakes his head. "Sorry. I heard something that could be a PR nightmare and automatically assumed. Carry on. But, uh, Emerson, come see me when you get a chance." Lane keeps moving and takes a seat a few rows behind us.

Aleks casts his eyes downward. "And now it's really official."

"Haven't you guys been married since high school?"

"Kinda. Well, not married since then but together since then. She's the only person I've ever been with, and so it's ... yeah. Been rough. Especially with still living under the same roof, but that's going to change soon."

"There's no chance of working it out?" Now is not the time to go into my "monogamy is bullshit" spiel, even if it's on the tip of my tongue. I'm reckless, not an asshole.

"We've been in couples' counseling for over a year. You know things are bad when even your therapist suggests you're a lost cause."

"They actually said that? Are they allowed to do that?"

He waves me off. "That's paraphrasing, but yeah, that's where we're at. Somewhere along the way, being married to a hockey player became too hard for her."

"At least you don't have kids?"

"That was part of the problem. She's ready for them now. I'm ... not. I don't know if I ever will be. And before you say anything, I know we should have had that conversation before we got married, but we were so young when we tied the knot we didn't talk much about anything. Eight years of marriage, ten of being together ... It feels like a waste."

I nudge him. "The minute you're ready to get back out there, I'll take you out and be your wingman. You don't even need to worry about me undercutting you because we're not in the same competition."

Something brief but telling crosses Aleks's face, but I don't call him on it. Again, not an asshole. "Sounds good, man."

"That's if, you know, my jailer will set me free." I thumb in Lane's direction.

Aleks laughs. "What's up with that anyway?"

"Team management is a teeny bit mad that I am a single gay man flaunting my gayness for everyone to see."

Lane pops up behind us. Of course he fucking does. Wasn't he sitting a few rows back two seconds ago? "It's not your gayness they have a problem with. It's the public nudity and sex."

"Which is my gayness. My dick is even gayer than my brain."

"Somehow, I think your dick is your brain," Lane says.

Aleks laughs again. "You know what? I'm starting to feel a whole lot better about my divorce now."

"Because I'm awesome and cheered you up?" I ask.

"No. Because if I thought my life was sad, I really only need to look at you. You're a hotshot famous hockey player who needs a babysitter."

"In my defense, when I'm left unsupervised, I make poor decisions. Fun decisions, but to the detriment of my career, it seems."

"And mine," Lane adds.

I turn to him. "Do you mind? We're having a private conversation."

"Oh, so conversations you want to keep quiet, but sex is okay to be put out there for everyone to see?"

"Yup. Keep up."

Aleks huffs beside me. "Is this what I have to look forward to being single?"

Lane reaches over the seats and squeezes Aleks's shoulder. "Just don't have sex in public, and you'll have no problem with me."

"Excuse me, I haven't had sex in public in weeks. Why haven't you left me alone yet?"

"Because the minute I do, I know you'll go out and do it again."

I open my mouth to protest but really can't. "Okay, fair."

"For the rest of the season, you have one job," Lane tells me. "Hockey."

Luckily, I've got that covered.

—

I don't have it covered.

At least, not tonight. We're down by one in the third, but the only reason it's one and not four is because our offense is kicking ass. It's a high-scoring game on both sides, and it's 6-5 on the scoreboard.

Aleks may be getting a divorce, but it's not affecting his game. Actually, he might even be on a streak because of it. Something to prove or getting out his marital anger, I'm not sure. But it works for him.

Me, on the other hand, my lack of action off the ice is making me too stiff on it. I need release, and by something that's not my own hand. It's not enough. I've let way too many Detroit forwards get a shot on goal, and our goalie, Glover—nicknamed that because he's usually so good with his glove—can only take so much.

Tonight is too much for him, thanks to me.

So when I let another guy past me, and he scores, the game is all but over. The minutes tick down to seconds, and then the finality of the buzzer seals it.

The usual disappointment of a loss cuts through me and the rest of the team, and we leave the ice with our heads hanging down.

We're on track to at least make the playoffs this season, unlike Tripp and Dex, who have no hope, so the loss isn't a big setback, but it still stings like a bitch and isn't a great omen for the rest of the road games coming up. We still have Pittsburgh, Washington, Columbus, and St. Louis to go before we make our way back home.

We do the media thing where we keep our chins up and our battered pride hidden away, cool down, shower, and then climb onto the bus to take us to the hotel.

When Aleks joins me, I smile up at him. "You played amazing tonight."

"Shame the rest of the team couldn't get on my level."

Ah, there's the guy I know. Confident and easy.

"It's not my fault," I say.

"Is anything ever your fault?"

"Hey, I totally own up to my mistakes and take responsibility for my actions. But this is actually not my fault."

"How so?"

"I haven't been laid in forever, and it's killing me. I need to be loose on the ice, not sexually frustrated."

"Sounds legit," Aleks deadpans. "Trust me, you can play good hockey without getting your rocks off beforehand. I speak from experience. Actually, my game has improved since Rebecca and I finally decided to call it quits."

"Celibacy is not for me. It's unnatural."

"How acephobic of you."

I reword for clarity. "For a healthy, allosexual male, it's unnatural for me to go this long without getting off with someone."

Snickers come from the guys sitting in the same general vicinity as us, and I guess I wasn't as quiet as I thought we were being.

I lift my head and address the whole group. "Don't snicker like you guys don't know what I'm talking about. How horny are all you monogamous people going to be after these eight days?"

There are murmurs of agreements between the guys with wives and girlfriends, though I know not all of them are faithful.

I settle back in my seat. "See? Unnatural."

The ride back to the hotel is short, and when we all get off the bus and wait for our gear bags to be unloaded from underneath, I keep an eye out for Lane. But when I don't see him, I figure he must have gone straight up to the room. I didn't see him enter the hotel, but he could have easily slipped by us.

That's the other thing I hate about this arrangement. On the road, I'm now rooming with Lane. If I wasn't already sexually frustrated enough, sleeping in the same room as him was torture last night. Maybe that's why I played so shit today. I was up half the night listening to him breathing. Wanting to climb out of my bed and into his. Telling myself the sooner I stop being a dickhead toward him, the looser the collar might get.

Ooh, him putting me on a leash sounds hot.

No. This is my problem. I have to stop thinking about Lane in that way.

When I get up to the room, and he's not there either, that side of me that always does what it's not supposed to gets a little too excited about maybe, possibly, being able to get out tonight. I won't need long. Just enough time to get my dick sucked.

I'm still contemplating it when the door clicks and opens.

Lane enters with a small bag, and he throws it at me. "You complained, and I delivered."

"What is—" I reach inside the bag and pull out ... a vibrator?

"You told the entire bus you needed to be fucked. So there. Go fuck yourself. You're welcome."

I blink at him, stunned. "You going to leave me alone to do it, or are you finally giving in to your urges to stay in here and watch?"

"It's cute you think I'm leaving you alone for a second. If I go down to the bar and give you twenty minutes to get yourself off, you're going to disappear on me. Bathroom is right there." He points. "Have fun."

Fun? Oh, he has no idea how fun I'm going to make this.

Chapter Seven

Lane

Hello, boundaries, don't mind me.

Is it professional of me to buy Oskar a vibrator? Technically, I don't have any directions except for keeping Oskar's ass out of headlines—there was nothing about keeping *things* out of his *ass*—so if this helps, then I'd say I'm doing my job exceedingly well.

Might even be worth a raise.

I don't know what I was thinking when I got off the bus and searched for nearby adult stores on my phone. I'm running out of options considering I can't let him go out and I can't sleep with him, so this is my last-ditch attempt at keeping him quiet.

I took it as a sign of fate that there was a store a block away, but now I'm second-guessing my decision. Because as Oskar steps forward and leans in, I can't help imagining him using it.

"Warning, I tend to get loud."

I bet he does. "Act like I'm not even here."

"Actually, I plan to do the opposite." His stare flicks to the package and down to my crotch. "Go on, give me a hint. Thick? Thin? Long? Short? That way, I'll be accurate when I'm bent over, imagining you inside me."

And fuck, now I'm imagining that too. My cock thickens as I scramble to find *any* excuse for why I'm getting hard over a player. I'd say that it's not my fault, that Oskar's filthy mouth is outside of my control, but that kind of bullshit thinking doesn't hold up when Oskar's standing there gripping the sex toy I bought him.

I'm on thin ice, and even though I'm not going to cave and give in to him, I'm still dangerously close to the edge.

Oskar's gaze flicks up to pin mine. "That'll do it," he rasps before taking a step back and disappearing into the bathroom. The door doesn't close all the way, and even though there isn't enough of a gap to see anything, I can hear the exact moment the packaging is torn open and Oskar's pants hit the floor.

I glance down at the obvious outline of my dick, hating that Oskar knows exactly how easily he can play me.

Though, it's not like I've ever hidden that I'm attracted to him. Getting hard over a guy and acting on it are two very different things.

But as a low buzz fills the air, and the snap of a lid clicking open echoes off the tile, the line separating those two things gets real blurry. My cock twitches, and then a soft curse from the bathroom makes me throw all caution to the wind.

I drop back onto the bed, flick my belt open, and shove my hand down the front of my pants. The relief is immediate but nowhere near enough.

Oskar groans, louder this time.

"I can hear you," I call out. My tone is dry, as though I'm doing the roommate-ly thing and giving him the heads-up, but it's all bullshit. I want him to know I can hear because I know exactly what that knowledge will do to him.

"Oh, yeah," Oskar gasps and makes no attempt to silence it. If anything, his moans and gasps get steadily louder. And sure, vibrators feel incredible, but they're not *that* incredible.

I squeeze my cock, begging the damn thing to deflate. It's not right to think of Oskar bent over, pants around his ankles, ass stretched around the vibrator as he fucks his fist. It's not right to picture how his cock would look close up. Or what that perfect hockey butt looks like from that angle. Or how it would feel molding itself around my shaft.

My hips give a pathetic jolt, cock desperate for friction. I strangle it tighter, lock up my limbs to prevent any unwelcome movement, and try to ignore the throbbing in my balls. The deep, gravelly noises coming from the bathroom really aren't helping my situation.

No one would blame me for rubbing one out. Surely. I mean, first off, no one would ever actually find out. And second, Oskar is ... *Oskar*. Easily the hottest man I've ever met. It's impossible to take one look at him and not be picturing sex. His eyes hold a thousand ways to undress you with one look, and every piece of ink on his body is designed to draw you in. Make you look closer.

And yes, I've looked closely.

Approving those photos of him was one of my favorite days on the job, and those words *la petite mort* are burned into my mind. I envision following them down, as vividly as if he was right in front of me, warm skin under my lips until it disappears under the neatly trimmed hair at the base of his cock.

My hand has started moving without my consent, but when I try to stop, it won't listen.

This is messed up. This is so unprofessional.

I snort. Sure. Because I've been the epitome of professional this entire time.

Still ... with as horny as I am, I'll never get any work done, so it only makes sense to get on with it. It doesn't have to have anything to do with Oskar. We're not touching; we're not even in the same room. For all the jokes about treating him like a teenager, we're not actually fumbling hormonal messes. We're grown men with needs.

And I *need* to get off.

If a tree falls in the woods and no one is around, does it make a noise?

If a Lane comes his brains out and no one knows, did it even happen?

"Oh, fuck yes," Oskar moans, and this time, it sounds a lot less staged. His sexy tone has me opening my pants and pulling my cock out before I can talk myself down. The relief hums through my bones. I'm already leaking and so goddamn hard that I know it isn't going to take me long, but Oskar has a head start.

The constant buzzing and all those delicious noises he's making tells me he's getting close, and if I don't want him to find out about this—and I don't because I'd never hear the end of it—I need to finish first.

I roll my palm over the head of my cock, smearing the trickle of precum down my needy shaft. Each stroke is firm and fast, thumb flicking over the tip on every other pump, and it doesn't take long for my toes to clench. I spread my legs farther, hips pistoning up into my hand as I listen to Oskar's raw soundtrack filling the room, trying—and failing—not to picture him on top of me. Riding me. Taking complete fucking control as he gets us to the edge.

I bite my fist to hold back my own noises, not wanting anything to get between me and the vocal show Oskar's giving me. It would be rude to not appreciate his performance, after all.

"I'm so close," he gasps. "So … close …"

Shit. I thrust into my fist, racing him to the finish line, desperate to reach that moment, that high, before he works out I'm jerking off over him. It barely took me two pathetic weeks to reach this point. I'm a desperate, horny idiot, but when Oskar cries out, "Lane," I'm powerless not to follow. My balls pull tight, and the pressure in my cock builds to an unbearable level and then finally releases. I'm barely coherent enough to catch my cum as I shoot. Spurt after spurt, I unleash, and when I finally relax back into the bed, I only have a second to get my head on straight.

I jump up and tuck myself away with my clean hand while I grab a wad of tissues to clean up the mess.

From in the bathroom, I hear Oskar redressing, and I throw myself back onto the bed, grab my phone, and will my heart rate to steady as Oskar opens the door.

He crosses his arms and leans against the doorframe.

"Adequate performance," I say, heart still drumming a quick, dull beat in my ears. "I'd say a solid five out of ten for vocals."

"Is that your way of asking me to be louder next time?"

I pretend like I couldn't care less, but it'll be a long time before I forget the way my name sounded as he came. "Whatever gets you going." My attention is fixed on my screen, so I have no idea how he took that, but I'm too scared to check. In the heat of the moment, that seemed like a perfect idea, but if Oskar had walked out and found me with my cock in my hand, that's the kind of shit he could use to get me fired.

Sure, Oskar likes to stir and flirt and doesn't seem like the kind of guy to blink twice at witnessing sex. But if it's a choice between having a babysitter and having me fired for inappropriate behavior, I can't trust that he wouldn't go there. It would be an easy out for him, and I'd be handing him the ammunition.

I've been used by young, fun things before. I've gotten in way over my head. I know what it's like to be hurt by guys exactly like Oskar Voyjik. I can't let myself go there. Ever.

No pretty face is worth that kind of pain.

I force down a long inhale and remind myself that I got lucky this time. That was a risky game, and while I might like to play, I can't play with *him*.

No more letting my cock take the wheel.

Chapter Eight

Oskar

I can't tell, but I swear Lane's face is flushed. His cheeks are practically glowing in the low light. His chest rises and falls faster than normal, but I wouldn't say he's panting. I could say it looks like he's trying to cover up that he's out of breath. I have my suspicions about why—okay, maybe it's more a hopeful wish—but I haven't decided how to play this yet.

"Are you okay? You look ... hot."

"You just got off, and now you're hitting on me again? Do you have an off switch?"

I laugh. "I was actually worried about your welfare. And mine. Do you have a fever? Are you sick?" I approach and go to touch his forehead with the back of my hand, but he swats it away.

And when his eyes meet mine, it's a fight not to let my amusement show.

He totally jerked off.

"How did you like my show?" I taunt.

"Like I said, I'm doing whatever it takes to protect the team's image. If that means listening to you make god-awful noises that are so fake and over-the-top, then I will have to endure it."

"Mm. Endure it. Sure."

Yet, the next night when we arrive in Pittsburgh and I repeat some self-love in the bathroom under the watchful eye of Lane, I say his name even louder when I come and don't even catch my breath before I open the door, trying to catch him in the act.

The fucker has noise-canceling headphones on.

He points to them. "Picked these up at the airport today. Smart, huh?"

"Why are you the ruiner of fun?"

Lane lifts one headphone away from his ear. "What was that?"

"Nothing," I mutter.

"Do you think you're loose enough for the game tomorrow now?"

I hope it's enough. "Only one way to find out."

I have to admit that while not the best release I've had, I do feel more relaxed compared to when I was only using my hand to get me off. It's not my fault I have a high sex drive—I was born that way. And it's not like a sex addiction or anything like that—despite what the tabloids say about me.

I like sex, and I like a lot of it. That's all there is. There's no story here.

But if I can't turn around my game tomorrow, I'm not sure I'll be able to convince Lane of that, and then I'll have him on my ass—but not *in* my ass because noooo, that's not allowed for some stupid reason—for a lot longer than he needs to be.

I'm starting to get desperate. I'm even willing to forgo public sex if it means I can have actual sex with a person again. I have my kinks, my likes and dislikes, but I don't need to have them all to get off with someone. What I do need is the high from having someone worship me and make it feel like we could be more than physical. It never is, but in that brief moment where I have hands or a mouth or a dick on me, in me, against me, I let myself believe it's possible.

"Good luck for tomorrow, then," Lane says. "I'm going to go to sleep."

I should get some sleep too, but as I strip down to my underwear and get into bed, all I can think about is reaching between my legs and fingering my still-slick hole but being as quiet as possible for once. Would Lane know what I was doing? He's put his headphones back on, so he wouldn't be able to hear it. Would he be able to *see* it?

My orgasm might have given me small relief, but the more I think about getting off again, my mind drifts to what would happen if Lane caught me. Would he be tempted to join me, or would he storm out of here and tell team management that I'm some lost cause and a sex deviant?

It's not worth the risk. I need to turn around the public's image of me—and Lane's image of me—and I need to prove that sex isn't all I think about. So instead of doing the naughty thing I really want to be doing, I whine instead.

"I can't sleep."

Lane doesn't stir.

I throw my legs off the side of the bed and stand over him. He can't be asleep already. I flick his nose.

His eyes fly open, and he sits up, headbutting my abs in the process. Even though it feels like he's punched me, my cock still gets excited.

"What the fuck are you doing?" he says and takes his headphones off.

"I was trying to get your attention, but you couldn't hear me."

He glances around the room. "What's wrong?"

"I can't sleep."

Lane lies back and rubs a hand over his scruffy jaw. Right where I want to rub my cheek and neck all over him like a cat. I love beard rash. Weird, maybe, because most people hate the sting and then the red skin it leaves, but for me, it's part of the whole exhibitionist kink. Knowing people look at me and can guess what I've been doing is hot.

"You've been trying for five minutes. Just close your eyes." Now his hand runs over his dark hair. "Fucking hell, it sounds like I'm talking to a three-year-old."

"Maybe listening to you drone on and on and on will help me." I sit on the side of my bed. "Ooh, I have an idea. I'll ask you a question, and you can answer it in that lecturing tone of yours. You know the one that's really easy to tune out? It'll be like going to sleep with my very own white-noise app."

"Oskar," he warns. He sounds exhausted, but he wouldn't be the first person to get tired of me.

"Ooh, no Mr. Voyjik this time? Are we friends now?"

"Well, you did call out my name while you got yourself off last night—"

"And tonight, but you couldn't hear it because you decided to be rude. Do you go to a play or musical and then sit there with noise-canceling headphones on? It's disrespectful to the performer."

"First, I didn't buy tickets to your show. Secondly—"

"No, you funded the whole damn thing by buying me my ... props."

Frustrated Lane is so cute. "I'm going to regret buying that thing."

"I'm more interested in why you felt you had to drown out my sex noises. Why is that? Too sexually frustrated? When was the last time you got laid?"

"That's none of—"

"Wait, I'm not tucked in yet." I climb back under the covers. "Now, tell me a bedtime story. A sexy one about the last time you came. How hard you were, how much cum—"

"No."

"Can I get myself off again, then? Maybe that will relax me enough to sleep."

"Go for it. Bathroom is right there."

"I don't want to move for it though. I want to do it right here."

"No."

"Can we do anything fun?"

"Yes. Sleep."

I grunt. "This sucks."

"You're like a needy child," he grumbles. "Though, at least children don't fucking ask about other people's sex lives."

"If you want to get technical, they do ask where babies come from."

"Why do you hate me so much?" Lane asks.

"Hate? You think I hate you? Why would I be doing all this to get your attention if I hated you? Can you seriously not sense flirting when it's happening?"

"Except you weren't really flirting. You were taunting. There's a difference."

"There is?"

Lane sits upright and stares at me with his sexy lips parted. "This is genuine flirting for you? Is this like a daddy issues thing where you don't care what kind of attention you get, so long as you get it? Negative reinforcement and all that?"

I sit up too. "Wait, are you saying there are forms of *positive* reinforcement? What's that like?"

His gaze narrows. "I can't tell if you're being serious or not."

I try to keep a straight face as long as I can, but I break. "I'm not. Well, not really. And I don't have any daddy issues, thanks. My dad is awesome."

"Yet, he somehow managed to raise you to be ... you."

"You say that like it's an insult. I'm awesome too. So is my mom, actually. We're the picture-perfect image of an all-American family. Dad was military. Mom was a stay-at-home parent. We moved around a lot, but for a military guy, Dad didn't even blink an eye when I told him I was gay. All he did was tell me not to join the army. Still too homophobic for his liking."

"So you went into sports instead because that's such a better industry?"

I grin. "I don't like being told what to do. It's just lucky for Pops that I love hockey more than guns, or I would've followed in his footsteps to prove I could do it."

"No daddy issues my ass," Lane mumbles. "There has to be more to you than a penchant for trouble and great hockey skills."

"I'm also a smart-ass and full of shit. I'm, like, the perfect package."

"Who hurt you?"

I frown. "Huh?"

"If it's not a terrible upbringing that makes you wear that mask of arrogance, then what is it? Someone hurt you? First love broke your heart?"

I can't speak. Not because he hit the nail on the head, which he didn't, but because it's more like the complete opposite. There hasn't been anyone willing to look past the surface long enough for me to get hurt. Or fall in love. No one has cared to be deep with me, and after a while, it's easy to become shallow and go with the flow.

It wasn't some*one* who hurt me; it was everyone.

I try to continue to wear that attitude, but it's like in a horror movie when the protagonist removes the killer's mask and sees the real person behind it all. It takes away their power, and I've never had anyone do that with me before. No one has ever cared to look deeper. I both like and despise it in equal measure.

"Ah. I've worked out how to make you silent." Lane smiles. "There's some ammunition I can use later. Poor Oskar Voyjik and his crushed heart. What happened? He cheat on you, so you decide to fuck everyone else? Bad breakup?"

I fist my hand in the sheet because I don't want to let him see how much he's getting to me, even though he has it all wrong. "No broken heart here. I've never even had a boyfriend. Sure as hell haven't been in love."

"Then what does your attitude protect you from?" Lane's tone has lost the teasing edge and has been replaced with something softer. Serious. Too serious.

"Yeah, we're not doing this." I lie back down, determined to get my body to listen and go to sleep, but now I'm too keyed up and ... icky. That same gross feeling in the pit of my stomach that I had all through high school swarms my gut. Every new school, every new face

... I was always the shiny new toy. People obsessed over my looks, which made it hard to make friends because guys were generally jealous and girls wanted more than friendship. And when the novelty of someone new wore off and they all realized I was a boring guy who loved hockey and video games more than socializing and being the center of attention, they'd all drift away, and then I'd be alone. Until we moved and it started all over again. Eventually, I learned that if I acted out, people stayed interested.

"Struck a nerve?"

"Nope. Ignoring it. Getting into emotional baggage with other people isn't worth it."

"Why's that?"

Because it all sounds so petty. I don't say that though.

I hear Lane shuffle around, and when I glance over at him, he's on the edge of his bed, leaning toward me. "Oskar, if there's something that can help your situation, you should tell me."

"Telling you won't help. At all. In fact, telling you the real reason I don't get close to people will just make you laugh your ass off because it's ridiculous and shallow, and you'll think, 'Oh, no. Poor beautiful person is too beautiful.'"

As expected, Lane rolls his eyes. "And you're back to being a douche. That split second of vulnerability I saw gave me false hope."

"See? I'm never taken seriously, so why should I make the effort to be when it's easier to be a fuckboy and get away with it?"

Lane's face falls. "Wait, are you being serious?"

I sit up again and scoot to the edge of my bed until our knees are touching. "I completely understand that what I'm about to say will come across as a first-world problem, but believe me when I tell you, when people judge you on the way you look, it's hard to live up to their first impression. When everyone wants you for your looks but you still end up alone, guess what that means? Your personality is the problem."

"So you act out because you think it makes you more *likable*?"

No, I act out because if people want to hate me for being someone I'm not, they don't really hate me, do they?

I can't say that though. So I go for the easy target. "My dick is one of the things you like, isn't it?"

"Nope. Not going to let you turn this into a joke."

"It is a joke. Believe me. I can hear it in my own words. *Wah, wah, wah, people hate me because I'm gorgeous, woe is me.* But do you know how long it has taken for someone to ask me who I truly am deep down? From the moment I joined the juniors to exactly this moment. Right here. With you."

Chapter Nine

Lane

For the rest of our time away, I've been subdued. Given Oskar a little more leash. Maybe I shouldn't have. Maybe the whole conversation in our hotel room was fabricated, his way of manipulating me, and given how many times I've been manipulated in the past, you'd think I'd be able to pick it by now. But true or not, something has shifted.

I *want* to believe him, and doesn't that make me the dumbest person alive?

But do you know how long it's taken for someone to ask who I truly am?

I steeple my fingers and stare unseeing at the screen in front of me. If I thought I'd get more work done in the office while Oskar is safely at training, I was wrong. I'm as restless and distracted here as I was while we were traveling. Oskar was never supposed to be a person to me, just a job. A problem to fix. And now, unbeknown to him, he's gone and poked at my soft spot by showing vulnerability, and my whole being is screaming at me to fix it.

Fix it. A problem that likely doesn't exist.

Oskar plays people. It's what he does. And even though it's happened to me with men in the past, somehow, I've reached thirty-nine and *still* can't see what's right in front of my face.

I like to think I have my shit together, but if the familiar empathy swimming in my gut is any indication, I'm every bit as pathetic and easy to read as I've always been.

On the surface, his problems are ridiculous. *Oh no, I'm too pretty*. But somewhere along the way, he decided the person he is inside isn't good enough and created this whole other persona. Someone loud and attention-seeking. Someone untouchable. Someone who doesn't need people or to be taken seriously.

And maybe I'd call bullshit on all that, but ... well, I'm uncomfortably aware that I haven't exactly taken him seriously, myself.

I push away from my desk and approach the floor-to-ceiling window that overlooks the park across the street. The entire time I've been shadowing Oskar, I've either treated him like a child or swung in the complete opposite direction and took every chance I had to objectify him. Sure, he encouraged the behavior, but maybe that's because he's never learned to deal with it any other way.

I have a flash of Oskar ten years ago, building up unhealthy coping mechanisms to get attention from his peers. *Jesus* ... With a laugh, I rub my rough jaw and acknowledge the fact I'm losing here. Oskar's getting the better of me.

When Oskar was nothing more than a shameless playboy, I had no qualms treating him that way, but this shift, this acknowledgment that he's human and hurting, has made my job so much harder. Either my hunch that he's incredibly smart and playing me is correct, or I'm the first person Oskar has ever shown that side to, and I'm not sure what to think of that.

There's a light knock on the door.

"Hey," Keerson says. "I saw you were in today and thought I'd take you out for a charitable lunch."

"Charitable?"

His voice is laced with amusement. "For your Voyjik sacrifice."

This is the point where I'm supposed to point out that one lunch doesn't start to cover it, but the words won't come. "I have a question for you."

Keerson looks surprised by the abrupt change of subject, but he walks in and leans against my desk anyway. "Shoot."

"How were you with Oskar? With your interactions."

"Ah ..." He folds his arms. "Professional, I'd say. Why? Did he mention something?"

"No, nothing like that. Did you ever—I don't know—ask how his day was?"

"I tried to talk to him as little as possible. The less I talked, the less he talked, and a quiet Oskar is the only kind I want to deal with."

I completely understand where he's coming from and feel like shit because of it.

"Why?" he asks.

"I get the feeling he's lonely."

Keerson lets out a skeptical choking sound. "*Lonely*? That guy? I'd ask if you've seen all the same footage I have, but you're the one who showed it to me. He's rich, reasonably famous, and gets as much dick as he likes. Where's this coming from?"

"Maybe lonely isn't the right word. Isolated? He doesn't have a safe space to be himself? Just a feeling I get."

And if he's playing a part every day, I can only imagine how exhausting that must get.

"Nah, no way. He's manipulating you. It's what he does. Everything you see is all that man is." He lowers his voice to a mock whisper. "Don't let him sense weakness. He'll devour you."

My immediate thought is how much I'd like to devour *him*, but I push it away. It's not helpful, and I'm trying not to think of Oskar that way.

I thank Keerson for his help but decline lunch. "I need to be done here by the time they finish practice to pick Oskar up."

"You his chauffeur now too?"

"Every good babysitter knows you don't allow children to drive themselves."

"Fair point. Okay, well, will you be around tomorrow? I'll pick something up, and we can eat here."

"I'll text you."

Keerson nods, then taps the doorframe on the way out.

I turn back to my computer and the emails I'm quickly falling behind on. Who would have thought that trailing around a hockey star you want to sleep with would be detrimental to productivity?

My lips twitch as I remember Oskar's ridiculous bathroom show. After buying the headphones, he did away with the theatrics pretty fast, and the sounds he makes when he's not focused on performing are criminal. I only made the mistake of shifting my headphones to listen in once before I worked out very quickly what a terrible idea it was.

And if I want to switch to full-on professional mode, I need to do better than that.

As I'm skimming the subject lines to check for anything urgent, an email arrives from the team owner himself. With the subject *Oskar Voyjik*.

I know I'm not going to like whatever it says before I even open it, and when I see the words "progress report," my suspicions are confirmed.

I take my now lukewarm coffee with me and head for his office.

Technically, I'm doing my job. Oskar hasn't been in a single scandal since I took over, but assigning him a babysitter isn't a sustainable option when I have a whole team of players I need to keep my eye on. No. For this to work, Oskar has to actually *want* to change, and even after getting a peek at that softer side of him, I'm not convinced it's something that will ever happen.

Mick Alcott, child star turned business mogul turned hockey team owner, is perched in his office on the top floor. San Jose has a huge redevelopment plan in the works for a new arena and management offices that should be coming in the next year or two. I can only hope I'll be around to see it built.

"Mick," I say, forcing a relaxed tone. "Got a minute?"

He gestures to the chair across from him, so I enter and close the door behind me. "I assume you're here about Voyjik?"

"Who else?" We share a short laugh, and while that twinge of guilt tugs at me for joking at Oskar's expense, the last thing I want is Mick thinking I'm getting close to him. "I thought it would be easier to go over it in person than in an email."

"I can't believe you stepped in yourself."

"I know." I drop down into the offered chair. "But he's a handful, and my guys couldn't stay on top of him."

It's almost painful to get that much innuendo out with a straight face.

Mick makes a thinking noise, clearly hesitating over something.

"Everything okay?"

"Yes, yes ... Well, it's unorthodox for you to be living with him, isn't it?"

"Highly. Believe me, it wasn't my first choice." We share another of those short laughs. "Unfortunately, Voyjik being left unsupervised is like a red flag to a bull. I've already caught him sneaking out and had to literally drag him back home again."

Mick runs a hand through his thinning hair. "What do we do here? He's our best player, and between us, we can't afford to get rid of him. With where we're sitting on the table, we have a good chance at playoffs, but without Voyjik, we can kiss that goodbye."

I'm hesitant to bring this up, but it needs to be said. "Would that be so bad? It'll be short-term pain with him gone, but then next year, you might make it to the playoffs with a team that isn't dragging San Jose's name into the tabloids. His behavior reflects as badly on team management as it does on his image."

"Trust me, the GM and I have discussed it. The problem is, Voyjik's contract lasts for another two years, and I can't even convince Coach Bowman to consider a trade. If it came down to us telling him to, he might, but our only option is letting him go, and then we'd have to pay out the contract, which means less money to offer another player. Which puts us back at square one of not making playoffs."

"Morality clause." Every player has one. "It's an easy out for you, and if anyone's in breach of that, it'd be him."

"Yes, but letting a player go in bad faith draws headlines. That's the kind of thing that sticks around—"

"And threesomes in seedy alleyways don't?"

Mick takes a long breath, and when he talks again, the conversational tone has been replaced with something harder. "I understand what you're saying, but we have a delicate balance we need to maintain. With the new arena coming, we need to be profitable in order to fulfill contracts and keep our players happy. To do that, we need playoffs and solid ticket sales. And to do *that*, we need Oskar Voyjik. I'm only going to say this once because I don't like saying it at all: keep him under control. If that means living with him, fine, because one more—just *one more*—indiscretion and I may need to use that morality clause after all. Your only job is to turn Voyjik into a star player *off* the ice. If you can't do that and I'm forced to let go of our only hope at that Cup, there will be a domino effect. A PR department who can't do their jobs is worthless to me."

With every word, my gut sinks. When Mick's business side comes out, he's ruthless, and people become collateral damage.

Anything for the team.

I lie through my goddamn teeth. "I have everything under control."

Chapter Ten

Oskar

As I sit across from my agent, I pretend I have no idea what this meeting is about or why he came to pick me up and drag me out to a "working lunch." Considering he got on a plane so he could take me to lunch, I know it's serious, but really, isn't this all a bit dramatic?

He didn't say a word about why he's here in the car. We exchanged pleasantries, and he talked about how long his flight was, but that's it. And now he's sitting opposite me, drinks ordered, and he's still not saying anything. He's not looking at his menu but right at me like he's trying to intimidate me.

And it's working. I inspect the menu closely so I don't have to look at Damon.

Considering I've been on my best behavior—involuntarily—lately, his sudden appearance in my life is confusing, to say the least. If some other scandal had broken out about me, I'm sure Lane would have torn me a new one before Damon could set foot in the airport.

Our drinks arrive, and thank fuck because my mouth is dry. After I take a large sip, I'm able to compose that cocky demeanor I'm known for.

"Lane needed you to step in as babysitter for a bit, did he?"

Damon King is literally the king of queer athletes. He represents nearly all of the Collective as well as players in the NFL, MLB, and NBA. Every queer athlete wants him as an agent, and his roster has become so big that he's starting his own agency: King Sports.

And the glare he's sending my way makes me think he's on the verge of dropping me as a client. *That* would explain a sudden business lunch.

My cockiness drops. "It's not a big deal. You didn't need to come all the way out here to tell me to be a good boy. I *am* being a good boy. It's hard not to when I'm being guarded twenty-four seven."

His stare doesn't falter, and he remains silent.

"Why am I getting in trouble for one grainy CCTV sex tape when straight players are photographed in much more scandalous positions with women?"

Still nothing.

I relent. "Okay, okay. I get it. As a gay athlete, I have different expectations than the straight ones because we're always under a microscope so the homophobes can't point at our actions and say, 'See! They're all sinful sex maniacs. Next, they'll want to marry animals.' I still think it's a double standard, and it's stupid, but I understand until there's change, I have to suck it up."

Damon's phone lights up with a message on top of the table. He glances at it, ignores it, and then goes back to looking into my gaze with his telling green eyes.

I lift my hand and hold up three fingers. "Scout's honor. Best behavior from now on."

Finally, I get a reaction.

Damon leans back in his seat. "I'm really tempted to get up and say *good talk* and then go back to the airport, but I need you to know how serious a mess you've gotten yourself into."

I shrug it off. "Same shit, different day."

"No. Not this time. Do you really want to know why I got on a plane and came all the way out here?"

"Because you and your partner had a fight and you made the excuse you needed to yell at me to fly across the country?"

"Nope. Maddox and I had a fight *because* I had to get on a plane and fly across the country after being away to attend a press conference for one of my NBA newbies whose career is now over thanks to an injury."

I force a sympathetic look I don't feel because I get the impression that nugget about his other player is about to be used against me. So instead of acknowledging it, I go for the easy response. "Aww, you and Maddox fighting over little old me? If you've seen the sex tape, you know there's enough of me to go around."

"Oskar …"

Uh-oh. That's Damon's cut-the-crap tone. It's amazing how many times he has used it on me over the years. Usually after I did something that has gotten me traded or for an unflattering headline about me. Back before Ezra Palaszczuk went and settled down with Anton Hayes, we both split Damon's time with our sexcapades landing on tabloid sites and blowing up Twitter. It's been surprising how much Ezra used to take the heat off me. I'd never noticed until he wasn't there.

"What do you want me to say?" I ask.

"It's not so much what I want you to say. It's what I want you to acknowledge. No team is going to want you if you keep bringing bad publicity."

"Bullshit. There's always going to be a team that needs a good D-man."

"My NBA kid. He had his whole future ahead of him, but because of one fall—one accident—his career is over. You're here pissing away your future because you can't keep your sex life behind closed doors."

"How is that pissing away my future?"

"Because your team owner is threatening to terminate your contract under a morality clause. Do you know how hard it will be for me to pitch you to a new team after that?"

For the first time in my entire career of bouncing from team to team, real fear strikes through me.

It's one thing to hide behind the façade, letting people think I'm an asshole pretty boy whose only defining characteristic is his looks. It's another to let that bullshit actually affect my livelihood.

"Th-they said that?"

"Your PR rep called me to give me the heads-up because contrary to what you believe about Lane, he's actually looking out for *you*."

"He's only looking out for the team." Because I refuse to believe it's possible for anyone to care about me or my well-being.

"No. He's not. He didn't need to call me. In fact, contacting me first could be detrimental to the team because I might be able to find loopholes in your contract to cut them off at the knees if they so much as mention the word termination to you. It will give me time to prepare."

That ... can't be right. Can it? "Why would he risk that?"

"Because, like I said. He's not babysitting you, as you call it. He's there *for you*."

"But ... why?"

"I have no clue. If I had an ungrateful player who didn't fight for himself, I wouldn't waste my energy on trying to 'fix' him."

My mouth is dry again, and I don't know what to say to that. I don't understand why Lane would stick his neck out for me when all I've done is made his hair go grayer in the short time he has stayed with me.

Damon breaks into a small smile. "And that's the reason I got onto a plane. To see that face. You finally look scared, so now you have something to fight for."

"Lane?"

Damon's gaze narrows. "Your career. I don't have to tell you here not to have sex with your PR rep, right? You should already know that."

After what he just told me, I can't promise that.

"Tell me you know that." Damon sounds semi-panicked now.

"I know that I *shouldn't* have sex with him. Does that help?"

Damon sighs. "Not at all, but I'm going back home to grovel to Maddox and make it up to him."

"I hear blowjobs are a great apology."

He points at me. "Do not apologize to your team by offering to blow them."

"But that sounds like a fun time."

"Don't test me, Oskar. I love having you as a client—"

"That's because I make you lots of money."

"No. It's because I believe you have the talent to be one of the greats if you pull your head in and stop being so shameless."

To save my career, I have to stop pretending to be that douchey guy that gets me attention. But the problem is,

I've been pretending to be him for so long, it's hard to tell where he ends and the real me begins.

—

Damon drops me home in his rental car and heads back to the airport.

The urge to run away is strong because I don't want to go inside and own up to a lot of things I've done that has put my career on the line—purposefully hitting on Lane being one of them.

I need a change of attitude. I need to be the man both Lane and Damon think I am, but that isolated kid I was growing up, the one that's hidden deep down inside, doesn't want me to strip away those layers. Putting in work to get rid of an attitude I'm not even sure is a choice anymore and then still failing seems like a huge gamble to me.

Taking a deep breath, I force myself forward and push through the front door.

Lane is on the couch, his laptop open, and he doesn't even glance up as he says, "Meeting with your agent go well?"

I freeze in my place, unable to come up with something to say.

I'm hurt team management is talking about giving up on me, but at the same time, I understand it. While there's a double standard when it comes to the queer players and the straight ones and I think it's unfair, I've known that's always been the case. I've always known what expectations have been on me and what could happen if I don't meet them. I played with that line because it got me attention. Attention for all the wrong reasons, maybe, but it was attention nonetheless.

"That good?" Lane asks.

I think of what Damon told me. That Lane is looking out for me. But as I try to see past his own confidence, all I see is annoyance. Not protectiveness.

I'm not going to put myself on the line like that. I've already shown my hand to Lane once. I'm not going to do it again.

"I can't believe you tattled to my agent." I charge into the kitchen so I have something to do. Only I don't know what. My mouth is still dry, so I get some water to distract myself.

"It was the only way I could think to get you to see how serious your situation is. You won't listen to me, so I thought maybe you'd listen to him."

"Clearly you think I'm a lost cause, so why are you still here?" My voice is raised now, something I have no control over. Because if I break down what I actually want to do, it's not yelling at Lane.

It's to march over to him, fall into his arms, and ask him to protect me with everything he has. To care about me. To want to see the other side of me—the one he knows I have. And he has to know I have it because why else would he have called Damon? Why else would he have risked his job? I know I'm not worth it, but it almost makes me want to be.

Lane stares at me for a few moments and then says, "Because it's my job."

Ouch.

Why does it feel like he's punched me?

He says it's because it's his job, but what I hear is, "Because I only care about the team."

See? Damon's wrong. And for me to actually believe for a second Lane could care about me as a person, not just a hockey player ... I'm an idiot. Embarrassment washes over me.

"I can't do this anymore," I say.

"Can't do what?"

"Everyone's waiting for me to fuck up. To put that final nail in my coffin and lose hockey forever. Why won't you let me do it?"

Lane stands and turns to face me. "Because you don't want that."

"How do you know it's not what I want? How do you know I'm not ready to give it all up so I can become a fuckboy full-time. I have enough money to last me a lifetime. I don't need hockey." Except, I really, really do.

It's the rejection I don't need.

"Screw this," I say and throw my hands up. "I'm going out. Don't follow me."

I storm out of the house, determined to go do something stupid to blow this whole thing up.

Because when it comes to rationality, I don't have any left.

Chapter Eleven

Lane

That's what I get for meddling, I suppose.

I knew that tipping off Damon wasn't smart. Picking Oskar over the team is the kind of thing that would put me squarely on the chopping block if it gets out, and if Oskar clues in on that, with how angry he is at me, I wouldn't be surprised if he goes right up to Mick and spills. He has *no idea* what I've risked for him.

But not following him? Yeah, that I can't do. I grab my keys and march outside.

This is exactly the type of mood that's likely to send him spiraling to a point where he gets himself into trouble. Which would be the opposite of what he needs.

I'm pissed. At him, at myself. Like, fuck, why won't Oskar look out for himself? Why do I feel like I'm the only one actually fighting for him to clean up his image and keep his job?

And why? *Why* won't I let him burn it all down when he's so intent on doing it anyway?

Do I really love my job *this* much?

Or is it that something about Oskar won't stop drawing me toward him? The hint of a good person underneath all that ... *him*.

My gut gives a familiar flutter and stalls my steps on the way to the car.

Ah, *shit*.

That ... didn't feel good. The fluttering, my elevated heartbeat, the need to rush out and protect.

Nuh-uh. Sex is one thing, but this is almost like ...

I never learn.

As much as I try to hide it, I'm a goddamn bleeding heart.

I'm torn between climbing in my car anyway and heading back inside the house. The only two real relationships I've ever had were toxic as all hell, and I'm recognizing the red flags already.

Broken boy, inner sadness, my protective need to swoop in and save him from himself.

It's not Oskar, specifically, that I'm drawn toward—it's his vulnerability.

The last time this happened, I came home from work to find my house stripped bare by my boyfriend of a year, who'd told me he'd stopped using but had been lying the entire time. The guy before that was closeted ... and married. Only I didn't find out that last part until I worked out that everything I knew about him—including his name—was a lie.

Oskar has all the markings of someone who can't be trusted and who will discard me the second he gets what he wants. He doesn't need some knight in shining armor. He needs a therapist.

My keys dig into my hand as I force myself to turn and slowly walk back up to the house instead of making the mistake of hunting him down. If those protective feelings are already taking over, I need to take a giant step back. Oskar's his own person, and while I'd love to believe he's suddenly been given a reality check, I don't have my head in the clouds.

The only way to prevent myself from falling into familiar patterns is to do the complete opposite.

I trust him to make his own decision.

And pour myself a stiff drink while I wait for my world to implode.

The whole time I'm pacing, drink barely touched, I'm fighting myself over my decision. Not like it matters now—Oskar is long gone, and finding him in this city would be an incredible stroke of luck. But fuck if I'm not kicking myself.

In the split second I decided not to chase him down, I all but threw my job to the wind. Gave up my entire livelihood, for what? An entitled, cocky hockey player who would sooner see me lose my job than give up his childish ways.

He doesn't give a crap about me or the team.

And somehow, I put him first.

Because even if he is entitled and cocky ... I know now that it's not *all* he is.

And I hate him for showing me that side.

I can fight my instincts over keeping my ass in this house all I like, I can't stop that need to wrap him in bubble wrap and keep him here with me.

The next sip of scotch I take deepens the bitter feelings. I push the mostly full glass aside, then refresh my phone for the fourteenth time. I have notifications set up for all of the players' names, and every time I pick up my phone, I'm waiting to see *Oskar Voyjik* flash up on the screen.

It's only a matter of time. And while apparently past Lane was fine with throwing my job in, the selfish asshole made the decision for Oskar too. Because one more headline and he's gone. I'm gone. The team is left the mess of trying to replace him.

The weight of pressure bears down, and I resist the urge to pick up the scotch again.

Instead, I send a text to Damon King.

> No chance you've heard from Voyjik?

> No. And if I have to miss my flight home because something's happened, he'll be calling Maddox to explain why.

> I'm sure everything's fine. He just wasn't happy when he got back and now he's left again.

> Isn't your sole job at the moment to keep tabs on the man?

> I was caught off guard.

Lies. Total lies.

> Why don't you call him?

> Because I'm not dumb enough to think he'll answer. What did you actually tell him?

> The truth. His ass is on the line. We're all sick of the shit. He needs to sort himself out. Not to sleep with you.

I blink at the last line, not surprised at all that Oskar had that conversation but surprised that Damon mentioned it.

> Why do I feel like you're telling me the same thing?

> Because I am. He's hot and he's persistent when he knows what he wants.

> Noted.

I toss my phone on the couch and scrub both hands over my face with a scowl. Damon isn't telling me anything I don't already know, and I'd be offended over him doubting my professionalism if I hadn't already jerked it to the sound of Oskar getting himself off. And if I didn't want to do it again despite all my warning signals telling me to abort that hot mess.

But no. Fucking Oskar and his fucking emotions. He just had to go and put it out there, and now I can't close the door on how those vibrant blue eyes dulled at whatever memories he has.

I'd almost be relieved to find out he was playing me and none of it was real.

I pace some more, pick up my drink, and set it back down again. And as I cast my eyes around the room, it sticks out to me that there aren't any photos. Sure, he's younger than me and has social media accounts full of them, but while I don't have a lot of ties to people, I have some Polaroids from a snow trip I took with my PR team back in Dallas framed on the den wall. I have a picture of my college buddies from back in the day, even though we've all lost touch over the years. And once upon a time, I had a photo of my parents and me on my desk with the hope that they'd someday come around and accept me for who I am. That never happened, and I got sick of staring at the stupid picture where we all looked so happy, so I threw it in the trash. But I still *had* it.

Oskar has ... nothing.

It's not only photos missing; there are no books, no trinkets, nothing decorative. His place is minimal and staged, but there's literally nothing in it that screams Oskar.

Stop trying to psychoanalyze him, jackass.

He's probably got hard drives full of his personal sex tapes hidden under his bed. Or, knowing him, stills of them printed off and plastered over his bedroom walls.

My mind gets stuck on his bedroom.

Surely there'd be something personal in there, and I can't help wondering what kind of thing a guy like Oskar finds important.

Of course, it'd be completely inappropriate for me to go snooping. Even in the name of finding out more about the guy I'm supposed to be babysitting.

But given I've failed at my job multiple times already, does any of it really matter? By the end of the night, there's likely to be photos or videos of Oskar's dick being shared all over the internet. Hell, maybe he'll even take it all the way and go live as he fucks someone.

I clench my jaw at that thought, and I wish I could say it was because of how it would destroy both of our careers, but nope. That nasty feeling taking hold is straight up jealousy over the thought of someone else getting to have him that way.

Before I can follow that line of thinking to places that would only get me in trouble, my phone gets an obnoxiously loud alert.

> I've spoken to him and he made me promise not to tell you where he is. So I won't. But I'm sure you'll be getting a call soon.

Almost as soon as I've read those words, a call lights up my screen.

"Hello?"

"Hey, is this Lane Pierce?"

"It is ..." I say hesitantly, not recognizing the voice.

"This is June from the San Jose training facility. I thought you might like to know that Oskar Voyjik and Aleksander Emerson are here."

I hurry to thank her and hang up, unsure what to do with that information. Oskar ... isn't out? He's not blowing up both our lives?

None of it is computing in my brain.

I trusted him and gave him space, and somehow—*somehow*—he made an actual decent choice. But enough playing chicken with both of our careers, and enough of this animosity between us. This shows Oskar wants to do better, doesn't it? This shows the guy I knew was hidden deep down is in there. I'm almost dizzy at the realization.

Time to make amends. Time to show him we can work together and turn around his reputation.

Starting right now.

Chapter Twelve

Oskar

I was in my car and halfway to a bar, prepared for some afternoon drinking that would lead to a night of poor decisions and drowning myself in a dick or two, when the reality really set in.

I've pretended I don't care about anyone or anything but myself for so long that I've actually started to believe I don't deserve anything real. Even with the threat of trades, the constant shuffling from team to team, I'd still have the only thing I've ever loved: hockey.

But now they're threatening to take it away from me, and I couldn't resist coming to the one place that makes me truly happy.

The sound of my blades gliding over ice is both relaxing and anxiety inducing. I can't let them take hockey. They can't fire me.

At the same time, they can't tell me who I can and cannot sleep with either. The public thing, fine. I understand that. But having Lane follow me around to make sure I keep my dick in my pants is ridiculous. I thought it would be a lot more fun than it is.

Aleks is doing laps, getting in a workout, but I'm taking my time.

Feeling the ice beneath me, the cool air on my face. It's like I'm already saying goodbye because I can't trust myself to stay on the straight and narrow. Which is a dumb saying anyway.

Aleks laps me and jumps in front of me, facing backward. "I thought you said you wanted to skate, not do ... whatever it is you're doing."

"I'm so happy I called you out here for this."

He does a hard stop. "Why did you call me out here?"

Honestly, it was so I wasn't tempted to do exactly what Lane expects me to. Maybe I should have picked a different teammate. One who isn't going through a messy divorce and would jump at the chance to go out if I asked him to.

"Lane thinks my place on the team is in jeopardy. So after a chewing out from my agent, I yelled and stormed out of my own house because Lane is always there. Because I can't be left without supervision, it seems."

"So ... you called me because you can't, in fact, be left without supervision?"

"Maybe."

Aleks starts skating backward, so I follow him, pushing forward. "What kind of jeopardy are we talking here? Trade?"

"Termination," I mutter under my breath.

He stops again. "Fucking, what?"

"Hence ..." I wave my hand around the rink.

"Though, why are you moving so slow? You should be killing it. Hitting the ice so hard and fast, you get it pregnant."

I cock my head. "Does that even make sense?"

"Sure, why not? Come on, I'll race you." He takes off, but I yell after him.

"What are we, five?"

"You act like it sometimes," he yells back. "And that's exactly why you're in this mess."

Asshole. I take off after him, chasing him around the rink as fast as I can and possibly cutting corners to catch up to him.

Maybe. Definitely not cheating.

But the guy is smaller than me, sleeker. He's light on his feet, and he's goddamn fast.

The game of chasing him lasts until we're both sweaty, breathing heavy, and my legs are aching.

Aleks clings onto the side railing, coming to a stop, and I slam right into him. "I give," he breathes, trying to gulp in gasps of air. "You got me. You win."

"That's the problem with you forwards. You don't have the stamina of us D-men." I pin him against the boards.

He turns his head to look over his shoulder at me. "Ooh, an extra five minutes of ice time. Such stamina you have."

"Five minutes." I scoff. "I'm on the ice at least ten more than you during any given game."

"You wish."

"Admit it. I'm better than you."

"Again, you wish."

I shove him, and he pushes back against me. He tries to turn to get the upper hand, but I won't let him, and then I'm too busy laughing to see him make his move.

His lips seal over mine.

I've had my fair share of straight guys taking a walk on the gay side with me, and it's gone to shit every time, so while my urge is to push him away, I hesitate because I don't want this to blow up in our faces. I don't want him to feel like I'm rejecting him because he's ... him. That has the potential to cause problems on the team. I just want him to know that I can't go there with him.

I promised myself I would never hook up with a "straight" guy again. I might not have a lot of rules when it comes to my sex life, but that one's a hard line.

It's a quick two or three seconds before I pull back, and he must see it written on my face because he lets out a curse.

"I'm so sorry I did that. I thought ..." Aleks shakes his head. "I think I read into that."

I glide backward, putting some distance between us. "Yeah. You did." I want to reassure him somehow, but I've got nothing.

That's something else I've learned over the years with bicurious guys. If you tell them it's okay or forget about it or anything like that, it gives them the impression it wasn't a big deal and they can do it again.

But when he says, "I think I'm done," and skates toward the exit, I force myself to follow him because this is the last thing I need—to start a feud with a teammate.

"Aleks, wait ..."

He doesn't. If anything, he moves faster.

The back of his neck above his practice jersey is bright red, and even though I chase after him, even off the ice, he's still faster than me.

I catch up to him in the locker room, where he's already stripped out of his jersey and shoulder pads. He has nothing but skin underneath, seeing as he didn't realize I was going to suggest we skate in full gear—I needed to feel the weight of my pads. Full gear grounds me. Feels more like a game or a proper practice. It was the reminder I needed that I love the game, and if I want to keep it, I have to turn my attitude around.

I look at Aleks's chest, his smooth body that under any other circumstance might tempt me to put my rules about straight guys on hold, and when my gaze travels back up, I find him staring at me.

"And I wondered why I was getting mixed signals. You're eye-fucking me right now."

I wave him off. "I eye-fuck everyone. I draw the line at actually doing it. Especially with straight guys and *especially* teammates."

"I'm not straight. I knew from an early age I was bi but found my wife before I was really old enough to explore it."

That explains the weird reaction when I told him I could take him out after his divorce because we wouldn't have the same competition.

"The teammate thing still stands. I ... I'm already in enough trouble without piling an illicit affair on top."

"Fair enough."

"Are we cool? Like, clearly you have all these deep, emotional feelings for me, and—"

He flips me off, and I smirk.

"Such deep, deep feelings," he deadpans. "But in all honesty, I think I just wanted to get that first kiss out of the way. Maybe even a first hookup. It's so weird being separated from Rebecca that I have all this anxiety about dating. I figured—"

I don't let it get to me. I *won't*. "Use the slutty fuckboy as a training course to gay sex. Got it."

"No. It's not even that. That you're a man didn't really factor at all. It doesn't with me. I figured getting that second first-ever time out of the way would help. But I realize it was crossing the line and blurring our friendship, and we still have to work together afterward. So can we forget it happened?"

I let out a relieved breath. "As long as we're cool, I can do whatever you want me to do."

Aleks throws up his arms. "There you go giving mixed signals again."

"You wish I was hitting on you. You can't handle all of this." I wave a hand down my body and do a little shimmy.

"Well, yeah, that's the other reason I realized I made a mistake. You're a gorgeous guy, but damn, you're annoying."

My laugh is forced. "My confidence is my warning label. If you can't handle my attitude, you can't handle this." I put my hands in a V, framing my junk. And in a way, I'm not even lying.

The people willing to put in an effort with me have more of a chance of not walking out the next day after getting what they want from my body. Of course, this theory has never actually proven to be correct. Because they leave.

They always leave.

Or, I do before they can.

Self-preservation is a bitch.

"You're so charming," Aleks says. "What made me want to kiss you in the first place?"

It sounds like a joke, but I'm pretty sure I know the real answer.

"Because I'm familiar. You're comfortable with me. And hey, if my spot on the team wasn't on the line and you had more experience in the queer department, I'd jump on your dick so fast, you'd come immediately."

Aleks throws his head back. "Is this what dating guys is like? All crude remarks and sex?"

"What's wrong with that?"

He glances at me and smiles. "Nothing. I just want it."

I snap my fingers. "Ooh, here's an idea. Go out there and get it."

His mouth opens, but no sound comes out. He turns back to his cubby and says under his breath, "Nah. I'm still too nervous."

Okay, well, now I feel like a shit friend. I step forward, cupping the side of his face.

"What are you doing?" He tries to pull out of my grip, but I hold firm.

"Your first kiss with someone new should be a memorable and life-affirming one, and I couldn't pull my best work out there. Maybe getting it out of the way will settle your nerves."

Aleks bites his bottom lip. "And you're okay with that?"

"It's only a kiss, and if it's anything like the one out on the ice, it'll be like kissing my brother. Actually, I'm going to challenge my dick to try to get hard for you."

Aleks grabs my jersey and twists it in his fists. "Just kiss me and get it over with, you jackass."

"Ooh, name-calling helps." It doesn't. Everything south of the border is dead.

"Shut up." Aleks cuts off another retort with his lips on mine, and while it's ... fine, and nice, and I give him my best work, it really is like kissing my brother.

He's the one to break it, and as he does, he whispers a very faint "Thank you," but it's drowned out by the loud, booming voice at the door to the locker room.

"What the fuck is happening in here?"

Shit. Lane's found me.

Chapter Thirteen

Lane

"Can I talk yet?" Oskar asks from the passenger seat.

"No."

"But—"

"Shh."

"Lane, I—"

"*Not yet.*" My hands clench the steering wheel so tight they're cramping. I want to wait until I get him home before I unleash over all the sheer dumbassery that he's constantly getting himself into.

Aleksander Emerson? Can't Oskar keep it in his pants *for one fucking afternoon*?

Not only is Emerson Oskar's teammate, but he's about to go through a very public divorce with his high school sweetheart. They've been media darlings for years, and this ... no. This I absolutely *cannot* let Oskar get involved in. Aleks is already being pinned by the media for indiscretions that are complete bullshit, but even with Rebecca denying that's the reason for the split, no one will believe it.

Especially not if Oskar Voyjik's name gets mixed up in it.

My head is *pounding*. Not only am I going to have to do some hard-core damage control, every time I picture

Oskar's mouth on Aleks's, this hot, harsh feeling churns my gut.

"Come on, Lane—"

"I said *no*, Oskar. You do understand what that word means, don't you?" My voice is strained as I try to stop myself from raging at him. This is all on me. I'm the one who let him go out. I'm the one who gave him space. And, yeah, he didn't go and screw everything up, but he was well on his way to doing it.

"What's the difference between now and when we're back?"

"When we're back," I grit out through my teeth, "I don't have the possibility of running us off the road."

"Wow, you *are* mad."

My jaw clenches to keep from responding. I know what he's doing. He's trying to provoke me so we get this over and done with on his terms, but that's not happening. I'm so angry and goddamn jealous I can't even see straight.

And that's the kicker, isn't it?

I *should* be more pissed that Oskar is corrupting a teammate and willingly walking into another scandal, but all I can concentrate on is how desperately I want to replace Oskar's memory of that kiss with one of my own.

My approach of playing it cool, of teasing and getting under his skin, has backfired because I don't think I've ever wanted a man as much as I want Oskar Voyjik.

"Lane, let me—" His voice is softer this time, which only pisses me off more.

"Save it."

We're not doing the vulnerability thing again. There's no way in hell I'm going to show him that it works on me, speaks to a side of me I try to keep hidden behind a confident attitude and a cool façade. Oskar might be willing to let pieces of himself out, but I'm not going to reciprocate.

Not after ... *that*.

My teeth clench so hard my jaw aches as much as my hands.

It's almost a relief to pull into his driveway, except where I'd been hoping to calm down on the drive, to approach this professionally, that's gone completely out the window.

I throw open my door, climb out of the car, and storm inside.

Only a few hours ago, I'd made a choice that could have lost me my career, but I have another chance to hold on to it, and I'm not going to let Oskar get one over on me again. He's proven how little he respects my trust—I'm not fucking up my entire career for someone like that.

A minute later, Oskar strolls inside, and the carefree vibes rolling off him only fan the flames of my anger.

"What ..." I begin, trying and failing to control my tone, "did you think you were *doing*?"

"So I'm suddenly allowed to talk, am I?"

"Yes, and you better get started."

He pretends to inspect his nails, nose screwed up on his stupidly gorgeous face. He clicks his tongue. "The problem is it's been *so* long since you showed up, I seem to have forgotten everything."

"Cut the shit."

"Don't know what you're talking about ..."

"How about having your tongue halfway down the throat of one of your teammates?"

"Halfway?" He sneers. "Now, we both know that's impossible. My cock, however—"

"You're unbelievable." I scrape my hands through my hair as Oskar continues into the kitchen. No smart-ass reply, no challenging my assumption, just acting like this entire conversation is beneath him.

I storm after him. "Do you want to get fired? Is that what this is?"

"That's possibly the dumbest question you've ever asked me."

"Then what the hell is your problem?"

"I'm not the one with the problem. It's everyone else who wants to constantly act offended by my life."

Urgh. "Of course. You're the *victim*, right? You sound like you're in high school. Grow up."

"You treat me like I'm in high school, so I'm playing the part. Making your job easier."

"*Easier?*" I explode. "Both our heads are on the chopping block here. You screw up and you get fired, right before I'm shown the door as well."

Finally, his bored expression slips. "What?"

I let out a humorless laugh. "What did you think was happening here? That I'm hanging around because I enjoy your company?"

"Is that why you told Damon?"

"No, I told Damon because I didn't want you to throw away your whole damn career."

"But you could get fired for that."

I throw my hands out to the side. "At this point, I could get fired for any number of things. Like letting you leave tonight. If you'd gone to a club—"

"But I didn't."

"No, instead, you went to our practice rink, in broad daylight, with another player and then proceeded to hook up with him in the fucking locker room." That red-hot, sickening feeling comes back.

"No one saw us."

"*I* did. Which means anyone could have walked in there." I huff. "I was actually coming to pick you up and congratulate you on making a smart decision for the first time in your goddamn life, and then I had to see ... to see ..."

"Us hooking up?" Oskar helpfully supplies.

I advance on him until he backs into the fridge. The teasing is gone, and his eyes look sharper, darker, as they meet mine.

"Never again," I say.

His lips tremble. "Careful, Lane. You almost sound jealous."

"I'm your PR manager. I'm worried about the *team*."

"Yeah, because you were really worried about the team when you gave Damon the heads-up about me."

"I wrongly thought it might make you wake up to your actions."

"Except you're forgetting one thing." He laughs dryly. "I'm wide-awake to all the shitty things people do and I'm only playing their game."

I shake my head. "That's more excuses, and you know it."

He shrugs. "Too late to change now."

"It's never too late. And if I have to stay glued to your side for the rest of the season, I will. You and him won't be happening again."

"I never realized you were so possessive—you didn't have an issue watching me on camera with two other men."

He's right. As much as I might have wanted to sleep with him then, there was no jealousy because he was just another hockey fuckboy. Now ... I still want him, but it's shifted. Because while I *want* him, I want him to *need* me.

"Admit it," Oskar says. "You wish you were the one I was kissing."

I open my mouth to deny it, but I can't make the words happen. Not while I'm pinned in his stare. Not while he's less than a foot away. "There will be no you and Aleks."

He opens his mouth to say something, then slams it shut again. Heat burns in Oskar's stare as he curls his fingers into the front of my shirt and tugs me toward him. Our bodies collide, his warmth wrapping around me, sucking me into his presence.

"You know how you can stop me," he taunts, deep voice turning raspy.

And while I've been able to mostly ignore my attraction to him this entire time, I'm quickly losing the fight. I try to remind myself of willpower and professionalism, but my cock is putting up compelling counterarguments.

And then Oskar seals my fate.

He leans in, nose brushing my temple, heavy breaths at my ear. "For the team."

The team. Aleks. Both of our jobs.

He shifts, and I catch the faintest scent of sweat. "You want to stop me from going out and having sex with anyone else ... give me a reason not to."

God fucking damn it.

He's done it. Given me all the excuses I need to justify crossing this line I know I shouldn't be crossing. None of the flimsy excuses will mean anything if we're found out, but for now, they're easing the stupidity.

Before I can talk myself out of it, I reach down and close my hand over his rock-hard cock, then squeeze him through his pants.

"Be a good boy and open your mouth."

His jaw immediately drops, and having Oskar Voyjik in the palm of my hand—literally and figuratively—turns me on so bad my dick throbs. We make eye contact for a fraction of a second, something heavy passing between us before I tear my gaze away. I ignore whatever that was.

This is all about sex.

The team.

Our jobs.

I dive on his mouth, sealing both our fates with the filthiest kiss I can manage.

Chapter Fourteen

Oskar

I am so ... confused.

Not confused enough to pull back and ask what the fuck he's thinking though.

Lane doesn't kiss the way I've been imagining it. For some reason, I thought he'd be passive.

He has these hard edges to him, both physically and with the way he speaks to me, but whenever I've fantasized about this—about his mouth on mine—I've pictured something soft. Gentle.

There's nothing gentle in the way his mouth claims mine, the hardness in his set jaw as he controls the pace and the force behind it. His tongue is demanding and rough, and so are his hands as they grip my hips.

His fingers dig into my skin, and even though the part of me that wants to hit pause on this so I can work out why Lane is suddenly doing all the things I've been dreaming of since meeting him, the confident way in which he's taking charge of this has me becoming pliant in his arms instead.

I moan into his mouth and then whimper when he pulls away.

"I need you to say it," he growls.

"I'm sorry." That's what he wanted me to say, isn't it?

Lane backs me up, pushing me against the wall, and when his hand closes over my throat, I'm torn between being scared or coming in my pants. I think I am scared, which only makes my dick harder, so I guess it's a bit of both.

"Say you and Aleks aren't happening," he clarifies.

"Not in this moment, we aren't." I want him to grip my throat tighter, but instead, his fingers loosen, and I whine. "Aleks and I will never happen."

I should come clean and explain what really happened back in the locker room, but he doesn't give me a chance.

Lane's hand is back at my throat, his mouth is on mine, and his tongue pushes past my lips.

I melt under his touch, and all thoughts of telling him the truth about Aleks and me fade away. My dick is harder than granite, but when I try to push my hips forward, his free hand pins me to the wall, and he breaks his mouth from mine.

"I know you're terrible at taking direction, but if you really are as desperate for sex as you say you are, you will do everything I say."

"Whatever you say."

His lips quirk. "So that's the trick to getting Oskar Voyjik to do what I want him to."

"Have I made that some kind of secret? The promise of an orgasm is the only way to get me to do something. You could have already learned that ten times over if you'd listen to me when I talk."

"No talking."

"Yes, sir."

"That's words, Oskar."

I mime locking my lips, even though I want to ask what he's going to do with me.

He glances over my shoulder, out the window that's over my kitchen sink, and then pulls me off the wall and leans me against the counter instead.

Then his whiskey-colored eyes meet mine, and his lips quirk. "Your neighbor is on her balcony, watering her plants."

I turn to look when Lane's firm grip takes hold of my chin.

"Don't look. I want you on your knees, and you're going to suck me off while your neighbor watches."

"Why does this feel like a trap? Or a test? Am I supposed to say no here? To prove I'm not the fuckboy you think I am?"

"I know you're that fuckboy, and if I'm going to have to sleep with you to save our jobs, I'm willing to do it, but this is on my terms, and you're going to do what I say."

This still feels like a test, but Lane should know I'm not going to turn this down. "But—"

"No more words," he says, his voice doing that growling thing again. "Knees."

Damn, it's hot. This whole thing is one of my biggest fantasies. Blowing someone I shouldn't where someone else could see us.

I immediately get to my knees on the kitchen floor. The counters are high enough to shield me from Mrs. Huxley, but the challenge for Lane to keep a straight face so she doesn't know what we're doing in here drives a need inside me. The thought of having him slip, just a little—the look of pure need and pleasure on his face brings out my competitive side, and I can't wait to get started.

I reach for his pants to undo them, but he swats my hands away.

"Did I say you could do that yet?"

I groan because *nrgh*. His orders turn me on something fierce.

"Now, if you're a good boy and do as you're told, I might even let you touch yourself while your mouth is on my cock."

My lip trembles, and I breathe out the frustration that's building in my gut. It's the best kind of frustration where I yearn for permission—to follow whatever he tells me to do.

I wasn't lying when I said sex is the only way to get me to obey orders. I don't know where that need comes from. It could be that when I use my body for pleasure and let others use me, the praise gives me that acceptance that I've been looking for my whole life. All my life, I've worked to get attention. *Any* attention to fill that void of loneliness.

"Take your cock out," Lane says, and I immediately start on getting my jeans open. Lane gazes out the window and lifts a hand to wave at the neighbor. "I think she's almost finished. We might want to hurry this up." Lane opens his fly and shoves his suit pants and underwear down his thighs.

His dick juts out, and my hands freeze in trying to free my own because Lane Pierce has an amazing cock. Of course he fucking does.

It's not the longest I've seen, but it's disproportionately thick compared to the rest of him. It has a perfect mushroom head that's red and leaking, and his shaft is super veiny.

I don't think I've ever fallen in total love with a cock before, but I want to marry it.

The guy it's attached to, I could take or leave. He's hot, and I love seeing him flustered and annoyed, but he's always too serious.

Though in this situation, that's a bonus.

"You still haven't done what I said." Lane hasn't even glanced down at me.

"How did you know?"

"Because you stopped moving completely. If you want my dick instead of just staring at it, you need to do as I say."

I fight with my jeans, pissed at myself for wearing my tightest pair today, but finally free my cock. I need to stroke it to give a moment of relief, but the second I do, Lane takes a step back.

"Did I say you could do that?"

I complain. "You said if I was a good boy. I'm being a good boy."

"You can't touch yourself until I come down your throat."

"Then why did you tell me to take my cock out? Now it's out there, all lonely, wanting attention, and I'm supposed to ignore it?"

"Yes." Lane crooks his finger under my chin and lifts my gaze. "Because if you want this—if you want to have sex for the foreseeable future—you'll do what it takes. I'm putting everything on the line for you. You can follow a simple direction for me."

I nod eagerly.

"Now, how are your deep-throating skills?"

"Top-notch. And I'm offended you're even asking. You saw the CCTV footage."

"It was too grainy to tell. All I saw was a fuckboy on his knees for someone who wasn't me. Just like when I saw you with Aleks. You make poor decisions, and I'm done trying to do this the professional way."

"So, you're stooping to my level?"

"Yes. Get to it. Give me your best fucking blowjob, and try to make Mrs. Huxley suspect what I'm doing standing at the kitchen sink without a dish to be seen. Let her know how desperate you are for me that you got on your knees and didn't care who saw."

Lane really knows how to push all my buttons.

I practically dive on his cock. He's so thick that my lips have to stretch wide to fit him all in my mouth. I don't take my time easing into it, and as his fat head hits the back of my throat, I almost gag and choke, but I get it under control.

My eyes are already watering, and my abandoned cock is complaining, but the sooner I can get Lane off, the sooner he'll let me come.

I glance up at him between my lashes to see if he's got the look of lust and sex across his face yet, but he's as stoic as he was when we started.

He must have had Botox because how is this not the hottest blowjob of his life? It's mine, and I'm not even on the receiving end.

Then he glances down for a split second, and I see it. The heat is in his eyes, but his mouth is drawn into a tight line. I can work with this.

I bury my face in his groin, relaxing my throat so he can fit, and then alternate between sucking him and squeezing his balls with my hand.

I can't see his face anymore, but his breathing quickly becomes stilted and erratic. He groans, and even though I can't see it, I can picture him biting into his lip to try to stop his face from telling.

His hand weaves into my hair, but it's the sounds that get me. He complained about me being loud on the road, and here he is, providing my ears with an encouraging porn soundtrack that drowns out my wet slurps.

Lane's grip tightens, my mouth fills with a faint salty taste, and I know he's close, so instead of alternating between my sucks and squeezing his balls, I hold them firmly.

They draw up tight, ready to unleash, and I can't wait to drink him all the way down.

"Don't pull off." He grunts.

Then he fills my mouth, finally letting go, and I can't get enough of it.

When I glance up again, I want to gloat. Because there he is, head thrown back, mouth open, and letting out a cry so loud I imagine what would happen if Mrs. Huxley heard it.

And fuck, fuck, fucking fuck. That thought alone—the image of Mrs. Huxley looking through the window and seeing how tense his whole body is while he orgasms, I fucking come.

Untouched.

I keep him in my mouth while I unleash all over my clothes and the floor, but when I shudder, Lane pulls out.

"Are you oka—oh." He sees what's happened, and I expect to get in trouble for— "Did I say you were allowed to come?" Yup, there it is.

"All you said was I'm not allowed to touch myself. And I didn't."

He steps away from me completely and pulls up his underwear and pants. "Did that at least tide you over for a while?"

I stand and reach for the paper towels hanging out on my kitchen counter to wipe myself down. "Depends on your definition of a while. A couple of hours? Yes."

"Keeping up with you is going to be a challenge."

I release a breath of relief because I was expecting him to do that annoying thing guys do after sex. Particularly straight guys, though Lane is very much not straight. But the whole, "This was a mistake. We shouldn't have done it. Wah, wah, wah." Calm down, it's just sex.

"We're doing this, then?" I ask to be sure.

"Desperate times call for desperate measures."

"Aww, you're desperate for me. That's actually really sweet."

"If you want to be deluded enough to take it that way, have at it. I'm done trying to get you to see it my way."

"On a scale of one to never hooking up again, where do you lie if I do a victory dance?"

"An eighty-six."

"Okay, fine. Internal gloating it is." And I'm going to be doing that for at least the next twenty-four hours. Or until I'm ready for another orgasm. Whichever comes first.

Chapter Fifteen

Lane

I've officially lost my mind.

I always expected it to happen at some point; it only seems fitting that being around Oskar twenty-four seven has accelerated the process. The sun was barely up this morning when he crept into my room and slid into bed beside me. I should have lectured him on respecting *some* boundaries, but my morning wood turned needy in a second flat, and I'd ended up pinning him to the bed while I rutted against him until we both came on his deliciously tattooed abs.

I'd wanted to spend time licking the mess off him, but I'm unsure how to play this, and I didn't want to linger on anything more than the sex until I figure it all out. Apparently, coming affects my mental capacity because I let Oskar go off to the training arena *solo*. Well, not completely solo. I'm sure *Aleks* will be there.

I sip my coffee, picturing how easy it would be for me to put the PR heat on Aleks instead. I never would though. I'm not about to ruin a man's life, but thinking about it is fun.

After I saw him and Oskar kiss, I called him to find out where the hell his head was at. Aleks confirmed he's bi, and I warned him if he plans to come out while going through a divorce, it would be a PR nightmare. I already have one too many of those.

Maybe getting fired for sleeping with Oskar wouldn't be so bad if I got out of handling that mess.

My gaze travels out the kitchen window to where Mrs. Huxley is in her backyard, tending to the garden, and my cock gives a slight twitch.

Hmm. First time that's happened with a woman before. Apparently, after yesterday, my body has created a Pavlovian response to her. Oskar came untouched. Just from sucking my cock while he thought someone was watching. She wasn't, of course, but he didn't know that. I'm trying to be creative, not completely stupid.

I'm going to have to come up with a few different scenarios to feed his exhibitionist kink because he's not going to believe the neighbor line again, and I can't risk us *actually* having public sex. It's risky enough without an audience.

But Oskar needs an audience.

And apparently now so do I, because I missed the hands-free show, and that's something that I *need* to see.

A flicker of doubt hits me again, but I shove that shred of morality way down deep. It's started now, and putting an end to our arrangement will mean absolutely nothing if we're found out, so I might as well get everything out of it that I can.

Which means while Oskar is gone, I'm going to have to think carefully about this. He's getting sex to keep him out of headlines, but that's not enough. His image has been dragged through the mud, which means we need to get back in control of the narrative and show the world more of who Oskar is. And while we're doing that, I simply have to ignore the saintlike persona we give him.

This is all business.

Well, *and* sex.

But definitely nothing more than that.

There are still a few hours until Oskar is back from the rink, even though today was a light skate before their game tomorrow, so I have time to come up with a plan before I need to run him through it. First, I need to do something I'm completely dreading but should probably get out of the way.

> How are you? Safe flight? Btw I had sex with Oskar. Just thought I'd give you the head's up on the off chance it gets out.

The reply comes through before I've even exited the message.

> You what?!

> Should I have used the phrase "we had public relations" instead?

> Dear god, tell me it wasn't in public.

> Relax, I'm reckless, not a lost cause.

> I don't think you get to claim that when it hasn't even been twenty-four hours since you said that would never happen. It's Oskar! What were you thinking?

> That everything else has failed so it was time to move on to plan X. This is plan X. Triple X if you want to get technical about it.

> This isn't a joke, Lane. Fuck! At least tell me this isn't going to happen again.

> I wish I could but it will definitely happen again.

> If management finds out, you'll be in as much shit as he is.

> Well aware, thanks. I'm risking everything for this idiot.

> I'm sure it's a real sacrifice.

I cringe and tuck the phone away in my pocket. That went about as well as I could have hoped for. *Way to make friends, Lane.*

Still, I did him a professional courtesy, and Damon isn't going to tell anyone because it would get his client in as much trouble as it would me. He's a locked box when it comes to his client roster and their secrets.

Now. Oskar. The sex is a smart move because it means I'll be able to control the situations where he gets off and make sure none of them lead to scandal. It's crossing all sorts of lines, but it's both consensual and effective, and with only a few months left of the season, I only need to keep Oskar in line until then. Maybe during the summer, I'll look for another PR role or hire someone else to manage him, but at least I'll have a couple of months to figure it out.

With any luck, Oskar's attitude will have turned around by then, but I'm not going to hold out on that.

The sex could help though. I agreed we'd continue, but I didn't specify how often. My smile turns filthy as I consider the possibilities. Sex once a week, and Oskar can earn bonus rounds. Good publicity will lead to positive reinforcement. I almost laugh at myself because it sounds like I'm training a dog.

I dump the rest of my coffee down the sink.

It helps to think of Oskar as purely a work problem because it desensitizes me to him. All it took for me to throw myself at him was a hint of jealousy, and that's without actual feelings involved. But is it worth protecting myself when I feel like dirt for treating him that way? I don't want to play into his issues and make them worse, especially not when I think that under all the bullshit, Oskar is actually a good guy. He just doesn't know it. I want to help him bring that side out, but doing that without getting emotionally invested might be impossible.

There has to be a middle ground though. A way to keep the sex detached without treating him like a walking sex doll.

He already has a wealth of issues over being treated like a fuckboy, but I know by the time we walk away from this that my issues are going to get me into trouble too. How I keep being attracted to the same type of man is beyond me, but it explains how I'm still painfully single.

I *want* a relationship, but I'm always attracted to the guys who don't.

And Oskar isn't even exhibit A. Maybe N. Or Z.

I swear I've gotten worse over the years, not better. In high school, it was being used by my crushes for rides to school or lunch money. My college boyfriend more or less used me as a sugar daddy, and through the years ... there have been a lot of mistakes.

I can already tell Oskar will be added to the list.

I still don't have my answer when Oskar's front door slams open a few hours later.

Here we go.

"You told Damon?" he snaps the second he catches sight of me at the dining table.

I don't answer right away, which I'm sure is driving him nuts. Instead, I finish reading over the media release Keerson has sent me before setting my laptop aside.

"How was your skate?"

"Great until I saw a million missed calls on my phone and got blasted by my agent for being a dumbass."

"Aren't you used to that by now?" I ask.

His sweaty hair is plastered to his forehead, and I take it he didn't shower before getting his ass home. That's how pissed he is. "You're avoiding my question."

"Because it's a ridiculous question."

"How is it? We said we weren't telling anyone."

"And we aren't. But Damon is your insurance policy. If it gets out, you can bet your ass he'll already have a story in the works." Pity I don't have the same safety net. Pointing out that I did it for Oskar will go straight over his head though, and I don't want him looking into the action anyway. My protective side will stay well hidden because I'd be willing to bet he's the kind of guy who'd use it to his advantage. The others were.

"It doesn't mean I want my agent knowing about us."

I laugh. "So, you don't care that the entire world sees your cheap hookups, but you draw the line at one person knowing you had sex with *me*. Wow, Oskar. I'm feeling the love."

He flips me off, then walks into the kitchen and pours himself a drink of water from the fridge door. "It proves his point that I'm incapable of making a single smart decision."

"Did you tell him it was a choice between me and Aleks? Because I can guarantee he'd agree with your choice."

Oskar's face screws up for a second before he drains the glass and sets it in the sink. "You're like a dog with a bone."

"It's called damage control."

"And I'm the damaged one?"

"I thought that was obvious." But even as I say it, I eye him. His attitude isn't as big today. That mask of false bravado is missing, and he looks tired. It could be his usual post-training look, or maybe—just maybe—he's actually stressed about what he found out yesterday. "I've had an idea," I say, softer this time.

"Is it to give up on this hot-mess express before you go down with me?"

I don't fall into the pity party with him.

"Sit down." I kick out the chair next to me, and to my surprise, Oskar does it without argument. "I've been playing with your schedule for the next few months and trying to work out some promotional ideas for when we're home and then teeing you up with anything happening in the cities you travel to."

He points at the screen. "This one is *before* a game."

"Yup."

"You've clearly never played a game of hockey if you want me to help out at a youth center instead of having downtime. I'll be wrecked."

I give him a dry look. "And yet you have no issues with going out, getting drunk, and screwing some guy in the VIP area bathrooms the night before a game. I don't think an hour of volunteering will kill you."

His eyes cloud over as he remembers the time I'm referring to. Some jackass got a grainy shot under the bathroom door and thought recording the audio would give him five seconds of internet relevancy.

Oskar gives in way too easily. "Fine. But if we lose, it's on you."

"How about I promise to make sure you're relaxed before you get to the game?"

"*Before?*"

"We'll hire a car with a privacy partition."

"And like that, I'm suddenly on board."

"Of course you are." I laugh, and it takes a second for me to notice Oskar watching me. "What?"

He pulls his stare away. "Nothing."

"Well, that sounded like a lie."

He nods back at the screen. "All of that seems so phony though. Our fans know I don't do this shit. It'll be transparent as fuck that I'm only going through with these things to make the team look good."

"Yeah, no one will doubt that. But you know what the point of this is?"

"What?"

"We'll keep you way too busy to have a chance to fuck up. Then if you're not fucking up anymore, they'll have nothing to talk about. Suddenly this 'phony shit' to create a positive image is real because you don't have time for anything else."

"Yeah, maybe." He shoots me another odd look, then stands. "Email that through to me. I'm going to go shower."

Then Oskar leaves, and I know something is up.

Because I'm pretty sure that's the first conversation we've ever had where he didn't hit on me. And I'm not at all paranoid that now I've given him what he wants that he's lost interest.

I mean, I knew it would happen eventually.

I just didn't expect it to hit so soon.

Chapter Sixteen

Oskar

Even though I showered back in the locker rooms, I was still feeling dirty when I arrived home. Not because of blowing Lane, but because practice was terrible. Nothing was finding my blade.

I've had off days before, but this is all new levels of suckage.

Didn't help that Damon chewed me out for the second time in twenty-four hours right afterward as well.

Shit's getting real. Too real.

I never let anything get to me—the rumors, the bad press, the fans who say I'm not as good as I think I am. Though that last one is easy to ignore, because please, I am that good. But my point is, I have thick skin. I can take a hit, physically or mentally, and my game has never suffered.

Because of that, my confidence in my future as a hockey player has always been solid, but I'm realizing that maybe it's been *over*inflated.

I'm not infallible.

And now I have to work for what I want.

I thought that getting off with Lane yesterday might have made me less tense, but all it's done is make me realize just how much trouble my career is in. If Lane Pierce is willing to risk his job to keep me in line, how much danger am I in here?

Once I'm done showering for the second time today, I head downstairs to find Lane where I left him.

"You lied," he says.

"I lie about a lot of things. What specific lie are you talking about?"

"According to Keerson, your practice was a mess."

Accurate, but still, ouch. "Off day. They happen."

"Explains the attitude though."

"What attitude?" I go to my kitchen and pull out a protein bar from the cupboard.

"You're ... weird."

"Way to boost my ego. *You played shit today. You're weird.* What, you think now that we're hooking up, you can be blunt about everything?"

Lane's gaze narrows. "I've always been blunt with you."

Doesn't mean it doesn't hurt. I don't say that though. "True."

"Want to talk about it?"

"About why I did so badly today?"

"Or ... anything else that might be bothering you."

I take a bite of the protein bar, talking with my mouth full. "You're my orgasm buddy and PR rep, not my therapist."

Lane stands. "This is what I'm talking about. Where's Oskar Voyjik gone, and who is this grump who hasn't so much as made a joke about having my cock in his mouth?"

I straighten. "Let me get this right. I'm a smart-ass, and you tell me to stop being a smart-ass. I'm not a smart-ass, and you tell me something must be wrong. Is that what I'm hearing?"

"Yes. Since when do you do anything I say?"

I drop the protein bar wrapper on the kitchen island and approach him until I can lean in close to his ear. "I think I did a fucking good job of it yesterday while I was on my knees for you."

His body coils tight, but then he places a strong hand on my chest and pushes me back. "Nice try with a deflect, but it won't work."

"Then what will work to get you off my case?"

"I'm not even on your case. I'm asking if you're okay after a hard practice. That's all."

Then why does it feel like more?

I don't like that Lane has learned to see through my act already. He hasn't been here that long. But with him in my living space, Damon breathing down my neck, threats from the owner of the team, it's all ... too much for my brain to handle.

And for once in my life, I'm not dealing with that by going out and blowing shit up. Because for the first time in my entire career, I'm worried about the fallout.

For a hockey player, doubt is worse than superstition. It has the ability to get in your head and not let go.

My playing is what has saved me in the past, and sure, one bad practice doesn't mean it's all over or that it'll happen again, but I can't go into tomorrow's game in this headspace. I just can't.

Thank fuck we're playing Vegas tomorrow because I need to see Tripp. Maybe he'll take pity on me and let me slapshot a few past him.

"Do you have anything planned for the Vegas trip?" I ask. "Publicity-wise? Can we get the Mitchells in on that action?" At least with them there, it would be more believable. People would totally believe do-gooder Tripp

Mitchell and his husband dragged me to some kind of charity thing.

"Yes, actually. It's already organized. Tomorrow morning, you get out of the early skate because you'll be doing it with the Rainbow Raiders. It's a junior team in Vegas that Tripp Mitchell has strong ties to."

"Sounds good." Well, it sounds doable, but I don't say that.

Lane is surprised by my words too. "Okay, who are you, and where is the Oskar Voyjik I know?"

"What would the Oskar Voyjik you know do instead?"

"Flat out say no. Or barter. Maybe say he'll do it if I give him an orgasm first."

My lips quirk. "Ah. I get it. Didn't take you long to get addicted to me. You want me to want you again."

"And there he is. All is right with the world." Then the asshole pats my chest and asks what's for dinner.

How can Lane Pierce be my least favorite person and my favorite at the same time?

—

As Lane and I enter the rink on the outskirts of Vegas, my best friend—or, I guess the closest thing I have to a best friend—smirks over at me from where he's on the ice with a bunch of kids.

He hands the reins over to his husband and skates toward us. "So it's true."

"What's true?" I ask.

"That your babysitter signed you up to do all this positive PR crap."

"Please, I am doing this out of the goodness of my own heart, and I'm offended you would think I'm here for anything other than the kids."

"What a load of shit," Tripp says.

I turn to Lane. "Having to deal with Tripp Mitchell's brand of mean wasn't on the list of things I needed to do today. Make it stop."

Lane slaps my shoulder. "Sorry, but I can barely get you to do what I want. You think Tripp is going to listen to me?"

"Trippy!" Dex, Tripp's golden retriever of a husband, calls out. "We need you."

The group of teenagers around him all say, "Oooh," and make kissy noises as Tripp makes his way back over to them.

Kill. Me. Now.

"What was that groan for?" Lane asks.

"I didn't realize it was out loud. I don't know what to do with these kids. They're teenagers. They're, like ..." Scary.

"Your mental age?"

"You know, just because something is true, that doesn't mean you have to point it out."

Lane laughs. "You'll be fine. You have about half an hour to get comfortable with them before the reporters show up."

"Mm. Can't wait."

His hand lands on my shoulder. "If it helps, I have complete faith in you. You can do this. Because, well, you literally have no other choice."

Asshole.

I throw on my skates, grab a stick, and head out there, skating up to Tripp to ask him what he wants me to do.

"Have fun. Dex and I love coming here because it's not about winning. Think of it like a good old game of pond hockey, where you let other people score on you because it'll make them feel better about themselves."

"I literally do not understand any of the words that came out of your mouth."

"Pretty sure you know what it's like to let people score on you."

"Not *on* the ice."

"It's really simple. We want to build these guys up while pushing them to be top of their game."

"Okay. So no yelling obscenities at them like my junior coach?"

Tripp touches his heart. "Your life makes me so sad."

"Thank you. So much. I love when you hug me with words." And unlike Lane, Tripp doesn't actually realize how horrible my teen years were. I have every right to find these kids scary; teenagers literally don't give a fuck about anything.

"Hey, everyone!" Tripp yells out. Everyone on the ice stops and pays attention. "Oskar Voyjik from San Jose came by to smack-talk Vegas."

That's really going to win me points. Thanks, Tripp. As expected, the kids all scowl at me.

"Who wants to see a shootout between him and Dex? Player who gets the most shots by me wins. Vegas versus San Jose. It could be a preview for tonight."

"Oh, you are so on," I say.

Tripp's in full goalie gear already, but Dex is like me—in jeans and his team jersey, gloves, and that's it.

The teens clear the ice, and their coach or someone who works at the rink brings us three pucks each to put at our feet.

Dex looks at me. "Who wants to go first?"

"Ladies first."

"I was thinking brains before beauty, but if you insist. You can go first."

"Am I the brains here, or are you?"

Dex cocks his head. "Did you really just ask that? Even I know I'm the dumbest person in this room."

"I'm not so sure about that."

I can tell I've confused him even more. "Who are you, and where is the Oskar asshole I know?"

"I wasn't finished. You somehow got Tripp to marry you. If anything, he's the dumb one here."

Dex bursts out laughing, but when Tripp calls out, "I can hear you! And so can the people in the stands," we break apart.

"Visiting team shoots first," Dex says.

Flashbacks of the shitty practice yesterday try to take hold, but I shake them off and do what I do best. Dex might be an expert at scoring from beside the net, but I do my best work from afar.

I skate forward and prepare for a slapshot. It moves like a bullet, right past Tripp's head into the top of the net.

Even if I am the enemy team, the kids are good sports and cheer for me. I turn and give them an obnoxious bow, which makes them cheer louder.

Dex goes next and also scores.

"Hey!" I complain. "Clearly, that's favoritism at work. He let his husband score, or there'd be no ... cuddles later."

Dex shakes his head. "Dude. The kids are teenagers, not five. They know you mean sex."

Oops.

I glance at Lane, who's in the stands, and he's facepalming. Lucky he gave me this warm-up time before the reporters get here.

"Besides," Dex says, "Tripp isn't that nice. Even to his husband. When it comes to hockey, he's in it for the W."

"So am I." This time, I go for a quick wrist shot and get it through the five-hole. I fist pump in the air and dance on my skates.

"Don't count your Easter eggs before they're snatched," Dex says.

"You mean ... don't count your chickens before they hatch?"

"No. Easter eggs. That's the phrase. Don't count your Easter eggs before they're snatched."

"Umm ..."

"Because if you do, then you get upset when your sister snatches them. So you have to wait until the next day so you know how many you really get."

"Oh, honey."

"What?"

"Did your sister tell you that was the phrase?"

"Yeah, why?"

"Maybe, uh, you should take your shot. The kids are waiting and all that crap."

He gets started, but as he tries to shoot, it's like the lightbulb goes off above him. He misses the goal and turns to me. "Phoebe stole all my chocolate!"

When he gets back, I pat his shoulder. "Sorry, buddy. But that revelation will be nowhere near as devastating as seeing this go in and you losing. On your home turf."

I take off with the puck, fly down the ice, and try to deke out Tripp, but he doesn't fall for it, and my shot hits his pads.

When I get back to Dex at center ice, he smiles.

"What was that again? Complete devastation I'd be feeling?"

"Yeah, yeah. You still have to get this one in."

"I've got this in the bag."

He doesn't. When Tripp catches the puck in his glove, I take another bow to the crowd, and then Tripp tells them all to come down to the ice and try to get one past him.

They rush the ice, and I have faced many big guys in the NHL. I've been flattened by them, pushed into the boards, and gotten into fights with them. None of that is as scary as twenty teenagers coming at you with admiration in their eyes.

But as they pull up to a stop beside me, offering me high fives, I have to admit they're not so bad.

"Even though you're from San Jose, you deserved that win," one of them says.

I'm actually impressed by their sportsmanship. I know people in the league who'd throw a hissy fit over losing a shootout.

"Thanks, man."

The kid's face falls. "I'm nonbinary."

Fuck. "Sorry. Ah, thank you, awesome person."

They light up, and offer their fist for me to bump.

We spend the next hour playing hockey with the kids, and I hate to admit it, and no way will I actually do it aloud, but ... this is actually cool. It's been a long time since anyone really looked up to me like this.

Sure, there are fans, but they come across like a hockey fan. Dex and Tripp, Ezra and Anton ... Hell, basically everyone in the Collective has dedicated fans who love them. I've never had someone come up to me and say I'm an inspiration. Mainly because my antics off the ice are anything but inspiring.

The time goes so fast I don't even notice the reporters show up or take photos. Only when we're leaving the ice do I see them talking to Lane, and when I reach him, the reporter says, "You look so cute out there with the kids. I have all I need. Thanks." Then he walks away.

"They didn't want to ask me anything?"

"I handled it for you. Ready to go? You've only got two hours of downtime before you need to get to the arena."

That's a relief. Playing hockey with the kids, easy. Talking about it? Not so much. "I can shower back at the hotel."

"Why bother when you're going to get all sweaty again?"

"Is that an invitation?"

"Only if you do one thing for me."

I groan and throw my head back. "What?"

"Admit today was fun."

"Never."

"I saw your face out there. You loved every second of it."

"Lies."

"You're allowed to like it, you know. You don't have to be this arrogant 'I don't give a shit about anyone but me' asshole all the time."

Except that's just it. I do.

It's all I know how to be on the outside.

Chapter Seventeen

Lane

This plan is going down the drain fast. I'd expected Oskar to pout and half-ass it. I clearly didn't give him enough credit.

After the initial hesitation, he shone out there, and I hate how much I liked it. Those kids looked up to him in a way I'm not sure he's experienced before, and seeing the hesitance melt away as he lost track of everything else but being on that ice was ... yeah, I'm not getting into that.

It's clear Oskar loves hockey. That's never been the issue.

I hold open the hotel room door, and Oskar eyes me as he passes.

"No point pretending to be a gentleman now. I'm already putting out."

I laugh. "We both know the gentlemen aren't the ones you're attracted to."

Oskar walks over to his luggage and grabs some underwear and the bag his suit is in. I love seeing him in that thing. "Am I showering, or are we getting sweaty?" he asks.

"That depends on you."

"Why? You're going to let me call the shots this time?"

I chuckle like he's adorable. "Fuck no. It depends on whether you'll tell me what I want to hear."

"Hard pass." He heads for the bathroom, and when he gets to the doorway, he pauses to throw me a teasing look. "Besides, I'll be taking Aleks out to dinner with Tripp and Dex tonight. Thought he might like to meet some of the Queer Collective before he decides to join. What do you think? Will *he* make me say I've had a good day before he blows me?"

My eyes narrow, a hot feeling building in my gut. "I know what you're doing."

"Showering?" he asks innocently.

"Trying to make me jealous."

"Oh, I don't think I even need to try. Your face is practically red."

"I'm not jealous. I'm pissed off. There's a difference." Just don't ask me what that difference is. "You're supposed to be taking this shit seriously."

His stare runs over me before it catches mine. "Then *make me*."

Oh, Oskar. Wrong thing to say to me.

He hooks his bag over the door, then walks into the bathroom, leaving the door wide open. If he thinks I'm going to give in because he's naked, he's still got a lot to learn. Including the fact I will call every one of his bluffs.

I take my time stripping off my clothes and then follow him in.

The shower is already going, filling the room with steam, and Oskar glances up from where he's pushed down his boxer briefs. He meets my eyes in the mirror.

"Coming in?" he asks like he's won.

"Nope." I step up behind him, not close enough to touch but close enough to see his body in the reflection.

And while I've seen the majority of it in those photoshoots he did, it's nothing compared to the real thing. The *full* real thing.

I refused to look when he opened the door to me naked the first time, but now I don't have those same reservations.

He has hard muscles and tattoos everywhere. Twin birds sit on either side of his pecs, a huge flower surrounded by smaller ones in the center of his torso, a flock of tiny birds over his abs, and the one line above his pubic region *la petite mort*.

I've seen all those before. The one I haven't seen …

Running between one hip bone and the next, right above his cock, are the words, *Welcum to the fun zone.*

I bark out a laugh. "Wow. Your tattoos really are like an instruction guide for sex. Just how dumb are the guys you hook up with?"

"Well, you're one of them. Why don't you tell me?"

I almost quip that this has nothing to do with his winning personality, but making this about looks with everything he's told me doesn't sit right. His personality is his defense, and I need to work *with* him on that, which doesn't include putting him down. So I swallow back my pride at letting him get the final word in and decide to tease him instead.

"Feel free to join me in the shower, but nothing's happening until you admit you liked today."

"I didn't *not* like it?"

I smile at his hopeful tone. "Nope."

He acts unaffected, even though his cock is saying otherwise. "You're really not that irresistible. I can get through one shower without wanting to fuck you."

"Pity." I lean in closer. "Because when I have a man in the shower with me, all I want to do is eat his ass."

I don't wait for his reply before I head into the shower and duck under the spray. Water runs through my hair and into my eyes and cuts out most of the sound in the room. I have no idea what Oskar is doing, if he's left or planning to join me, but a moment later, I hear a soft splash as he approaches.

His shoulder softly bumps mine, knocking me out from under the showerhead as he takes my place. For a few minutes, we don't say anything, just pass the bodywash back and forth, silently fighting for the water as we wash ourselves from head to toe. I greedily watch him wash his cock, and then he turns around and dips his hand into his crack.

"I like to clean everywhere," he says.

"Always a good idea. You never know what might happen."

"Especially when I'm going out with Aleks."

This time, I'm prepared, and I try not to let it show how his taunt makes me want to punch a wall. "It's astounding you think I'm letting you and Aleksander Emerson loose in Las Vegas. I'm going with you."

"I don't recall inviting you."

"Not your choice. You know what is your choice though? Whether or not you're relaxed for the game or sexually frustrated."

"You're really sticking to your guns, huh?" Oskar's tone is more amused than pissed off.

"Willpower of steel, remember?"

"And yet you're currently naked in a shower with me. Does that mean I win?"

"It means I let you win *here*, so long as you let me win when it comes to our careers. Believe me, I'm good at this game."

"I've been playing games my whole life, and believe *me*. I play to win." There's a slight edge to his voice, and I wonder if he's thinking back to the shitty situations he's been in.

And like usual, that need to protect strikes hard. Even as I try to push it away, I'm already working out how to distract him from all that. "What's the prize?"

He isn't expecting that question. "I haven't figured that out yet. But I'd start with a rim job."

"You know what to say. Just three little words." I tick them off on my fingers. "*I liked today* or *I enjoyed myself* or even better—*you were right*. That's it."

Oskar holds up his hand, three fingers raised, and I think he's about to do it. "Go"—he folds down his thumb—"fuck"—his forefinger is next—"yourself." Then he gasps, pretending to be shocked over his middle finger still standing.

"Looks like I'm going to have to," I say, turning back to the water.

Oskar reaches for my cock, and I swat his hand away. "Consent, Oskar."

"Consent? You followed *me* into the bathroom." Despite his complaint, he doesn't try to touch me again. He crosses his arms and leans against the tile, clearly pouting. I take the moment of silence to check him out. My gaze runs from his wet, slicked-back hair down his gorgeous scruffy face, over his chest, his water-slicked abs, the glorious cock, and his strong legs.

Oskar shifts, and his voice comes out as a rasp. "If you eye-fuck me any harder, my prostate will feel it."

"I'm more than happy for your prostate to get involved."

"Then—"

"You have to say the words."

"You're an asshole."

My lips hitch up on one side. I hold his stare. I'm desperate to give in and touch him anyway, but I'm trying to get him to stop lying to himself, and he needs to admit this more than he needs an orgasm.

"Fine," he huffs. "I maybe enjoyed it. Can I touch your cock now?"

"Not if sex is going to be as half-assed as that confession."

"What do you want?" he almost whines. "I said it, and you're still being a dick."

I take two steps, closing the small distance between us, and press my body up against him. My arms cage his head in, and this close, he has no choice but to meet my eyes. "I want you to drop the act."

"What act?"

"That you don't care about anything."

"You give me way too much credit if you think my attitude is all an act." He ruts his hips against mine.

"Not really. You're just incredibly stubborn." My lips find his exposed neck, and for all my talk about willpower, I'm quickly losing this game. Not only is he sexy and naked and willing, but after today, I'm more attracted to him than ever. Seeing him genuinely happy isn't something I ever thought I'd witness.

He gasps as my lips work over his skin, leaving rough red marks behind. "Ah, yes," he mutters, hands closing over my ribs. "That feels ... damn ... so good."

My head is getting foggy with want, and this time, I rock my hips into his. My kisses are getting rougher, and I want so much more. I'm getting desperate, and Oskar's killing me with the noises he makes.

"Say it," I growl against his ear. "I need my mouth on your hole *now*."

His grip on me tightens. "Fine. *Fine*. I liked it. It was fun, and I forgot what I was even doing there, and you were right, okay?"

I pull back, grin almost splitting my face. "I was right?"

"What? No. My brain is swamped with horniness. Practically drunk. People say dumb things all the time when they're drunk. I didn't mean a single word."

I want to push him and make him admit it, to hear those perfect words again and again, but relenting to me the first time took a lot out of him, and I know when to push and when to back off. And right now, Oskar needs to be rewarded.

I push off the wall and trail my hands down his sexy body to wrap around his cock. "I'm going to make this so good it'll be all you can think about tonight."

His blue eyes light up with a challenge. "I'll be out with Aleks, so you really better bring your A game."

And I know he's only trying to push my buttons, but it's working anyway. I grip his cock harder, almost painfully. "I can guaran-fucking-tee that bumbling baby bi can't give you what I can."

"Oh yeah?" he asks, shifting his legs farther apart. "And what makes you so sure?"

"Because I know how to give you exactly what you need." I walk out of the shower to where I've dumped my clothes and return a moment later.

"What are you ..."

I lift up my phone, crossing to where the counter is opposite the shower, and water drips all over the tile as I open my camera and hit Record. "We're going to make a little sex tape."

Oskar's surprise is genuine, and as he hesitates, my PR heart warms. It's possible I might be changing his habits. But that's not the part of me that's driving this, and while I don't want to ruin the illusion by pointing out that (a) it will be deleted as soon as this is over, and (b) there's so much steam in here you won't be able to make out much anyway, I also don't want him to worry.

I join him back in the shower and press him against the wall again. "Trust me," I say against his ear.

And when I pull back to see his tiny nod, he's looking at me like ... nope. I'm not reading into things.

Sex. That's what we're focused on here.

"I hope neither of us gets out of here and fumbles that recording," I say. "It would be a shame if we accidentally sent it to everyone."

He lets out a long, shaky exhale.

"I probably should have paid more attention," I say, kissing my way down his body. "But I couldn't wait to get back in here with you. Now I can't remember if I opened my camera app or social media."

His abs contract under my lips.

"Oh no. What if I hit the go live option? What if thousands and thousands of people are currently watching?"

His wet hands slap against the tile.

"Seeing you squirm for me. Seeing all the filthy, filthy things I'm about to do to you."

"Holy shit," he gasps, and he already sounds wrecked.

I tilt my head back to look up at him, then drag my tongue over the head of his cock. "All those people watching *you*. About to see me completely fucking own you."

I've never seen someone's pupils dilate so quickly.

"Turn around."

I barely shift back in time for him to spin and plant his hands on the wall. Then his delicious ass is hovering right in front of my face. My eyes almost roll back in my head, and I can't stop myself from reaching down and giving myself a few pumps. The water pouring over me makes the action sound pornographic, and Oskar glances over his shoulder.

"No fair." He tilts his ass back more. "I've been good."

The *crack* of my hand finding his ass cheek echoes through the room.

Oskar strangles a cry. "Do that again."

I chuckle. "I'd rather do this."

My hands close over his firm glutes, and I spread his ass wide, then bury my face between his cheeks. Oskar might be the king of promiscuity, but I know sex. *Good* sex. Not just quickies and orgasms—which are great in their own right—but from everything I've seen and everything that Oskar's told me, I'd be willing to bet that the amount of real, mind-blowing sex he's had could be counted on one hand. And I plan on erasing every one of those times from his memory.

My mouth closes over his hole, sucking gently, then following it up with a long lick from his taint to the top of his crease. He tastes like Oskar but stronger, sexier, and I can't stop my moan from slipping out.

My cock is aching to be touched, but I ignore it, reaching between Oskar's legs to wrap my hand around him instead. It's no surprise he's so proud of his cock—he's a perfect handful, long, smooth, with perfectly proportioned balls. I dip my head between his legs to suck one of his balls into my mouth.

"Lean forward more," I tell him, and he immediately follows the instruction.

I spit in my hand and start to rub his hole as I suck on his balls and slowly ease his cock back between his legs. I want it all. Just one part of him isn't enough, and when Oskar's hips rotate the tiniest bit, I know he feels the same.

The delicious gasp he lets out when I wrap my mouth around the tip of his cock, how he trembles when I nip at his balls and presses his ass back as I slip a finger inside him ... it's all making me want to stand up and replace my finger with my cock.

But to do that, I'd have to stop and find a condom, and there's no way I'm moving away when I've got him right where I want him.

My mouth travels up and down, wanting to devour every inch of him. Between the water, spit, and his precum, I've made a mess that I can't stop chasing with my tongue.

"Can't wait to watch this back," I tell him, and *fuck*, I wish that was a possibility. "To see you bent over like this." I drag my teeth over his taint as I keep lightly stroking his dick. Oskar's vocals are magic, echoing off the tile. "I'm going to get myself off every night to the sounds you're making. While you're at practice, I'm going to watch the way you begged for me, and you'll be on that ice, skating with your teammates, knowing I'm touching myself over you, desperate for you ..."

He whines. "Lane ... I need ... Damn it, I need ..."

"You're so loud. I bet the people in the next room can hear us. I hope they don't call the front desk. I hope the front desk staff aren't on their way up here to find out what all those filthy sounds you're making are from."

He pounds his fist against the tile. "Fuck me."

"No."

"Please. I need you inside me."

"Fine." But not how he thinks. I press my face into his ass, and my tongue finds his hole. It's already soft from being worked open, and I push inside easily. Eagerly.

His gasps and grunts are everything I need to hear as I work him deeply with my tongue. I start and stop, draw him out, tease him over and over. I keep my grasp on his shaft light and his cock pulled back to hold off his orgasm, even as I knead his balls roughly with my other hand.

"Asshole," he whines. "Such an asshole."

I'm smiling the whole time.

Sex with Oskar is fun.

I let his balls go to spread him open more, pressing my face as deep as it will go. My short beard is rubbing against his ass, and a small part of me hopes I leave him with a dull burn that he feels all night. Something to keep me on his mind while he plays and then is out with his friends.

Eating his ass shouldn't be as addictive as it is, but in my defense, he's a hockey player, and the thing in my face is easily the sexiest ass I've ever seen. My cock is desperate to get in on the action, but I refuse.

I *am* conscious that he has a game soon, so while I'd love to play with him all night, I reluctantly bring his cock back to the front and start to stroke with purpose. My tongue spears in and out, and I press a finger in to rub his prostate, and he pushes back against it before fucking into my fist. I've lost track of what he's saying—it's all nonsensical words and noise by this point, and I love every bit of it.

Until—

"I'm ... I'm—" His groan cuts off his words as his whole body tenses right before he lets go. His orgasm paints the tile, spurt after spurt, until he shudders and goes boneless.

I give his hole one final swipe with my tongue before I stand up behind him. "I could be wrong, but it looked like you enjoyed that."

He presses his face to the wall. "I'm usually an awesome liar, so I hate that I can't deny it."

"Your brain cells aren't all firing, so that's understandable." I almost make a joke about there only being one of them, but I don't have it in me to insult him right now. So instead of those words, I drop a kiss on his shoulder. "Better get ready for the game."

"I want to suck you off first."

"Nope." I press my aching cock against his ass, hating the next words about to come out of my mouth. "You're going to go to dinner, and when you get back, my cum is going to be your dessert."

Chapter Eighteen

Oskar

I'm still on a high from having a good day and an even better afternoon in the shower that, when I hit the ice, I'm unstoppable.

Almost to the point I suspect Tripp of taking pity on me for having a full-time babysitter and letting me score. Not only am I blocking any attempts on our own goal by making sure Vegas can't even get into position to take a shot, but I've even got myself a Gordie Howe hat trick: a goal, an assist, and a fight in the same game.

I didn't even start the fight, so I only got five minutes and McGillan got ten, giving San Jose a power play that put us solidly in the lead.

Vegas is falling apart in frustration, and it fuels me. I mean, aww, poor Dex and Tripp. But no, seriously, this game is amazing.

It's the best playing I've done in a while, and that's saying something because I've got serious beard burn in my ass, *and* I always play great. The terrible practice is forgotten, and I'm at the top of my game. If only I could go out after this and celebrate the way I normally would.

Instead, I'll be forced to behave myself with my watchful prison guard hovering. His promises of what will happen after will have to get me through. And as much as

I might pretend to pout about it, I'm looking forward to blowing him again.

Dancing into the locker room after an epic win helps keep up my energy. Everyone is on a high, and even though we'd usually be going out as a team to celebrate, they all know I have other plans.

"Remember to thank Tripp for us," Jarett says.

"Because that won't rub salt into the wound or anything. They're having a really shitty season. I'm going to go easy on him."

"Really?" Jarett asks.

"Fuck no."

We all laugh, but honestly, I won't be gloating. The Collective is about supporting each other. Even if we sometimes might be *overprotective* of each other.

We cool down, shower, and dress, and Aleks approaches me, his face ashen. "I'm ready."

"Are you sure?" I look him up and down. "You look like you're about to wet yourself. The Collective is a no-judgment zone. Well, unless you deserve it. Then we will rip you to pieces."

"You're making me feel so much calmer," he deadpans. Then he glances around the locker room. "It's not the Collective I'm nervous about. It's …"

"Everyone else? You don't have to tell anyone you're not ready to."

"Going out with you tonight instead of them might tip them off."

I sometimes forget what it's like to be worried about people finding out about me. I've been out for so long it's part of my identifier. People see me as Oskar Voyjik: gay hockey player with all the depth of a fuckboy.

"Want me to text you Tripp's address and we can go separately?"

He thinks about it but then says, "Screw it," and turns to the team. "Hey, guys. I won't be going out with you either. I'm going out with Voyjik."

There are some confused glances, but it's mostly shrugged off.

"Because I'm bi," Aleks adds.

"That makes more sense than what I was thinking," Rosky says.

"What were you thinking?" I ask.

"That your fifth PR rep abandoned you, and because Aleks is old and responsible and whatever, he's been put in charge of your ass."

In perfect timing, Lane enters the room as the press conference ends, and I can't resist.

"I've already told Aleks he can be in charge of my ass anytime he likes."

Everyone laughs. Except for Lane.

Mission accomplished.

"I still have my very own babysitter." I gesture toward Lane.

"You know you wouldn't need one if you knew how to keep your dick in your pants," Jarett says.

"It's a constant fight." I reach for my fly.

Everyone's used to my antics, so they turn back to their cubbies to finish getting ready to head out instead of acknowledging me. They all learned quickly that responding urges me on.

Aleks leans in close to me. "Can you please be there for every time I come out?"

I grip his shoulder. "I'm there for you anytime you need the focus taken off you and put on me. Just say the word. I'm good at causing a scene."

"So I've heard. And ... saw."

I can't be sure, but I think Aleks is referring to my awesome sex tape in the alleyway.

"Ready to head out?" Lane's gruff tone sends shivers down my spine, and there's no way I'm going to make it all night without claiming my prize. I want his cock in my mouth, and I'm going to spend the next few hours teasing him to move up his timeline.

I don't want to wait until we're back in the hotel room.

The three of us leave together and get a rideshare to Tripp's apartment. He lives so close to the Strip, I can't deny it was smart for Lane to come. What wasn't smart for him was cutting me off so he could slide inside the car before me so I couldn't sit in the middle next to Aleks, who got in on the other side.

I don't think Lane realizes how much his jealousy act turns me on.

On the ride to Tripp's, I widen my legs so our thighs are pressed against each other.

He glares at me, but hey, this is his fault. He voluntarily sat between two hockey players in the back of a Mazda 3. It's cozy. Only made cozier by me taking up more room than I really need to.

I wink at him, so his frown deepens.

I love it.

We arrive at Tripp's way too soon, because I've never had this much fun in the back of an Uber before. Oh, wait, that's a lie. I once hooked up with an Uber driver when playing an away game in LA, but I dunno, this might even be better than that.

That was sex. This is like fore-foreplay. It's a lead-up, and sometimes, that can make the payoff even more explosive.

Plus, I dunno. I like being around Lane. Teasing him. Messing with him. I like knowing that I can affect him when he's normally so in control. *I'm* the one who makes him slip.

I'm not worth it, but that doesn't seem to be stopping him.

When I enter Tripp's apartment, both he and Dex look sullen.

"Okay, let's have it," Tripp says. "Let the gloating begin."

Lane follows me in and then Aleks. Surprise flits through Tripp's eyes, but he schools it fast.

"Instead of gloating, I figured I'd offer the Collective a present. New blood."

Tripp's gaze ping-pongs between Lane and Aleks. "I don't think PR reps are included in our arrangement. Lane's always welcome, but he can't officially join or anything."

"It's me," Aleks says and then screws up his face. "Can I come out publicly already?" he asks Lane. "Then at least everyone will know, and I won't have to awkwardly fumble every time I blurt *I'm bi*."

Lane looks sympathetic but says, "We want you to be legally divorced before you say anything, or people are going to think you left Rebecca for a man. And I know it's not the thing you want to hear, but it's probably best if you focus on dating women first before you even think about being seen with a man, or the public will come to their own conclusions."

"That's such bullshit," I mutter, and everyone agrees.

Even Lane. "I know it is, but we don't want to be perpetuating stereotypes that all bisexual men will leave their female partners for other men because they can't make up their minds. Or worse, that he's saying he's bi to hide that he's actually gay. That misconception needs to be changed. So the plan is divorce. Date a couple of women. You don't even need to go on second dates. I can arrange for you to date some B-list celebrities, and then after a few, you can come out and date whoever you want."

"It sucks that I'm ready to take that leap and tell the world. No, I'm *available* to take that leap. I've been ready for years but saw no real point in it when I was happily married. Maybe I should've done it sooner, and then there wouldn't be all this red tape with coming out."

"I understand," Lane says. "I really do. But being a public figure—"

"I know." Aleks sounds so dejected. "I just wanted to point out that it sucks."

I slap his shoulder. "Welcome to the club of sucky double standards purely because we're awesome. And on that note, let's celebrate the glorious win tonight by drinking all of Tripp and Dex's expensive whiskey."

"Oh, so fun for me," Lane says.

"Babysitting is your job here, isn't it?" I drag Aleks to where Tripp keeps his liquor.

I pull out a bottle of Jack Daniel's and glasses from under the counter.

"No Macallan tonight?" Tripp asks.

"Nope. Not enough of us here to induct Aleks. Could you imagine Ezra's face if we did that without him? He loves those things."

Tripp nods. "True. I used to think it was because he was expanding his hookup pool, but now that he's with Anton, he's still just as excited to welcome new members." He gasps. "Could ... Ezra be ... thoughtful and supportive?"

We all contemplate it for a moment.

I shake my head. "Nah. Not possible. Must be something else."

"Agreed," Tripp and Dex say in unison.

Aleks looks from one to the other. "You guys seem fun."

"We are. And don't worry, Ezra will throw you your own welcome party when the time comes."

"When I'm allowed to." Aleks side glances at Lane.

"Hey, we're both on Lane's leash now. Ooh, kinky." I smile at Lane and lift a glass in his direction. "Come on. Live a little. We promise to be good boys for you."

I love the way Lane looks like he's trying to decide between yelling at me, spanking me, or fucking me right here in front of everyone.

And even with all that, I'm sure I pick up a twinkle of ... tolerance? Amusement?

Dex whispers to Tripp, "I know I'm usually slow, but he's trying to tempt Lane into a threesome, right?"

Tripp snorts.

"Even I'm not that stupid to think Lane would break his rules for me." Lies. My goal is to get him to break *all* of them for me, and I'm off to a great start.

Instead of playing my game, Lane reaches for the glass of whiskey. "I'm going to need this tonight."

"He's getting used to me, I swear."

Tripp pats my head. "I've never known someone to be proud of almost being tolerated, but you pull it off."

"I have really low standards for my friends. And hookups. Actually, I just have really low standards."

Everyone in the room says, "We know."

And even though we're all joking around—myself included—it does sting to realize I am actually at that point.

Lane makes me see that I really don't have much self-respect. I've known it for a long time, but it's finally hitting home how sad that is. I thought I was happy and living my best life. But as much as going out and hooking up with randos who didn't give a shit about me was fun, I'm realizing I never once got the validation I needed from them.

I don't think I'll ever have that.

And that's kinda depressing.

Maybe Lane's right and I don't have to be that persona all the time. Maybe it's time to pull back. It's scary even contemplating it, but I originally started doing it to protect myself, and now it's risking my entire livelihood.

I hate to agree with Lane, but ... it's time to grow up.

That's so fucking gross.

My gaze seeks out his, and I regret it instantly. His face is pinched with concern, like he's picked up on the change in me, and of course he has. It's rare I try to hide my moods because no one cares enough to pay attention. Except him. He catches everything.

I quickly look away.

We carry our drinks out onto Tripp's terrace and take seats surrounding his automatic gas firepit. The thought crosses my mind that it would be better to step back from Lane and this messed-up system we have where he'll get me off if I do all the PR things he wants me to, but at the same time, it's probably the only reason I haven't self-destructed yet.

Putting myself out there like I did today with the Rainbow Raiders was daunting, but I'm glad I pushed through and did it, and the only thing that got me there was the promise of another orgasm from Lane.

I could put blind trust into him and do whatever he says because it will be good for my image, or I could keep using his incentives as a reward for putting myself out there time and time again.

When our eyes lock again, his promise to feed me his cock for dessert flits through my mind, and I decide I need to take baby steps.

Just because I've decided to pull in line and grow up, that doesn't mean I'm ready to leave my fuckboy status behind completely.

That's obviously all this need is.

It has nothing to do with the fact I'm starting to like having Lane's attention.

Chapter Nineteen

Lane

I'm not superstitious—not like a hockey player, anyway—but even I'm hesitant to jinx this. I think ... I think this might be working. I noticed the shift after the game in Vegas, Oskar lost some of that extravagant personality he always puts on, and now he's almost subdued.

Well, subdued for him.

He's humming when I walk into the kitchen and pull out a stool at the counter. "Nice sleep?" I ask.

"Yeah, it was okay."

"You're in a good mood."

"I'm always in a good mood." He flashes me a smile from where he's frying eggs. "Breakfast?"

"I didn't know you could cook."

He winks. "There you go underestimating my pretty face again."

"It's less because you're pretty and more because it's been about a month now, and I've never actually seen you do it."

"Yeah, well, we're on the road half the time, and I'm usually too beat from the season to do much more than order in. Plus, my babysitter has been keeping me fed." Oskar's back is to me as he cooks, but even without being able to see his face, I can tell he's relaxed. There wasn't the usual derision on the word *babysitter*, and his shoulders aren't tight like usual.

My stare slides over his back muscles, which bunch and smooth out as he moves, and it makes me want to crowd up behind him and slip my hands down his sweats. I don't though. Because I have restraint.

We haven't had as much sex as I'd assumed this week, but after Vegas and his shift in mood, I've left it up to Oskar to initiate things. Unlike him, I can go long stretches of time before the itch becomes too much, and he knows where I'm at with everything. He has the green light, and I'm leaving it up to him to decide when to use it.

If he can keep it in his pants without me having to keep him satisfied, that's a *good* thing. Fewer chances for us to get caught. Fewer opportunities for me to get hooked on him. It's good. *All* good. Except for the part where I picture him getting it from somewhere else and end up blind with jealousy.

Luckily, I keep those moments to myself.

"Even though you didn't answer me, I'm going to assume you want some," he says, that low voice way too sexy for this time of the morning. "How many eggs?"

"Three. I'll get the coffee."

"I'd assume you're being nice, but I feel like it's more of a self-preservation thing."

"How so?" I ask.

"Because you don't trust me not to poison the food, and I don't trust you not to poison my coffee." The teasing look he throws my way makes me a little too happy. "Guess we're just going to have to take that risk."

"I like risks."

"I know. That's why you're here."

I pour our coffees, and Oskar steps closer than he needs to take it from me.

"The chances of you offing the star player on the team are slim though. Whereas I've wanted to get rid of you since you started this job as my shadow."

"Get rid of me?" I cock my head. "Or get under me?"

He laughs as he steps back and hands me my plate. "Eat this and find out."

I retake my seat, and Oskar pulls one up opposite me. The smell of bacon and eggs makes my stomach growl, and even if I really thought there was the possibility for him to lace it with something, I'd probably still take my chances.

I lock eyes with Oskar as I spear a piece of egg and pop it into my mouth. His lips twitch, and then he grabs his coffee and takes a slow sip, still watching me over the cup.

"How are you feeling?" I ask.

"Good. You?"

"Completely fine."

"Give it a minute, then."

I marvel at how ridiculous he is, then set my fork down. "We haven't argued as much this week."

"I'm happy when I'm not horny."

I narrow my eyes because we both know that's bullshit.

"What? You were expecting a heart-to-heart or something?"

"Or something. You're definitely not ... *you*."

He throws his hands up. "First I'm *too* me, now I'm not *enough* me. What do you want?"

That's a good question. Obviously as his PR rep, my answer is for him to keep doing what he's doing, but as me ... I *like* Oskar. And I hate that I like him. I give him the realest answer I can.

"I want you to be you but without all the media attention."

"That's an oxymoron."

"Big word."

He taps his temple. "I'm smart if you haven't noticed."

"I didn't." I smile at him through a bite of bacon. "At least until this week. You've been making smart choices."

He shrugs awkwardly. "I don't know what you want me to say."

"I'm interested to know why."

"You want me to spill all my secrets? Open up? Be vulnerable to my jailer so I can see that you've cared all along? I've seen that movie, and it's called Stockholm syndrome and isn't as romantic as people think."

Damn him, he gets an actual laugh out of me. "Fine, don't talk to me. We'll eat breakfast in complete silence. That won't be awkward at all."

"What about you? I'm always the one sharing. You tell me something."

"Like …"

"Well, even big bad babysitters have to come from somewhere, right? What lab did they make you in?"

"One in Texas."

Oskar blinks. "Southern boy? No way."

"*Deep* South. I basically have sunshine in my veins."

"That explains the sunny personality, then, though not your lack of accent. What about your parents?"

"What about them?"

"What are they like?"

"I haven't seen them in a long time." I keep my tone light and airy, but I don't think I pull off the nonchalant act. It's hard to do when it comes to my parents.

Oskar's cocky expression dims, which makes me think he's come to two conclusions: dead or disowned. "Why?"

"The gay thing." I keep my voice light because even though it was fucked-up, I've long worked through my issues with them. "And at least they cared enough to fill up my bank account before they shoved me out the front gate."

Oskar drops his fork loudly onto his plate. "Assholes. Want to invite them to a game and I'll shoot a puck at their heads?"

"Aww, I didn't know you cared."

"No one should have to go through that. Even you."

"I detect a level of affection buried under all that animosity," I tease. "But it's okay. I have a great life."

He lifts a skeptical eyebrow. "At what point during getting your college degree did you stop and think, 'following around a professional hockey player to make him behave himself sounds like my idea of a dream job?'"

"Never. Obviously. It was more, 'following around a professional hockey player sounds like perfect spank bank material. Go, future Lane!'"

My insides thrum happily as he laughs. I watch him practically inhale the rest of his food before throwing back what's left of his coffee. "This has been fun, but I gotta go. Are you driving me in today?"

I hesitate over the question. The answer should be *of course* because letting him go anywhere alone is dangerous, so I'm unnerved when my answer is, "You go. Keerson has been trying to get me to go out for lunch, and, well, you've done well this week. I think you've earned a day off without your babysitter."

He stares at me like he's waiting for me to go on. "Wait. You're serious."

"I am."

"This isn't one of those situations where you say I can go and then follow me, is it?"

"No."

"Even though *Aleks* will be there."

I try really hard not to clench my jaw. "As much as we both like to pretend I'm in control of you, if you really wanted to go and screw up, you would. With or without me. But remember ..." I stand and round the counter to stop in front of him. Then I tilt my lips to his ear, "If you choose Aleks, this thing with us is done. And no amount of teasing and flirting and fucking yourself in bathrooms will change that."

His stool makes him a fraction shorter than me, and I love the look in his eyes when he glances up at me. "Noted." He grabs the front of my shirt and tugs me in closer. "But if you're not going to follow me, how would you ever know?"

"Because ..." My eyes fall closed for a second, unable to believe these words are about to come out of my mouth. "I'm choosing to trust you. For an entire day. To make your own decisions. Keep yourself out of the headlines and be back here for dinner, and I'll make it worth your while."

"Oh, *really*?"

"Don't get too excited," I point out, stepping away. "You have to do it first."

"I think you're underestimating a hockey player's need to win."

"Maybe, but I think I'm estimating your need for trouble *just* fine."

He gets up and grabs his plate, but I take it from him. "I'll clean up. You go."

"I could get used to all this domestic shit. You cooking for me most nights *and* cleaning now? Plus orgasms on top? Heaven."

I sigh as he slaps me on the ass and bounces away to get ready.

Then I spend the morning hoping I haven't made the wrong decision again.

"You're game," Keerson says. "A whole day? You do know the trouble Oskar can get himself into with that much time at his disposal, don't you?"

"We'll see."

"Quick, let's email the PR department and place bets on what he's going to do to make our lives hell." He grabs his phone, and I pluck it from his grip.

"No need. Oskar has been on track the last few days, so I've given him a few hours off. He knows if he wants any more than that, he'll need to play nice." I don't bother getting into the real reasons with Keerson. How Oskar found out his talent isn't enough to coast on for the rest of his career. I think seeing an actual consequence outside of the multiple slaps on the wrists he's had has been a reality check for him, and ... I'm not convinced Oskar *wants* to be that guy.

Which is not a thought I should be having. Tempting my protective side is an idiot move.

Keerson stares at me, disbelief all over his face. "He's really got you fooled."

"I guess we'll find out."

"This isn't like ..." He lets out a quick burst of air. "I know you're a professional, and you're one of the best

PR bosses I've had—way better than the last one—but ... you don't want to sleep with him, do you? Like, it's Oskar Voyjik, so you probably do, but you *wouldn't* is what I'm saying ... right?"

I chuckle. "You don't need to worry about me." I've already crossed every possible career line there is.

"Phew. *I* think he's hot, and I'm straight—I can't imagine how it is for a gay guy."

"The same as any other man. I have a type, and I have self-control." And maybe if I keep telling myself that, it'll be true at some point. "Both mine and Oskar's careers are tied together. If I don't want to be his shadow for the rest of his time in the NHL, then I need to make sure he can be trusted to make his own choices. Otherwise, what's the point of all this?"

"I guess, but ... man. That's a big ask. I barely lasted as long as you have now, and by the time I was done, I was ready to smother him with his own pillow."

"Oh, I've been there, trust me." I've also smothered him with my cock a few times, which has been fun. "But I get enough of Oskar in my day. How's the family?"

Keerson is easily distracted and fills me in on everything from potty training to new words to his wife's morning sickness. And as sweet as it is when he talks about them, it makes me happier than ever that kids are not in my future.

We're almost done with lunch when my phone dings, and I'm hit with a sinking feeling. I only have one email account set up with a notification sound—the others get too many emails to bother—and there's only one thing I use that email for.

Google alerts on the players.

I take a deep breath and hold it as I open the notification, hoping and begging that it will be any other name

but the one I'm expecting. One glance at the subject line dashes all my hopes to hell.
Oskar Voyjik.
Motherfucker.

Chapter Twenty

Oskar

After taking the millionth selfie for the day with kids from this LGBTQ youth center I found online, my cheeks hurt. And as annoying and long as today has been, I'm glad I came here after practice.

When Lane forced me to go to that hockey rink with the Rainbow Raiders, I realized that I'm not doing enough. My aversion to teenagers because of how miserable I was when I was one shouldn't have stopped me from doing all this community crap, but I figured with the way my image was in the media, they wouldn't have wanted me anyway.

I was wrong.

Kimberly is the director here, and her face lit up when I walked in. Aleks wanted to come too, but I told him Lane would be pissed if he started hinting at his sexuality. Not that volunteering at an LGBTQ charity automatically means he's queer, but I told him he shouldn't risk it anyway.

Look at me thinking about Lane's job and being responsible.

Plus, I sort of wanted to do this for myself.

I was planning to come here with my shadow to show Lane I'm using some initiative, but when he trusted me, I wanted to prove to him that I can take his trust seriously.

Eww, who am I?

Kimberly approaches me as the last kid finally gets his photo. Some of them here don't have a phone, so Kimberly took them on hers, and that's just sad. What teenager doesn't have a phone? Then again, from what Kimberly told me when I came in to volunteer, some of these kids don't even have *homes*.

Because of people like Lane's parents, who promise to love their children no matter what and then abandon them for being something they can't change. That's not love.

I wouldn't be where I am today if my parents hadn't been supportive. I know for a fact I'd be a statistic. Because when you feel all alone, your parents should be the ones to tell you that you're not.

Kimberly smiles at me. She's around fifty and looks like she's run ragged but in a good way. If there is a good way to look bone-tired. "I'm sorry they've been a lot to handle today. If you come back to volunteer, you won't be so shiny and new."

"Don't worry about it. The kids have been really great."

"I see you ignored my come back to volunteer talk though."

I did, but maybe not for the reason she thinks. "I'd actually love to come back, but I'd need to set it up with the team's PR department so they can find something in my schedule. And can I ask, does the center have restrictions on donations? Say, if I wanted to donate new phones with a prepaid amount on them, is that okay?"

"It is. Any and all donations welcome. Though if you want to get them something they really need, clothes, books, and your basic needs is a good idea."

I make a mental note to get all that stuff too. Maybe some jerseys from the team as well.

"I'll go home and talk to my PR guy."

Something that looks like disappointment crosses her face. "No problem."

"What is it?"

"What's what?"

"You look like Lane when I make him a promise."

"Who's Lane?"

"Oh, my PR manager. He wants me to 'clean up my image.'" I dramatically roll my eyes. "Please, I'm a saint."

She doesn't laugh. "Well, I guess *that's* my problem. You seem to only be here for your sake, not the kids. I don't want them to get their hopes up about you coming back and then have you never show. Or worse, show up a couple of times, get your positive publicity, and then walk out on them. They're not a gimmick to be used like that."

Well, shit. "Sorry, I didn't mean it like that at all. Well, I did. But no. I want to come back. I'm going to come back. And I promise I'm not using them for publicity."

"Sure." She nods, and then her smile is back in place, though it doesn't seem as genuine as before. "We look forward to seeing you again."

She so thinks I'm never coming back.

Whether it's reverse psychology or she's seen so much in her life that she doesn't have faith in humanity anymore, it works. Because I will be coming back. And I won't even take credit for it.

Suck on that, charity lady.

—

I expect to be grilled about where I've been all afternoon when I walk through the door, so I have my story all straightened out: male strip club, soliciting hookers, and buying illegal substances.

Only when I pull up out the front of my house and jog up the stairs to the entrance, the door swings open like Lane had been waiting for me that whole time.

It's just gotten dark out, so I'm a little late, but the porch light is on, so I can see every contour of his face. Where I'm expecting anger or disappointment, I'm met with ... something I can't decipher because I don't think Lane has ever looked at me like that before. Like he's genuinely happy to see me.

I don't like it. It's weird. So I throw on my cheeky smirk, put up my hands, and say, "Hey. I promise I only did half of the things you didn't want me to—"

I'm taken off guard by him slamming against me and practically bruising my mouth with his. His tongue forcefully enters my mouth, and my dick is already hard. I have no idea what this is about, where it's come from, or why he's doing it when he can't be sure what I've been up to the last couple of hours, but I'm not going to stop it to taunt him.

Sex is definitely more fun than taunting him. I mean, it's borderline, but shutting up is the smart way to go.

He pulls me inside, and I kick the door closed behind me. We don't part as we stumble through the house, discarding my shoes somewhere along the way. My T-shirt goes next and then Lane's.

He tries to break free of me, but I'm not ready for that yet. I tighten my grip on his hips and hold him against my raging hard-on.

"Get naked for me and bend over the back of the couch," he murmurs against my lips because I refuse to stop kissing him too. Well, until now.

I pull back, and that's when I notice the lube and condoms on the kitchen counter. "Mm, someone's desperate for me. Someone had a plan for when I got home." And fuck, that makes me feel all warm inside, just the thought of Lane waiting for me with anticipation building and the intention of taking me as soon as I walked through the door. Maybe even worried about when I'll get here.

Why is something so domestic making me feel more cherished than any grand gesture from all those rom-com movies?

Ever since hitting it big in the NHL, my life has been that shiny dream most people could only wish for. Hockey gave me money, the notoriety, and the means to do whatever I wanted whenever, so my everyday life has been anything but ... normal. And for the first time ever, I get a glimpse of what actual couples do.

I've never understood the appeal of it. Until now.

I do as he says and strip off the rest of my clothes and bend over the couch so my ass is sticking out.

It feels like an eternity for him to get the supplies from the kitchen counter. I look over my shoulder to see him standing a few feet away, condom already rolled down his thick cock, and he's covering himself in lube while staring at my hole.

"Hurry up," I whine.

His brown gaze meets mine, his lips quirking at the sides. "And when have you ever been in charge of what we do in the bedroom?"

"We're not in the bedroom."

Lane steps forward and smacks my right ass cheek. "Don't be a smart-ass."

My cock leaks at the sting on my skin and the growl in Lane's voice. "But when you do that, it only makes me want to talk back more."

There's another whack on my other side this time, and precum lands on the back of my couch. Thank fuck I was smart enough to get leather. I can't wait to paint it with the load already simmering in my balls.

I want release.

Lane presses his cock against my stinging ass while one hand grips my hair tight and pulls my head back while he uses his other hand to dip lubed fingers down my crack to tease my hole.

All the nerve endings around my ass fire, sending sparks of want down my spine and into my feet. My hips move on their own, rubbing my aching cock against the back of my couch.

His hold on my hair tightens as his fingers breach my hole. He doesn't even start with one but two. I love the pain, crave the sting, and he's giving it to me everywhere. My ass, my hole, my hair. It's so hot.

And then he leans in close to my ear and says the one thing that can make this hotter. "Oops. I forgot to close the blinds that cover the front window."

I look and almost come on the spot at the sight of the bare window and headlights as cars drive by the house.

"If anyone in those cars were to look in here, they'd see you bent over this couch with me behind you."

I can't breathe. My heart's beating too fast, and my whole body buzzes.

There's a tiny voice of reason in the back of my head asking if this is really worth the risk—something I've never had before—but he's driving me so crazy, it's easy to block out. I don't care if I'm caught. That thrill of someone possibly watching gets me harder than any other fantasy I have. But for the first time, I'm thinking of someone other than myself. It doesn't matter if I'm seen like this—I'm in my own home and with only one guy, which is better than in an alley with two other men—but Lane could lose his job if this is exposed.

I'm about to tell him to close the blinds when he replaces his two fingers with his cock.

I'm barely prepped, and he goes slow, but he's so thick the sting is intense. I cry out in pain, and he stills.

"Are you all good?"

I love that he checked, but it's unnecessary. "So good. I love it. I love your cock. Keep going."

"You sound like it's hurting."

"Only in the best way. I promise I'll tell you if it's the wrong kind of pain."

Lane pushes in more, and I almost lose it.

I have to grip my cock hard to get it to calm down.

"Did I say you could touch yourself?" Lane rumbles.

"If I don't, this will all be over in about two seconds."

"It's cute you think that if you come too fast, it'll all be over. It's not over until I'm coming inside you. So unless you want to be fucked until your oversensitive prostate wants to grow legs and run away, you better hold off."

I snort. "Well, with an image of a runaway prostate in my head, I think I'm all good. You really know how to talk sexy to me."

"Well, it worked, didn't it? You're no longer too close to the edge. Now, focus on outside. On every car driving by. Maybe one of your neighbors is walking their dog and happens to glance in here."

"*Urgh*. Now you're bringing me back again."

Lane pushes inside me the rest of the way, bottoming out.

There's this push-pull he's doing, putting me so close to spilling that I swear it's all over, then distracting me with pain or his words until I'm calmer before doing it all again.

It's a sweet, sweet torture, and I never want it to end.

I close my eyes and breathe deep as he begins moving in and out of me in smoother motions, stretching me wide, lazily brushing my prostate.

"Open your eyes," he orders.

"If I close them, I can imagine every single person that goes by watching."

"Whatever fulfills your attention whore fantasy."

He thinks that's an insult, but it really isn't. I *am* an attention whore.

I close my eyes again. "Now, I need you to let go. You need to fuck me like you're putting on a show because, in my head, you are."

"Oh, you want a show? I'll give you a show." Lane doesn't hold back.

He moves in and out of me hard and fast, only getting harder and faster with every thrust. I have to white-knuckle the back of the couch to prevent me from crushing my dick. The slight brush of leather against the head of my cock only adds to the sensory overload, and I can't take much more.

I feel him everywhere. From his commanding presence behind me, the way he moves inside me, the goose bumps he causes to race all over my skin. I've never been so … owned. There's fucking to get off and have fun. And then there's this.

It's everything I've fantasized about but never quite found. The way he's turning me inside out, not only physically but the way he's making me a better person on the inside. Even if I hate it when he tries to drag my baggage into the conversation, there's no denying I've taken more steps to cut the outside act with him more than anyone I ever have.

And as he continues to own me, that sense only grows.

Lane might be the best thing that's ever happened to me, whether I'm willing to admit that aloud or not.

"You're so tight," Lane says. "Now it's my turn to worry about coming too fast."

As much as I'd love to hold out forever, I know it's not going to be possible. "I'm close too. Tell me when you're about to lose it. I want to come together."

"You better start jerking yourself because …" He stops to take a breath. "It's … oh fuck, I'm coming."

My hand flies to my cock, and I jerk fast. Lane's thrusts turn wild before slowing right down, but even then, he changes from short and shallow to hard and deep. He's breathing heavy, slowly coming down, but it's not until he says, "Come, Oskar," that I finally unleash.

It's been so long since I've been turned inside out so thoroughly, I shouldn't be surprised by the amount of cum that decorates the black leather in front of me.

My muscles turn to jelly, and I flop forward, resting my chest in the mess I made while the last few drops hit the floor.

Lane silently pulls out of me and walks away, leaving me exposed, used, and dirty. And yeah, I fucking love that too. When he returns, I flinch because I'm not expecting the warm cloth that runs between my thighs and over my ass, cleaning out all the excess lube.

"Turn around for me," he instructs, his voice losing the edge he had while inside me.

I stand upright and then turn, resting my ass on the back of the couch next to my mess. Lane leans over and licks any cum off my softening dick while wiping down my chest and the couch with the cloth. It feels a hell of a lot like looking after me, and I'm realizing that's a running theme with us.

"Now, I'm definitely not complaining," I say, "but what exactly prompted this little romp?"

He stands again. "I saw what you did today. With the LGBTQ youth shelter. You deserved a reward."

And even though my chest dances with happiness that I made him proud, the rest of those fuzzy feelings about us being domestic and almost like a normal couple die a horrible death.

Because this wasn't an "Oskar is irresistible" thing. This is still an "I need to keep Oskar on a leash" thing.

That shouldn't hurt as much as it does.

I think I'm getting in way too deep here.

Chapter Twenty-One

Lane

Oskar's lying stretched across the other couch, holding his phone high above his head while I work opposite. We'd been as close as two people could be barely half an hour ago, which has to be the only reason all this distance feels wrong.

From where I'm sitting—right beside where we had sex—I have a direct line of sight out the front window, but no one can see in. I know because I checked before Oskar got home. With the porchlight on, all you can see in here with the lights off is shadow.

"Why do I feel like you're ignoring me?" I finally ask.

"How am I supposed to know why you feel what you feel?" His voice is dry, giving away that something's up.

I'd thought things were good. Oskar made a choice today I never would have expected, and the fact he didn't go out to lunch or come here to sulk—or worse, head to a strip club—speaks volumes about where he's at.

Oskar is actually *trying* because he's scared of losing the one thing he truly cares about: hockey.

But while he was happy and relaxed right after we had sex, it's like something tripped in his brain, and that contentment disappeared.

"How was it today?" I ask.

He grunts but doesn't answer.

"Oh, goodie, one of those nights. At least with you ignoring me, it's quiet around here."

Oskar flips me off.

Okay, I'm done with this. I set my laptop aside, then push to my feet and reach over to steal his phone.

"*Hey*."

"Tell me what's going on."

He scowls. "Why? As we've established, therapy isn't in your job description."

I perch on the side of the coffee table, right beside his head. "Did I overstep earlier? Should I not have done that?"

"If I didn't want you to fuck me, I wouldn't have let you fuck me."

"Then where's this attitude coming from?"

He closes his eyes and tucks his hands behind his head. "News flash, I always have attitude."

But stupid me assumed he was changing. Growing. And there I go proving I can't be trusted in these kinds of situations. Both hands scrub over my face as I resist the urge to shake him. Maybe I should have thought things through more, taken a step back today and planned out my next move instead of getting home, scrambling for supplies, and then spending the afternoon pacing the living room as I waited for Oskar to get home so I could pounce on him.

Seeing him being kind and putting himself out there was such a turn-on, I forgot for a moment that I was supposed to be more calculated in my moves.

My laptop dinging alerts me to an email coming in, so I leave him to his weird mood and open the web page.

I still have too many to count left unread, but something about the subject line of this one catches my attention.

Fundraising volunteers needed—LGBTQ players encouraged.

It's from someone named Richard Cohen from Montreal's PR department.

I open the email and skim through the details. A training facility is being opened in Vermont for hockey players ranging from pre-K to eighteen, focusing on readiness for college. The kicker? It's all not-for-profit, and their plan is to supply everything for kids who wouldn't otherwise be able to afford it. Hence, the fundraiser.

It's a great idea—hockey is expensive, and there's a lot of gear involved before you even factor in the cost of training. It's why hockey has always been considered a rich man's sport. Opening the door for talent that wouldn't otherwise get that chance is a game changer.

The email is asking for pro-league volunteers to attend a fundraising day and highlights that LGBTQ players are not only welcome but wanted, as the center wants to send a firm message that *You Can Play* isn't just words.

Before I let my excitement get the better of me, I check what Oskar's schedule looks like. Having an event like this during the season isn't ideal, but the center wants to be up and running for the summer, so it doesn't look like there was much choice there.

This is the kind of thing that would be perfect for Oskar.

The problem is that it's the day before an away game. Normally players take the day for light training and conserving their energy, but his game is in Montreal, so it wouldn't be that far to travel.

I grab my laptop and move to the other couch. Oskar doesn't move, so I lift his legs, sit down, and drop them over my lap.

"Read this."

He skims through the email, and even though he tries to hide it, I swear I catch a hint of excitement. "Could be cool."

"I'm going to reply that you're available."

"Whatever."

It takes a deep breath to stop from returning his attitude. As I'm replying, Oskar picks up his phone and types out a message. It's distracting, and I keep glancing from what I'm doing and over toward the smile he's wearing.

"Aleks?" I ask, not able to keep the disapproving tone out of my voice.

"The Collective, actually. Foster said he's doing that thing. The others are looking into it."

The knot of jealousy lessens. "Good."

We're quiet for a moment, and I can feel him watching me.

"If you have something to ask, just ask it," I say.

"I need your help with something."

That gets my attention. "Is it an orgasm? Because you've already had one of those."

"No ..." Something about his tone makes me glance over. He looks ... uncertain.

Shit. It's such a fine line with him. On one side, I can view him as a petulant hockey player and protect myself; on the other, I see the real him. The one who wants to try and doesn't know how. And as much as I'm holding back, I always find myself slipping onto the side of compassion. It's the side my dumb ass *wants* to be on.

I set my laptop down and turn my attention on him. "Sorry. Let me try again. What do you need my help with?"

"New strategy? Pretending like you care?"

"This might be a complete shock to you—it was to me—but I do care. So how can I help you?"

I'm sure he's going to throw back a taunt, the thought definitely crosses his mind, but at the last moment, he breaks eye contact and clears his throat. "I need to make a donation. But I need it to be anonymous."

Okay, that I can do. "How much?"

"Not money. Phones, day-to-day supplies, shit kids with nothing would want."

Motherfucker. There he goes, making me cross that line again. I rub a hand over my short beard, trying to hide the way my lips twitch happily because the last thing I want is for him to think I'm laughing at him when I'm actually laughing at myself and how one good deed is making me light up inside. "First step is making a list. So why don't we do that, then go pick it all up? The mall is open late tonight, so there's no reason to wait."

He springs upright, the renewed energy making me lighter. His hair is the same chaotic mess it always is, and I can't help reaching over to flatten some of it down.

Oskar freezes for a second but doesn't acknowledge me, just pulls out his phone and starts typing.

"Okay, phones and clothes are a good start. What else?" he asks.

"Practical things. Deodorant, shampoos, bodywash. Think like you have nothing and work your way up to the big things."

He types away, clearly excited but trying to hide it, and we scrape together a list that looks easy enough to obtain—for someone with money. Oskar calls the shelter he was at today to find out how many people are staying there and then gets changed, ready to head out.

Before we reach his car though, I put a hand on his arm to stop him.

The words are harder to get out than they should be. "After my parents kicked me out, I was too embarrassed to go to my friends, and I wasn't out at that point. The shelters in the area were full, and there weren't as many back then, but one of the ones I went to had a woman who let me sleep in the office overnight. The next day, she put me in contact with people who set me up with an apartment to lease in a building full of people in similar circumstances to me. She helped me with my college application, dropped me at the library on the weekends, kept me motivated through the rest of senior year ... I was still in an incredibly privileged position, but she didn't make me feel bad about having money where the others didn't. So ... thank you. What you're doing will make a difference to the people there, and I thought you should know it isn't an empty gesture."

Oskar shifts, looking uncomfortable, before he forces out, "You okay?"

I give his shoulder a playful punch. "I just had incredible sex, my hockey player is behaving himself, and we're about to spend the night doing something charitable. I'd say I'm better than okay."

He unlocks the car and crosses to the driver's side. "Don't tell anyone that somewhere in amongst the black sludge in my chest, there might be some semblance of a heart. I have an image to uphold."

"You better be careful, then, because at this rate, your wayward reputation is going to be more or less ruined. Another couple of weeks and you won't need me anymore."

And isn't that some shit?

Oskar's finally doing everything he's meant to be doing … and there's a small selfish part of me that wishes he wouldn't. Because with the way he's going, I won't have an excuse to stay.

Chapter Twenty-Two

Oskar

After killer back-to-backs where we very narrowly take the wins, I have a rare day with no practice. I've spent the morning lying on the couch, alternating between icing everything that hurts and putting heat on it, and every time Lane looks at me, he tries to hide his amusement, but I know he's laughing on the inside.

I don't hate it as much as I should.

"I heard Caleb Sorensen say when everything hurt, that's when he knew it was time to retire."

"Fuck you. That word isn't allowed in this house. Also, hockey is pain, so that excuse from him was bullshit. He really retired to follow his famous husband on tour."

"Someone's protesting a little too hard about how much pain he's in. Do you have any other plans than feeling sorry for yourself today?"

"Yeah, I have to hit the weight room at some point, but that's it. We have two rare days off to prepare for this next road trip."

"Which has another back-to-back up first," Lane adds. "And then the fundraiser in Vermont, followed by the game in Montreal."

I groan. "Don't remind me."

It's that part of the year where there are only a few weeks left of the regular season, so we're all exhausted yet scrambling for those top spots to head into the playoffs.

"We should do something fun today."

My ears perk up. "Sex? I'm ready." I dump my ice packs on the floor and go to lower my sweats.

"I was more thinking of going out to have fun."

I sit up, my excitement growing. "Strip club? Ooh, BDSM club? Do you want to pass me around and watch me get used by a room full of—"

"Why, when I give an inch, do you take a mile?"

"Firstly, your dick is impressive, but no way is it a mile long. And secondly, you say fun, I think sex. What else could it be?"

"Get changed out of your sweats and find out."

Hmm, to get up or to keep lying here feeling sorry for myself. It's a tough one because the first intrigues me, but my couch is really comfortable. And why, when I joke about being shared, does the thought hold little appeal anymore?

I stand. "Okay, show me this super-fun time." After I change and we get in the car, Lane drives us to the mall and parks right outside ...

"Dave & Buster's? I think we have different ideas of what constitutes as fun. I can't believe I put on underwear for this."

"Come on. Where's your childhood spirit?"

"Thinking about hookers and debauchery." I lean forward and stare up at the sign through the windshield.

"Sometimes, I think I give you far too much credit."

Me too, Lane. Me too.

"I figured being a military brat, you didn't do much of this as a teenager," he says, and he's right.

I was never invited to parties, didn't have many friends. It felt like we were never in the one place long enough for me to make connections. Much like in my hockey career where I keep getting moved.

"My guess from what you've told me is you didn't do a lot of things most kids did. So I brought you here to do all those things."

Damn it. Why did he have to go and make this a good thing? I was prepared to hate it.

"Okay, let's get this over with." I get out of the car and head for the entrance.

Lane follows me inside and says, "Where to first?"

"Bar. Duh."

"Nope. No drinking."

"How is any of this going to be fun if I'm not at least a little buzzed?"

He turns to me. "Are you trying to tell your PR agent that you could be an alcoholic?"

"Yes, because I drink so, so much. All the time," I say dryly.

"Is it bad I half wish you did have an addiction of some kind? At least then it would be easy to handle the media. The threesome in the alleyway was because of a sex addiction. Send you away to rehab, come back out all fresh and acting like a choirboy." Lane taps his chin. "On second thought, would you be willing to fake an addiction? It would make my job a lot easier."

"No," I say immediately. "Especially not a sex addiction. I think celebrities who are caught out sleeping around one too many times are too quick to jump on that for an excuse. It adds to that stigma about sex being shameful when it's not."

"Sex addiction is real, by the way."

"I know, but someone needing it and doing it through any means necessary and someone enjoying it with as many people as he wants are two completely different things."

Lane nods. "I agree with you, and I was only joking about the addiction thing."

"Were you?"

"Sort of. But no, really, you're right. We need to clean your image up with the truth."

I open my arms wide. "Please tell me how this is the truth?"

"Take away hockey, sex, and booze—"

"Kill me now. Just end it. I don't want to live anymore."

Lane backhands me in the chest, and I pretend his pathetic slap hurts, but I can't keep a straight face.

"Stop being dramatic," Lane says.

"I can't help it. It's who I am."

"No. It's not." Lane's words are said with such conviction, like he knows that's not the real me, but that's not possible. He moves closer now, almost pressing against me to the point if people were looking, they'd probably take notice of our proximity. "Here you can be you."

I lower my head and my voice. "You say that like I'm not always who I am. I *am* hockey and cheap hookups."

"But that's not *all* you are," Lane says, and he's so confident, I almost want to believe he's right. In my experience, people only hang around for two reasons: my looks or my ridiculous, over-the-top, fun nature. Sure, those people aren't worth being permanent, but I'm not worth it either, so it works. But Lane doesn't think that personality is me, and he's trying to bring out some good person he thinks exists. If I do that, what then? Am I pretty enough for him to stick around for, or will he get bored of me like everyone else?

"I don't know what else I am," I admit.

As if admitting to something he has wanted to hear all along, Lane softens. "Well, why don't we figure it out?" He looks out at the arcade. "Maybe Oskar Voyjik is a slut, great at hockey, annnnd ..." His gaze moves around the room. "A Skee-Ball champion."

I glance at the games and then back at Lane. I have no idea what Skee-Ball or bowling or video games have to do with who I am on the inside, but we're here now, and I'll give it a go. "You're on."

But it becomes apparent quickly that Skee-Ball is not my game.

"Skee-Ball champion, you are not." Lane laughs when my first two tries earn me absolutely zero points.

"I can get it," I say. "I just need to practice." I roll another ball, and it goes nowhere near one of the holes with a score on it. "Or not. I think you need to be extra talented to score as low as I am."

Lane takes his turn on the ramp beside me, and just when I think he's gone too far left and will get zero like me, the ball shoots up the ramp and lands in the hole in the top corner, scoring one hundred points. "I guess I'm not that talented."

"Why won't my stupid balls get in my stupid hole?"

Lane snorts, and I turn to him, wondering what's so funny.

He shrugs. "You want your balls to go in your hole. It's an ... interesting image."

"I thought *I* was supposed to be the immature one?"

"Oh, come on. One snigger at balls in holes, and suddenly, I'm more immature than you?"

"No. Bringing me here and making me play stupid games that I suck at means you're more immature than me."

"You really hate losing, don't you?" Lane asks.

"I'm a *hockey player*. We all hate losing."

"Okay, Mr. Hockey Player. How about we play some air hockey? Maybe your hockey talent extends off the ice?"

Spoiler: It does not.

No matter what I do to try to stop the little air puck thingy from going in my goal, Lane shoots it right past me. Seven times in a fucking row.

He leans on the table. "I think that's what you guys in the biz call a shutout."

"How are you so good at these games?"

"Well ..." He rounds the table and approaches me. "You weren't the only one with a not-so-fun school experience. I don't exactly know how the popularity chain worked while you were growing up, but while you were moving around the country playing hockey everywhere and being all 'Go, Sports, Go,' us nerdier, non-gorgeous gay kids would go to the arcade on weekends with our other equally nerdy friends because being good at something made us feel better about being losers." The sadness in his stare, the soft tone in his voice ... they make me want to kiss it away and have him go back to gloating.

I swallow hard and then screw up my face. "Eww."

"Eww?"

"Yeah. I almost felt ..." I fake gag. "Sympathy for you there."

"Oh no! What's the world coming to?"

We're smiling at each other before I realize it's happening.

"What did you want to play next?" he asks.

I glance around. "There has to be something here I'm better at than you, and we're not leaving until we find it."

"Or until you can't put off weight training any longer."

I snap my fingers and point at him. "Or that. But there has to be something." One of those old-school games where you have to throw balls at clowns that fall catches my eye. "The clowns." I point.

"Are you sure?" Lane asks in that kind of way where I immediately know I've picked wrong.

He kicks my ass at that, human-size Hungry Hungry Hippos, and even good ol' pinball.

"I think I've worked out something else that you are," Lane says when we're almost out of time to play.

"What's that?"

He steps in so close I can feel his breath on my lips, and then his eyes flutter, his gaze locking with mine. "You're an even bigger loser than I was." Then his lips quirk, and I can't help myself.

I burst out laughing, and somehow, even though he's insulting me, it makes me feel somewhat accepted. Warmth fills me, and I'm lit up with a weird kind of connection I've never felt before. It makes me soften toward him. Makes me want more. It's strong and fierce, and so fucking terrifying.

Chapter Twenty-Three

Lane

"You okay?" I ask Oskar as he buttons his shirt. It's a deep blue, the kind of color that really suits him in a way that makes me want to take it right back off him again. I should get out of bed and dress as well, but I'm too busy basking in postorgasmic bliss.

"I think we both know I'm better than okay." He winks in an overly sleazy way, and I give him a blank look.

"Not what I meant."

He doesn't reply, and I eye the tension in his hands and arms as he does up the final button. Oskar shakes out his limbs and drags a hand back through his hair, disturbing the style I fucked it into. Ever since we landed in Chicago, he's been a little off.

"You're way too stressed for someone who's had two orgasms already today. Do I need to blow you again?"

That finally gets a smile. "Screw you for offering that right as we need to leave." He adjusts himself. "You'll be doing it the second we're back though. You know how horny I get after a win."

"And a loss," I mutter but finally slip out of the sheets because he is right. We need to leave for the game.

He points at me. "Don't even put that out there. Quick …" He raps his knuckles on the wooden side table while I pull on my clothes.

As far as hockey players go, Oskar's not overly superstitious, but I've noticed a few things lately that have been sort of adorable. We're getting close to playoffs, and San Jose is in with a decent shot as long as we can win at least half of the remaining games. Apparently, that can make even the most laid-back players cautious.

Someone pounds on the hotel room door. "You ready, Voyjik?"

Aleks. I temper my annoyance at the interruption. Oskar is going through something, and I wanted him to get it off his chest before he goes out there tonight, but I think Oskar would rather abstain from sex for a year than admit he might be feeling the pressure.

Oskar grabs his suit jacket and slings it over his arm. "You coming?"

I sit on the end of the bed to pull on my shoes and socks before I'm ready to get out there.

Before Oskar, I was at every single game like a good PR manager should be, but since taking on this new role of babysitting, I've been having Keerson watch the home games while I've caught up on work and delegated rising issues to my subordinates.

I've always paid attention, but with following Oskar everywhere he goes this season, I've spent more time focusing on him than the general game, and I've finally taken notice of Oskar in his prime. I thought everyone who'd sing Oskar's praises before my self-imposed assignment with him were kiss-asses. I'd thought people were exaggerating his importance on the team as an excuse to dismiss his poor behavior. But I was wrong.

From the second Oskar hits the ice in every game, a special kind of magic takes over. Plays happen. We have more time in our offensive zone. The morale even seems to be boosted. It finally makes sense why San Jose is so determined to keep him.

I follow Oskar out into the hall, where Aleks gives me a friendly wave. It's so hard to resist my urge to stare him down, to make it clear Oskar won't be going anywhere near his dick, but Aleks is a San Jose player too, and it's my job to be approachable.

"Good luck tonight." I manage a quick nod back, then pull out my phone and walk ahead of them, blocking out their conversation. On the team bus to the arena, I sit as far from them as possible and try not to glance over every time Oskar's laugh fills the space between us.

He's rowdier than he was back at the hotel, and where some of the other guys have headphones in and are trying to block everyone out, Oskar's only getting louder. That personality he's taught himself is on full display.

I'm starting to recognize it for what it is: fake.

The broad smile hides his nervousness, and the false cocky attitude and snide remarks divert attention away from him in a way I'd never noticed before. I used to think of Oskar like gravity, constantly drawing people in, but that's not totally accurate. No, it's more like his exuberance creates an invisible barrier between him and everyone else. They can get close but never past it.

Except me. For some reason, Oskar's let me in, and that's not something I'm going to take lightly.

So fuck Aleks.

We pull up at the arena, and the players follow their coaches down to the locker room while I head upstairs. It's still early, but a handful of the WAGs who travel with the team are here, and the bar is already open. I order a drink and wait.

The arena fills up slowly. First some of the diehard fans in the front rows, then gradually more and more people show up to take their seats.

My gaze drifts over the space as I sip my scotch and snags on the DJ booth over the arena. It's not as high up as the one in San Jose, but unlike the team box, it's relatively obscured from view.

A wild idea takes root in my mind.

I pocket it for later as both teams file out onto the ice for a warm-up skate. My gaze is immediately drawn to Oskar. There's something so sexy about him in that uniform, which doesn't make sense to me, considering the majority of his body is hidden beneath the bulky pads. His strong legs are obvious even from up here though, and I greedily watch them as he speeds up and slows down before turning in a sudden stop.

"Lane, how are you?"

I jump at the familiar voice and glance over at Mick, completely surprised to see him here. It's not that owners don't travel with their teams sometimes, but more that *he* doesn't. I hurry to pull my shit together and shake his offered hand.

"I'm great. Surprised to see you out of San Jose."

He gestures to the arena around us. "We're getting close, and I wanted to experience a different atmosphere."

The reasoning seems flimsy but is probably half-true. I wouldn't be surprised if he was here talking business with Chicago's owners or other businessmen, but that kind of thing is well above my pay grade. Mick has no need to be following up on me when Oskar's been coasting under the radar the last few weeks. He gestures to seats toward the glass window and sits beside me. "Think we'll take out the win?"

"Oskar's confident. Chicago has come off two good games though."

"True, but we're ranked higher than them."

He's right, but I'm not sure that's a good thing. Chicago needs to win most of their remaining games to make the playoffs, so I can imagine they're going to go out there and play hard.

"Speaking of Voyjik ..." Mick says, and I immediately tense. "He's been quiet lately."

Suspicion prickles the back of my neck at the way Mick's casual tone doesn't sound so casual. "He has been. He's trying."

"I have to say, the complete one-eighty has given me whiplash."

I force a laugh. "So first he's too much of a problem, and now he's being too good?" No wonder Oskar hates it when I do that to him.

"Of course not." He takes a long sip of his beer. "Just want to know what magic you've pulled on him."

"No magic. I reasoned with him."

"And that worked?"

I shrug. "Seems to have, doesn't it?"

"It does." He gives a quick shake of his head. "I never thought Voyjik was the type of man who could be reasoned with."

I play up the smug angle to try and get him to drop the conversation. "I simply reminded him how easily he could lose the one thing he loves. Oskar is hockey. Completely. And the thought of losing that—and, yes, of having me shadow him every waking moment of his life—has helped reframe his perspective."

"Well, at any rate, I'm glad it's working. I never thought we'd see months go by without Voyjik's bare ass splashed all over the internet."

I laugh at that, partially from what he says but mostly from relief because the fishing tone he was using has completely disappeared. "I have to agree with you."

Mick holds out his drink, and I knock mine against it.

"How long do you think you'll need to continue shadowing him?" Mick asks. "As much as I love that this plan has worked, it's not the greatest message for the team to have our PR manager out of action on one player. It also weakens some of the argument that Voyjik is a changed man."

That's the million-dollar question, isn't it?

If my professional self were to answer, it would be easy. Oskar understands the position he's in; he's putting in the effort, and with all his focus currently on hockey anyway, there's no real reason for me to keep this up. I should be loosening the reins, pulling back, giving him freedom to prove he can do this on his own.

The emotional, private side of me says fuck that. I'm not done with him yet.

The scary part is it's not even entirely about the sex. Oskar hasn't completely opened up to me yet, and I want him to. I want him smashed open like a walnut. I want him to break down that huge-ass barrier he surrounds himself with and let me in willingly.

I clear my throat as the pregame show starts and lift my voice above all the noise. "I'm being cautious. I think we should ride out the rest of this season, and then we can work out where to go from there."

"I don't know, Lane." Mick's eyebrows pull together. "We've got Emerson's divorce that needs to be managed, and I wasn't happy with how Carlov's two-week ban was handled by Keerson. The sooner you're back full-time, the better."

"I disagree," I bite back. I shouldn't have, but I can't stop my mouth.

A heavy silence falls over us, despite the roar in the arena all around, and it's like I can *feel* his disapproval from here. His annoyance at being argued with.

"It's probably best you're free for playoffs," Mick says. "We'll need all hands on deck to make sure the team is focused and talked about for the right reasons. Voyjik isn't our only player."

"Could have fooled me."

We hold stares for a moment, because while I knew we were getting to that point, I'd told myself I could drag this out until the end of the season. I'd counted on having that time. A few weeks isn't enough.

Enough time for *what* I'm not really sure. I just know the weight sitting on my chest is making me feel reckless.

Mick shifts. "I'm glad we agree. Game's starting."

I turn to the ice and pretend to concentrate when really, I'm trying to devise a way for Oskar to get enough attention that he's not in trouble but still clearly needs me. And how fucked-up is that? He's finally taking the steps everyone wants him to, and I'm sitting here selfishly wanting to jeopardize that to keep him all to myself.

It's not like I can tell Mick the only reason he's stopped sleeping around is because he's doing it with me instead, can I? I'd actually like to keep my job.

No. There are no options. Oskar wants me as much out of his business as Mick does, no matter how much he might enjoy being railed by me. Sex is easy to come by for Oskar Voyjik, and I'd foolishly hoped I could offer him something else.

Now, it's too late.

I lean forward, elbows on my knees, as the game gets started.

My scotch is forgotten, and instead, I give Oskar my full attention. I let myself watch him shamelessly, drinking in every powerful move, every steal, every time he rams another player into the boards. He belongs out there. It's beautiful.

The stress of playoffs might be building, but you'd never know it with the way he moves. It's like he can do no wrong. With the first line change, Chicago sneaks one past our goalie, but as soon as our first line returns, Oskar sets up the perfect assist, allowing Aleks to sink one in the back of the net.

They hug, along with half of the team, but my stare only follows them. The reminder of their kiss causes this pang in my chest, and I clench my jaw hard against it.

Just a few weeks.

Once I'm out of the picture, Oskar can do whatever and whoever he likes. Though with Aleks's divorce, I'm sure I can interfere between those two, at least for a little longer. My lips hitch in a half smile as I picture all the ways I can cockblock Oskar without him even knowing.

Game passes quickly below, and we're approaching the end of the first period with the score tied up at one apiece when Chicago takes off on a breakaway. Oskar flies after Rostel, pushing fast to catch up, Aleks right behind him. Rostel makes the shot—my heart hits my throat—but the puck rebounds off the crossbar.

I barely have time to exhale before it happens.

Rostel and Oskar both go for the puck, but with Aleks's momentum, he can't pull up in time. All I see is a three-way collision. A mess of jerseys and limbs, someone hitting the ice.

Aleks slams into the boards and is straight back up again, but Rostel is sluggish when he pushes onto his hands and knees. Oskar is facedown on the ice.

I wait, one second, then two ...

The hell, Oskar? Get up.

Play stops.

He's faking. He wants the penalty. Any second now ...

Aleks starts toward Oskar, but the ref gets there first. Bends down. Signals for help.

Rostel staggers to his skates, and when he shifts, all I see is the smear of reddish pink over the ice.

Aleks is frozen, hands gripping the top of his helmet. The team gathers closer. The crowd is on their feet, craning necks, noise getting louder.

And I'm too goddamn far away. Helpless. Panicked. Gut in knots, hands clenched, every part of me willing the asshole to *get to his fucking feet*.

He doesn't.

Chapter Twenty-Four

Oskar

"Did I get possession?" I croak and roll over.

The bright lights of the arena make me squint, and the ice underneath me is cold, even through my layers, and I'm hit with an overwhelming dose of pain that almost makes me pass out again.

Aleks appears above me, eyes wide. "Only you would be worried about that right now. You've got bigger problems than possession. Taking a skate to the face, for one."

"Wha'?" I'm disoriented, and when I sit up, the team trainer, Zee, appears out of nowhere and gently pushes me back down.

"Stay still."

There's a flurry of action, and out comes the dreaded neck brace.

"No, I don't need this." I try to bat away the hands fixing the collar to my neck as someone else shoves something against my cheek. "It's just a little cut."

"You lost consciousness," Zee says. "You know what that means."

"Nooooo," I complain. Not concussion watch. "It was from the skate. I didn't hit my head. I'm fine."

Coach joins in on the fun, appearing next.

"Put me back in, Coach. I'm good."

Coach purses his lips and shares a glance with Zee. They almost look ... worried?

Oh, fuck. Maybe I'm not good? That's when I realize I still only have one eye open. I can't open the other one.

I stop struggling against not getting up and resign myself to the knowledge that I'm out for at least the rest of the game.

There are murmurings of plastic surgeons as they take me off the ice, but none of that is as terrifying as the words that follow. "He might lose his eye."

A pro hockey player with only one eye and no peripheral vision? There's no such thing. I swear to the hockey gods that I will disown them if an injury takes me out. I've been working so hard on reining in my attitude, and to go out this way ... *No*. Panic clogs my throat.

It won't happen.

It *can't* happen.

Oh shit, what if it happens?

What has been the point of behaving if it's all for nothing?

I'm quiet and introspective as the team doctor bandages my face and management discuss what to do. My face and neck have the familiar sticky feeling of blood.

"If it was only a matter of stitches, I could do them right here and now," Doc says. "But the cut is right near his eye, plus isn't Voyjik known as one of the prettiest guys in the league? I don't want to be responsible for mangling his face."

"Mangle it," I say. "I don't care."

"No, he's right." It's a new voice. One I only hear when things are serious. I didn't realize Mick Alcott was here in Chicago with the team. "You make more money from your face with endorsement deals than we pay you."

That's so not true, but I'm not going to point out he overpays me and my salary is ridiculous.

"You'll go to a hospital here in Chicago, and we'll find the best plastic surgeon in all of Illinois."

"And my eye?" I ask because that's the actual only thing I'm worried about.

"It's too swollen to know anything for sure," Doc says. "We need to get you to the hospital to find out more."

Dread as heavy as an anvil hits me in the gut, and I know I'm going to be on edge until I get a definitive answer, but with four little words, not everything seems so bleak.

"I'll go with him," Lane says right before appearing in my vision.

"You should stay here and handle the press about the injury," Mick says, and my panic deepens.

"No. I'll keep Keerson up to date with Oskar's progress, and he can relay it to the media. I want to be there for firsthand information."

I can't be entirely sure, and maybe I'm reading into it because I want it to be true, but the direct tone and concern on his face makes me think that Lane isn't doing this for his job. He's doing it because he cares.

That warm-belly feeling floods through me again, the same one that got to me in the arcade when Lane called me a loser and somehow made me feel accepted.

I make a mental note to ask one of the doctors at the hospital if this heat in my gut is normal, because mushy, emotional warmth isn't something I've ever had to deal with before.

Maybe it's stomach cancer or something.

The wait is excruciating, even more so than the gash on my face. Though that doesn't actually hurt at all right now. "Drugs a good," I murmur, answering a question Lane didn't ask.

We were taken to a VIP suite in one of Chicago's top hospitals, which I didn't even know was a thing. We need to get on this VIP thing back in San Jose because my room looks like a hotel suite. Only thing is, I've been left here alone with Lane since we arrived and they pumped me full of painkillers, and Lane has barely said a word since.

It only makes me more worried about my eye.

If you strip hockey away from me, what's left? Hockey has been the only consistent thing in my life. It became my lifeline. My support.

The last couple of months, I've had it in my head that the end of my career will happen because every team in the NHL would get sick of my antics and think I'm not worth the drama. An injury was the last thing on my mind. Lane sits on the side of my bed, next to my good eye, and he grasps my hand.

"I know you're trying to reassure me, but quit it with the pity." I pull my hand out from under his.

He takes it back. "I'm not trying to reassure you because telling you everything will be okay would be complete bullshit when a doctor hasn't even looked at you yet. I'm just letting you know that I'm here for you because no matter what the outcome, you'll need a support system in place."

"You think I'm going to lose my eye, don't you?"

"I'm more worried about your mangled face. You've practically gotten away with murder because of your looks. You're going to have to learn to"—he gasps—"be friendly and bring out your real personality."

Why is it that when he insults me, I want to swoon?

I laugh, but it's hard because my face feels tight. "Shit. Does that mean I have to be genuine? I don't know how to do that."

Lane's hand squeezes mine. "Yes, you do. I've seen it. All you have to learn is how to show it to other people. From the couple of times I've seen you with your friends, I get the impression the Collective don't even know who you are deep down."

They don't. No one does.

And I'm starting to suspect that neither do I.

"No one likes the real me."

He's quiet for a moment before he says, "I do."

We're thankfully interrupted by them collecting me for some tests, including a CT to make sure I don't have a bad concussion. Because the laceration is so close to my eye, they want to put me under to stitch it up and get a better look at my actual eye to assess the damage and possibly repair it if they're able to.

It's going to be a long night.

It's tempting to ask them to sedate me so I can sleep through everything, not just for the surgery, but I already know the answer will be no.

Seconds tick by, and now that I'm alone and only with the doctors, I get a glimpse of my future without hockey.

It's fucking lonely.

I let the medical staff poke and prod me. I sign forms I can't even read because my bad eye is covered, and my good eye is blurry, but before I know it, I'm waking up in recovery with half of my face numb.

I ask the recovery nurse if they took my eyeball, but all she says is, "Don't worry, dear. All of your important parts are still intact." Then I have to wonder what actually came out of my mouth. I thought I asked about eyeballs, but maybe I said balls ...

"You can ease up on the painkillers," I say. "I think they're making me loopy."

"Sure, it's the painkillers that are doing that." Lane sounds close, but I have to twist my head to find him.

"Have they told you anything?"

"Only that you hit on every single male in your operating room before they put you under."

"Did I?"

Lane laughs. "No, actually, but that you even asked tells me all I need to know."

"What's that?"

"You're going to be fine. I was worried when they said you were on your best behavior, like maybe you were dead and they hadn't realized because you were so quiet, but you've reassured me you're not a corpse."

"Are you seriously kicking me while I'm down?"

Lane throws up his hands in defeat. "I can't win with you."

Just his presence is making every worry and thought somewhat calmer. He gives me the illusion that it's not only me who's injured but him as well, and that's comforting.

I reach for his hand this time, and he comes willingly. "Thank you for being here for me even when Mick told you to be there for the team."

Lane squeezes my hand. "I wouldn't be anywhere else."

A throat clears, and Lane pulls away as my surgeon steps up to my bed.

I manage to get out, "What's the verdict?"

My heart is in my throat until I hear the words, "The blade missed your eye completely."

I let out a loud, relieved breath, but his next words are the ones that bring dread.

"But because your stitches are so close to your eye, you'll be unable to play until they're completely healed, which can be anywhere from ten days to two weeks."

I'm going to be okay, but I still can't go back on the ice until the playoffs?

I glance at Lane. "So, I'm heading back to San Jose while the team plays the rest of these away games?"

"If you're up to it, there's still that charity fundraiser in Vermont." He turns to the doctor. "Would that be okay?"

"So long as his eye is nowhere near ice or blades or anything else sharp, and he doesn't mind looking bruised and worse for wear, then it's fine by me."

Lane's attention's back on me. "It's up to you."

If the doc had given me bad news, it would be the last place I'd want to be, but knowing I'll be back on the ice for the playoffs? Not only do I still have to work on recovering my image, but I actually want to do it. Stitches or no stitches.

I'm making a decision because *I* want to do it. It's not armor. Not defensiveness. The thought that my pretty face might be gone is giving me this heady kind of freedom I haven't had before.

People only stick around for two reasons.

Maybe with both those things gone, I'll find out who's around for real. That thought is terrifying. I could end up friendless and alone.

And for the first time ever, I care. If my friends write me off, if Lane walks away, I'm not so sure I could bounce back easily from that.

But I still want to try.

Chapter Twenty-Five

Lane

I've said it before, and I'll say it again: hockey players are crazy.

The wound goes from his cheek all the way up to his eyebrow, and either Oskar was in shock and didn't realize how bad it was, or ... hockey players are crazy. The only way I knew he was in pain as he was taken to the hospital was because of how tense he held himself. Otherwise, his only concern seemed to be his eye when I swear it looked as though his cheek had been sliced in half.

I hold back another gag at the memory. That was possibly the nastiest thing I've ever seen, and the panic that took over as I fucking ran to the locker room didn't help. But Oskar doesn't need to know all that.

After being released from the hospital, we rented a car and drove down to Burlington for the fundraiser event and checked into a hotel, but I'm starting to think we should have stayed in Montreal or even flown home.

Oskar looks terrible. Still hot. But ...

"You need to clean them," I say as patiently as I can for a *third* time. "Properly."

Oskar lifts his head from where he dunked it under the tap and flicks his wet hair back. "It's water. Water's clean."

I kick down the toilet lid, and with one hand on his shoulder, I push him down onto it. It's been twenty-four hours since the stitches went in, and if it wasn't for me reminding him today, he probably wouldn't have tried washing them at all.

I breathe heavily through my nose in an attempt to stay patient as I grab the soap and a washcloth. "You're also supposed to keep them relatively dry. You almost drowned yourself."

When I turn back to him, Oskar is looking up at me in a way that makes me want to pat his head. I step in closer, then tilt his face to the side, getting a better look at his injury. The area all around his eye is bruised like a motherfucker, and the stitches form a line all the way up his face, holding closed the deep gash. They've done an excellent job with them, but with something that big, there's no possible way it won't scar. Badly. It's going to be large and prominent, and I worry how it'll affect Oskar when he's gotten by on his looks all his life.

Every time I try to talk to Oskar about it, he laughs and says how he got the good drugs. The avoidance isn't a worry at all.

I wet the washcloth and gently start to clean the area, but the second I make contact, Oskar lets out a loud shout and jerks away.

"Fuck, I'm sorry." Guilt hits me for a full second before Oskar drops his hand from his face.

He smiles. "Got you."

That asshole. I punch his shoulder. On his injured side, so he barely sees me coming.

"Hey, I'm wounded, you jerk," he says, rubbing at where I hit him.

"And I'm trying to look after you, you jerk."

"You're just annoyed that you were fooled."

"Better than having my face slashed open." I turn his chin again, and this time, I hold his face as I clean it. He doesn't try his shit again, and the whole time I gently dab at the skin, my mind is spinning, wondering how the hell this kind of injury is going to affect Oskar's already fragile self-worth. I want to tell him that it doesn't matter, that the scar will give him that edge to make him even sexier, and that it's not fair he can take a skate to the face and somehow it makes me want him more than ever.

But focusing on his looks won't help, and every time I try to point out that his personality is what's important, he sneers and tells me I sound like a Lifetime movie.

I'm almost done when Oskar reaches out and runs his hands up my thighs. I'm only in my boxer briefs, so it's immediately obvious what his contact does to me.

"Stop it," I murmur.

"Stop what?"

I swear under my breath. "You're such a brat."

"You like it though."

His blue eyes flick up to meet mine, and I'm caught in his stare. My thumb lightly strokes his good cheek. "Yeah, I do." Then my grip tightens on his jaw, and I lean down so we're a breath apart. "But not while you're injured and can't do anything about it. Just remember that everything you do to tease me now will come back at you tenfold once you're better."

"That really isn't the threat you think it is."

And he's so lighthearted and matter-of-fact about it that a laugh slips from me. I straighten and drag my hand back through my hair. "What the hell am I going to do with you?"

"You could spank me again. Oooh, better yet, give me a pounding. My ass can take it."

"With how vocal you are, I don't trust you not to split your stitches open. We both know how you like to scream for me."

"I can be quiet."

"That's total bullshit." Smiling, I lean down and brush a kiss over his lips. "You sure you want to do this hockey camp thing today?"

His nod is immediate, and a bit of seriousness takes over. "I promised I would."

"No one would blame you for backing out."

"You're going to make me say it, aren't you?"

He already knows me too well. "Say what?"

"Urgh." Oskar huffs. "I *want* to go."

"There. That wasn't so hard, was it?"

He flips me off and stands up to take a piss while I pass back into our hotel room to find some clothes. We didn't share a bed last night, and even though we don't when we're at home, usually while we're away, we collapse after sex and don't move again. Last night, when I climbed into my bed, Oskar watched me with an unreadable look on his face. Tension flooded the room and existed long after we turned out the lights.

I'd wanted more than anything to crawl in beside him. To let him know I was there and that he could use me for support if he needed it, but without sex, I couldn't work out how to cross that line that I'm beginning to wish didn't exist between us.

"I still think you should wear a suit," I call out to him, grabbing my shirt and shrugging it on.

"Fuck no. This isn't a game. I'm not going on the ice. I'll be wearing my San Jose workout gear, and if anyone says shit, I'll remind them that I took a skate to the face and then ask them how their week is going."

I refuse to laugh, even though I *so* want to. Technically, what I should be doing is arguing and reminding him who's in charge here, but getting a chance to see Oskar in a tight San Jose T-shirt and gym shorts that show off those muscular calves isn't something I want to deprive myself of.

"You're going to milk this injury for all it's worth, aren't you?"

"If you have to ask that question, I'm going to start thinking you're not very good at your job."

"Tell me how many other PR reps managed to get you under their thumb?"

He snorts. "We both know it's another appendage that has full control over me."

Once we're dressed, ready to head out, I steer Oskar toward the mirror in our room.

"Other than your wayward hair, you look good."

He scrubs a big hand through the mess on his head, making it even more rumpled. "Something's telling me it's not my hair people are going to be looking at."

Then his gaze slides to his cheek. Needing to give him some of the comfort I wanted to last night, I step up behind him and prop my chin on his shoulder. He leans into me, and I can't help sliding my hands from his waist around to settle over his abs.

"It'll heal," I assure him. "Besides, you actually look like a hockey player now. With all those teeth of yours, I was starting to think you were lying to me."

"It does look badass, huh?"

"Badass. Rugged. Slightly unhinged." I turn my head so my lips are by his ear. "No one's going to call you pretty again."

His chest expands on a deep breath, and it feels like he melts against me. "Is it weird that all anyone could talk about was plastic surgery and it's the last thing I want?"

"Nope. Because they don't know you. As your PR manager, I should be encouraging you to go with that option …"

"And as Lane?"

I don't want to say it, but the way his eyes are pinned on my reflection makes it difficult to keep quiet. "I think you should keep your scar."

His lips part. "Why?"

"Because I know *you* want to."

Oskar straightens and turns so he can see me properly. "Yeah. I really fucking do."

"Then that's what's gonna happen."

"And if Mick pushes for the surgery?"

"We'll sic Damon on him. One of the smartest business decisions you ever made was signing him as an agent." I cross to the hotel room door and hold it open for Oskar.

He sticks close to me in the hall, stands so his shoulder touches mine in the elevator, and when we cross the foyer, his hand ghosts over my lower back.

The whole time, I try to keep my business face on. We're in public, and even though it's only a small hotel in Burlington, I have no idea how many others are staying here, considering the fundraiser drew a few volunteers. As far as anyone knows, I'm here in a professional capacity and not because I'm struggling to walk away from the man beside me.

As we collect the rental car from the hotel parking lot, we head south for the one-hour trip out of Burlington to a smaller town called Maybury. It's beautiful out here. Small and idyllic.

When we pull up out the front of a shiny new facility, I give Oskar's thigh a reassuring squeeze. "Your friends are all here. Might be a good chance to let them in a little, don't you think?"

"We'll see." He slides his sunglasses on and jumps out of the car, waiting for me on the sidewalk. We're early, but there are already a lot of people around, so I lead Oskar away from the large doorway with the welcome banner stretched over it and toward the side entrance, where Richard said he'd be waiting for us.

He's a fair bit younger than me with a thicker beard and a friendly smile, and from what I've gathered through emails, the people running this camp were friends of his, so he's organized the event in his downtime.

"Lane?" he asks as we approach.

I shake his offered hand. "I couldn't keep Oskar away."

"That's great, man. We're so happy you could make it. Beck's a big fan, and, well, so am I …" Richard's stare catches on Oskar's injury, and he cringes. "So sorry about that too. I caught the game, and I swear I could feel it through the screen. I had a few bumps and bruises when I played, but nothing like that."

Oskar shrugs. "All part of the game."

"Damn straight." Richard holds out his hand for a fist bump that Oskar returns right as Tripp and Dex Mitchell arrive.

They immediately steal Oskar's attention, replaying the hit to his face. Tripp goads him about having better aim next time, and Dex loudly exclaims Oskar should go to his next costume party as a pirate.

"Or the joker," Richard happily adds.

"Yes." Dex throws his hands up. "Oh my God. Idea! Tripp's birthday. Villain party. You're the joker, Tripp can be—what's that chick with all the vines?"

"Poison Ivy?" I ask.

"Exactly. And I could be ..."

Oskar, Tripp, and I exchange a look because I've never met anyone who exhibits less villain energy than Dex. None of us have a suggestion for him.

"Harley Quinn," Richard suggests.

Dex gasps. "I could *totally* do booty shorts."

"Great idea." Oskar slings an arm around Dex's shoulders. "You'd be *my* bitch for the night."

Tripp pins him with a look. "If you're trying to make me jealous ..."

Oskar leans in and runs his tongue up Dex's cheek.

"Yeah, that's enough," Tripp snaps, and Dex laughs, ducking out of Oskar's hold.

Richard opens the door. "Why don't you guys come in before someone gets hurt? Ah, again."

Dex bounces after him, still on a roll with this party idea, as Oskar and Tripp follow, shoving and jostling each other like a pair of fucking teenagers. I want to remind Oskar about his face, but there's no point wasting my breath.

I hold true to my previous thought: hockey players are crazy.

Chapter Twenty-Six

Oskar

This camp is state-of-the-art for something that's a nonprofit. Richie from Montreal's PR department has organized this whole benefit because he went to college with the owners of the camp, as well as Foster Grant, one of our very own from the Collective.

Richie gives us a tour of the main building, which includes the dorms, the admin offices, and a dining hall before moving on to the marquee set up outside where I spot Ezra, Anton, and Foster putting tablecloths over rented tables.

"Damn it," I say loud enough for everyone to hear. "We got here too early, and now I need to help set the place up? I thought it was my job to stand here and look pretty."

I didn't know it was possible to make this many hockey players silent at once, but I've managed it with one joke.

When I look at Lane to taunt everyone over being awkward about my appearance, the disappointment on his face is obvious, and I'm reminded that he wants me to make an effort with my friends or whatever.

This whole growing as a person thing is really fucking boring. Though, I might see his point. A little. This event and how many of us turned up is proof that the Collective will do anything for each other, yet I've somehow never called upon them for anything serious. I haven't confided in them. Haven't really talked about anything deep.

Because I try not to go there with anyone.

Letting Lane in has brought us closer. Not the physical side either. I'm connected to Lane in ways I don't completely understand yet, but I do know that he'll be there for me if I need him. I guess with the Collective, I've held back because what if I did need them but they didn't care? What if I called for them and no one showed up? What if I was the one member out of all of us who wasn't a priority? I've never had to test it out, and I have to say, I'm not liking doing it now either.

Ezra is the first to get to me, and he pulls me in for a tight hug.

"Whoa, who died?" I ask because he's hugging me and not giving me shit about how ugly I am. It hits a little too close to my chest. "Other than my modeling career."

When Ezra pulls back, he looks all serious and sympathetic. "I just didn't know how you'd be feeling."

I go to open my mouth to say I'm fine, but he keeps talking.

"Before, you could've rivaled me for sexiest player in the league, and now you'd be lucky to beat Tripp."

"Hey," Tripp whines while I laugh. My face still feels tight and sore from the stitches and bruising, but at least the almost serious moment has passed. "Redheads are hot."

"Not when they're stealing your soul," Ezra yells.

Other people helping set up the event look over here with varied expressions. From awe to confusion and everything in between, Foster being one of them.

Foster starts in our direction and brings two other men with him, and when he gets to me, he slaps my shoulder. "Have to say, you're less intimidating with all"—he waves a hand in front of my face—"that being mangled now."

I've heard the intimidating thing before. A lot.

"And I'm not now?" I ask.

"Not for your face anyway. You're still scary as ever on the ice."

Under his praise of hockey, I preen. When Foster mentions my looks, I hate it. There's barely a difference, but with hockey, it took years of dedication and work. I was born with my face. It's the whole reason I built up my personality so it'd be the first thing people noticed about me instead of my looks. One compliment is acknowledging my talent and my drive. The other is giving a silent high five to my parents for fucking each other, and that's weird.

"This is Beck and Jacobs," Foster says. "They own the camp. They're also really big fans and are going to embarrass the hell out of me, but I promised I'd introduce them to as many of my NHL friends as possible so they could have some pull with clients and investors."

"Aww, you want to use me for my fame?" I ask the two guys who are maybe one or two years younger than I am.

The dark-haired one's mouth drops like he's in trouble. The blond, who has a carefree look on his face, simply says, "Yep."

I chuckle. "Wow. No shame. You're my type of guy."

The blond leans in close to his partner and whispers, "Is it too late to change my hall pass to Oskar Voyjik instead of Zendaya?"

The growl from wherever Lane is hits my ears and makes me light up inside.

"Ignore Beck," Foster says. "We all do."

"Oh, I don't think I want to. I've never been someone's hall pass before." And while I'd normally be all over the hot blond, who has blue eyes and that All-American glow, I have no desire to go there.

"That you know of," Lane mumbles, his jealous streak showing once again. "How could you know when you don't even know most of your hookups' names?"

I rub my chin. "True. Next time I'll ask if I'm their hall pass before I let them fuck me."

"*No* hall pass," says the guy who must be Jacobs if the blond is Beck. He turns to his partner. "Besides, what happened to being mostly straight?"

"Hey, I might skew toward women, but have you seen Voyjik on the ice? Sexiest thing ever."

Him wanting me for my hockey skills and not caring about my mangled face? No, *that's* the sexiest thing ever.

"Can I please, please, please have sex with the camp owner?" Not that I actually want to. I just want to see Lane's reaction again.

Both Lane and Jacobs snarl, "No," at the same time.

There it is. That delicious jealousy that almost makes me feel worth something. I can barely contain my smile. "Sorry. My sex jailer says no." I thumb in Lane's direction.

"Sex jailer?" Beck asks. "I really want to ask what you did to get one of those, but I get the feeling it's a cult, and I promised Jacobs's mom that I wouldn't sign up for one of those."

Jacobs coughs and says, "Again."

Foster's friends are fun.

"Where do you need help?" Lane asks, trying to get this shitshow back on track.

Jacobs points to the tables. "We need help setting up the marquee for lunch, and then when the guests get here, we'll show them the grounds and the rink. Did you bring any San Jose merch for the auction later?"

I glance at Lane because I have no idea what he's talking about.

Lane obviously does though. "It's in the trunk of our car back in the parking lot, and Oskar still has to sign all of it. We've been a bit preoccupied with pain meds and stitches. We'll get them out and signed now."

Ezra whines. "He gets out of helping because of one little skate to the face?" He calls out to Anton, who hasn't stopped working since our arrival. He's fully into the charity thing. "Hey, babe! Can you throw your skate at my face? Apparently, it will get me out of helping."

Anton doesn't miss a beat. He keeps on working while yelling back, "I thought we already agreed it wouldn't make it through your thick head because your ego is like padding around your skull?"

Ezra slumps. "He loves me. I swear he does."

Tripp raises his hand. "I'll give it a try."

"No, you'd do serious damage. Anton wouldn't be able to stand it if he mangled my face as bad as Oskar's."

"I'm so glad all of my friends are so sensitive toward me over my near-death accident."

"Pfft," Ezra says. "Please. Death of your career, maybe, but your eye is fine, right? They say you'll be back for the playoffs. Therefore, you're fair game. Just because you aren't as pretty, don't think we're not going to treat you the same."

Jesus, there is something wrong with me because my admiration for Ezra just grew. "I know this will sound sarcastic, but that's possibly the nicest thing you've ever said to me."

Ezra cocks his head like a dog, and I can't blame him for being confused, but I ignore it.

"Shouldn't you all be working?" I ask, which makes them split into work mode.

Lane puts his hand on the small of my back and says, "I'll go get all the gear from the car you need to sign. Take a seat and rest."

"I'm not completely broken, you know." Though I am already exhausted, and it's going to be a big day, so I don't fight doing what he says.

Lane looks into my eyes, and a small smile crosses his lips. "I want to look after you."

And fuck, if that doesn't feel good. Someone to look after me. Care about me. Actually ask how I'm doing ... But while he disappears, the flies swarm back toward me. Even Anton.

"Collective meeting," Ezra says. "Now."

All of them are staring at me like they want answers to questions I should know but don't.

"Uh, my PR manager told me I have to take a seat and rest. Sorry."

"Nope. You don't get out of this that easily," Ezra says and grabs my arm to drag me toward one of the already set tables.

And then there they are, Anton, Ezra, Tripp, Dex, and Foster, with all their focus trained on me.

"So. I look scary now. It's pretty cool."

"Cut the shit," Ezra says.

"Umm. I'm not scary-looking?"

"Tell us what we want to knoooow," Tripp whines.

"What do you want to know?" I have no idea what they're talking about, but I get the sinking feeling—

"Are you having sex with your PR manager?" Foster asks.

Oh fuck. Yep. There it is.

I didn't think we were being obvious. "Why do you ask?"

"I have a sixth sense," Ezra says. "I know who exactly has had sex with who."

"No," Tripp cuts in. "It's because you've been here longer than five minutes, and you haven't joked with Lane about having sex. Therefore, you're actually having sex with him."

I rub my chin. "Well, damn."

"You are, then?" Dex asks.

I lick my lips. "Maybe."

Everyone around the table groans.

"No, it's not as bad as it sounds," I say. "It's ..." What is it? "He's helping me."

Tripp snorts. "Helping you come?"

And here it is. Here's the moment where I either need to seize this opportunity to let them all in or keep my mask in place. I take a deep breath. "He's helping me see that there's more to sex than doing it for attention or to make a headline. It's more than fulfilling an image that I need to fit. And ..." I hesitate.

I've already given more than I normally would, but there's something about Lane that makes me want to open up about him. Because he's amazing.

"It's actually kind of cute. You all know how I have a thing for public sex. Well, he's been giving me that ... without actually giving me that. He pretended my neighbor was on her balcony and could see into my house, and there was the time with the phone in the hotel room where he filmed us, but the steam from the shower actually blocked the camera from getting anything scandalous, and another time he turned the porch light on so no one could see in but told me they could. And even though I realized afterward there was no chance of being caught, that he came up with these scenarios for me ... I didn't call him out on it because ... he ..." I shake my head. "He understands me and still wants me anyway. Even though it's only physical."

Though, it's not only physical for me anymore, is it? And by the look of everyone else at this table, they don't believe it either.

"We love you," Anton says cautiously. "But do you realize this could completely tank his career?"

"Yep. And to start off with, I didn't care, but ... for once, I'm ..." It's so hard to get out. "I'm worried about how my choices affect someone else. Because I know it's wrong, but I don't want to stop."

Then Ezra looks over my head, and his eyes widen.

One of my gear bags drops to the ground by my side, and Lane's voice makes me flinch.

"Apparently we're common knowledge now?"

Oh, shit.

211

Chapter Twenty-Seven

Lane

When I went to grab the merch from the car, the last thing I assumed I'd be coming back to is a huddle of hockey players discussing my sex life. Actually, I don't think that's something I assumed I'd experience *ever*.

I'm still trying to work out how I feel about them knowing about us, but from everything Oskar has told me about how close they are and my pushing him to let them in and find his support network, it's not as though I have grounds to be mad about it.

"I assume you'll all keep this quiet?" I ask.

Five hockey players nod like kids in trouble, and when I look down at where Oskar is sitting, his gorgeous blue eyes are wide.

"I need help getting something from the car," I say, then turn on my heel, knowing he'll follow.

Before I'm out of earshot, I pick up the sound of jeers and *ooh, Oskar's in trouble* and *Daddy's mad*, and I can't help it—I smile. Just a little.

All because of idiot hockey players and *not* because Oskar shared a hard thought with them and admitted that he actually cares. About us. And wants it to go on.

"If you want to yell at me, you could have done it without demanding cardio first," Oskar pants, jogging up beside me.

Yell at him? I almost laugh. The farther we get from the camp, the lighter I'm starting to feel. There'd been *affection* in his voice. For me. Fuck. Oskar's in trouble, but not the kind he's imagining.

The trouble will come when I struggle to give this man up.

He's under my skin, this incessant need to build up and protect. To touch and comfort and care for. He wants something? I'm prepared to serve it up on a fucking platter, and there isn't even the tiniest part of me ashamed of that fact.

There is a car parked on either side of ours, blocking the view from the entrance to the facility, and it's still early enough that no one is around. I lead Oskar between our car and the SUV beside it before I suddenly turn and press him into the door.

Surprise crosses his face as I lean in, forearms pressed to the window behind him and body snug against his own.

"You don't want to stop?" I ask.

Oskar's eyebrows pull down. "What do you—"

"This. Us. You don't want to stop it. Why?"

"Who'd want to give up convenient sex?"

"No." I grip his jaw carefully, just firm enough that he knows I'm not messing around. "Don't do that bullshit with me."

"Who says it's bullshit?"

I want to kiss him, claim him, force him to admit that I'm the only one he wants. For this week, this month, who knows? But he's given me the tiniest window of opportunity, so I'm sure as hell going to take advantage of that. "I do. You want to keep this thing going? Tell me I mean more to you than an easy orgasm. Because you sure as shit aren't that for me."

It breaks my heart that he could be so surprised by that. He struggles for words for a full couple of seconds, then swallows roughly. "It's possible that I don't find you completely unbearable."

I give his jaw a warning squeeze. "Try again."

"*Urgh*, I take it back. You *are* unbearable. Completely annoying and a pain in my ass I could do without. All you've done is walk into my life like you have it all figured out and push me out of my comfort zone. Maybe I was happy with the way things were, did you think of that?"

"Were you?"

A frustrated noise leaves him. "No, damn it. But I didn't know that until you and your bossiness and the way you put me first and check that I'm okay and meet my every single need that I didn't even know I had." His hands grip the sides of my shirt. "I hate everything you've ever done to make me like you."

Happy nerves fizzle in my gut. "You like me."

"More every stupid day."

I can't hold back. My chest floods with something indescribable as I press a quick, hard kiss to his mouth but pull away before he can try and take things deeper.

"Here's what's going to happen. You're going to climb into that back seat, and I'm going to blow you, but you're going to keep that filthy mouth shut because one noise that could fuck up your stitches and I stop. Understand?"

"You really like torturing me, huh?"

I chuckle. "You have no idea. Now, get in the car and keep a lookout. We're very *public* here."

His pupils blow wide. "We could get caught."

"We could."

Then he surprises the hell out of me by cupping my face. "If we are, it could be bad for you. I don't want that."

"That's for me to worry about."

Oskar shakes his head. "Maybe I'm a little worried about it too."

Fuck, that softens me toward him. "You're beginning to see that your choices have consequences, but I've known that for a very long time. I knew what I was doing when I got into this."

"And you chose me anyway."

I turn my head to press a kiss to his palm, then pull open the door behind him. "I'd do it all over again too."

"Now, not that I'm complaining, but why *do* you suddenly want to suck my cock? Is this a reward for being a good boy?"

"Oh, you've definitely been a good boy." I quickly slide the driver's seat forward before nudging Oskar toward the back. "But it's mostly because I really, really need to touch you."

"Well, feel free to touch me whenever you like."

Oskar climbs in, and I follow him, pulling the door closed behind us. The windows are tinted dark, so there's very little chance of anyone seeing in, even without the cars on either side, but from in here, we can see *everything*.

I sink onto my knees between Oskar's spread thighs and yank his gym shorts down. His half-hard cock bobs in front of my face, and I almost groan. "I take it back. You were right. A suit would have been a terrible idea."

Oskar's laugh is husky as he runs his fingers through my hair. "Are you saying you were wrong?"

"I'm saying I'm always open to negotiation." Then I lean forward and wrap my mouth around his cock. I run my tongue over him, sucking him deep as I coax him to full hardness. The feel of him lengthening in my mouth makes me dizzy, and I bury my face in his pubes as he fills my mouth and pushes into my throat.

Oskar lets out a long, loud exhale, grip tightening on my hair. His legs shift wider, and I love the way he's struggling to stay in control. I pull back and dive back down again, ears strained for the hitches in Oskar's breath. The fact he wants to be vocal and can't is turning me on more than it should, knowing that he's having to control himself all because I told him to.

And, well, medical advice, but that's nowhere near as sexy.

I bob up and down a few times, slicking his cock up with spit before I pull off and let my hand take over. "How many people are out there?"

His gaze flicks around. "A volunteer." He gestures to the side. "She's over there."

"I bet she saw you," I lie, and his cock twitches in my hand. "Bet she saw how desperate you are for me and knew I was on my knees in here for you. Bet she's going to go in there and tell everyone that you're having your cock sucked, and then they'll all come out here and see what I do to you."

"Ah, fuck—" He bites off the rest as his hips leave the seat, fucking his cock into my fist.

"That wasn't very quiet."

"I'm *trying*."

"You are. And good boys deserve to be rewarded." My hand drifts lower to cup his balls, one finger sliding over the skin behind them. "Now fuck my face."

"*Yesss*."

I sink back down and open my throat as Oskar's hands tighten in my hair. He shoves me down onto him, hips tilting up to meet every movement, and when my eyes flick up to meet his, they're hooded and unfocused.

I pull off. "Don't watch me. I want your eyes on the window and everyone out there."

He shudders and shoves me back onto him but pulls his stare away. The whole time he uses me, his jaw is clenched tight, like he's fighting every urge, and the sounds building in his throat are hot as hell. His focus is on the front window, toward the facility, and I can only imagine the sexy thoughts running through his mind. It makes me regret blowing him and not being able to vocalize them myself, but then he rewards me with a taste of precum, and I hum around him. Everything about Oskar turns me on. Everything about him fits so perfectly into my fantasies.

I grip his thick thighs, the feel of his muscles bunching and flexing under my hands making my cock throb. Oskar's not being gentle, and his cock hitting my throat over and over is making it tender. My drool is leaking out of the corners of my mouth, and I'm really having to work to breathe. But I wouldn't have it any other way.

Making him feel good makes me feel good.

Even though I told him to look outside, I can't drag my stare from his face. The windows are fogging up, and his breathing is heavy, lips parted, sounds and curses starting to slip out.

"*Shitshitshit*," he gasps, trying not to move his lips.

When his cock slides into my throat this time, I swallow around him and slide my hand back to press a finger over his hole.

"Tell me to come," he begs.

I moan my approval and pull off with a deep, gasping breath. "Come down my throat."

Then I wrap my lips around his head before I miss it and jerk him off into my mouth.

Oskar's whole body tenses, hands forming fists in my hair as his cock swells. Then he comes, spurt after salty spurt hitting my tongue as he does his best to hold back his long groan.

When he's done, I pull off panting, cock achingly hard.

"Here ..." He's practically boneless as he reaches for me, and fuck if that doesn't make me feel proud.

"No. We have nothing to clean up with."

"I'll swallow."

I brush a kiss against his temple. "Stitches, remember? Waiting until I can get back to jerk off isn't going to kill me."

Oskar pins me with a look. "This is starting to become a trend with us."

"You like public sex. I like edging myself. Apparently."

"It makes me feel like a shitty ..." Lover? Boyfriend? There's a moment of awkwardness as we both fill in whatever he was about to say because I'm realizing that I have no idea what we are anymore.

"I promise it's fine," I assure him, ignoring the whole thing. "When it comes to you, I'm happy to wait."

I don't stick around to see his reaction to that, just climb out and hold the door open for him.

Oskar follows me, then starts to laugh. "Shit, your hair looks worse than mine."

I turn to the window to take in my reflection. Where my hair was smoothed back and neat, it's now sticking out in all directions. Exactly like someone has held on to it real good. The red, puffy lips don't help things.

Oskar's attempts to flatten it down don't really work, so fuck it. I ruffle it up until it almost looks purposeful.

Half of the guys here know what's happening with us, and the rest of the people coming today won't be here to see me.

"Come on, this thing starts soon," I tell Oskar, and he falls into step with me.

"They're all going to know what we were doing." The smile he's wearing tells me he doesn't give a fuck.

But he's right. And I don't give a fuck either.

We reach his friends, and some of them get it faster than others, but I can tell the exact moment it clicks. Well, with all of them except one.

Dex gives Oskar a sympathetic look. "How much trouble are you in?"

Tripp loses his cool laughing, and Ezra pats Dex on the back in pity while Foster and Anton exchange perplexed looks.

I just say, "A lot. And trouble tastes good on him." Then I slap his ass and walk away to set up everything he needs to sign.

I'm trying not to overanalyze where we go from here and what happens with us when I no longer have to babysit him. I'm going to focus on this moment. Because it feels goddamn perfect.

Chapter Twenty-Eight

Oskar

There is nothing more frustrating than knowing something could easily be fixed, yet no one is fucking doing it.

"I need to stop coming to games," I say from my cushy seat in the corporate box.

Ever since my injury, the team has been on a losing streak, and all I want to do is get back out there, but I'm not allowed.

Which is stupid because I'm fine. But then all the doctors have to say is if my wound tears, it could do damage to my eye because it's so close, and I retreat back into my injured reserve list hole. One close call with early retirement was too much for me.

The only thing keeping me borderline sane is that I'm healed enough to have sex again, provided we don't turn our bedroom activities into an extreme sport.

But that doesn't stop the frustration bubbling up inside. When Forsyth lets a Dallas forward past him without so much as an attempt at blocking or stripping the puck, I get out of my seat and yell, "Where's our defense? Come on!"

Lane pulls me back down into my seat. "There are sponsors here who pay a lot of money to get their logo plastered all over our arena. You might want to at least try to look like you have confidence in the team."

I scoff. "If anyone said we were playing great this week, I'd ask what drugs they're on and can I have some. We only had to win half our games. Half. And since then, we've won *none*. Which means, if we don't pull a win out of our ass soon, we're going to have to win every game from now until the end of the season. Do you know how much pressure that is? And do you know how frustrated I am that I can't get down there and put this in the bag for us?"

The buzzer sounds, signaling the end of the second period and the score 4-2 to Dallas.

"For fuck's sake," I mutter.

Lane glances around the corporate box and then stands, grabbing my hand and pulling me with him.

"Where are we going?" I ask.

"Somewhere where you can let out your frustrations without pissing off corporate sponsors."

My dick perks up at that. "Blow off steam? And where exactly do you propose we do that?"

"I got an idea while we were in Chicago, but it's risky. Especially when we only have fifteen minutes."

"Intriguing ... Will I get to touch you this time?"

He's been reluctant to let me do anything because of my face, but it's been almost a week, and it's looking better by the day. My surface stitches have been taken out and the ones beneath the skin should have started to dissolve by now.

"Even better, I was hoping you'd do all the work." Lane pulls me to the end of the hall to the emergency exit and down one flight of stairs.

When we get to a door, he knocks twice, but when no one answers, he uses his security pass to open up.

He lets me in first and closes the door behind him, and I take in the DJ booth and the glass windows that overlook the rink and the crowd.

"Are you sure you brought me to the right place?" I turn back to see him leaning against the side wall with his suit pants around his ankles and his underwear sitting under his tight, round ass. He has his jacket off and shirt lifted up so his hole is on full display.

"I've been tracking Roe's movements. He leaves the booth during intermission for anywhere between twelve to fourteen minutes, hitting play on a playlist while he has a snack and goes to the bathroom. If you want to take my ass, suit up and take it while staring at the crowd out there." He holds up a condom. "I'm all ready for you."

I'm ... speechless. "How are you real?" He's perfect for me.

"What?" He looks over his shoulder at me. "We really don't have time to get philosophical. Are you going to fuck me or not?"

I'm torn because the new me, the one who is open to whatever it is Lane and I are doing, the one who actually cares what happens to Lane's job, the one who is wanting more than sex, is telling me I should say no. The inner caveman sex fiend is screaming at me to do this.

Having sex in front of a full arena? That's ... like ultimate fantasy.

"Oskar?" The need in Lane's voice is what makes me break.

"Screw it." I go for my belt and fly, undoing my pants as I walk toward him and take the condom wrapper and open it. While I get that rolled down my cock, I lean in close to Lane's ear and whisper, "If we get caught, this is on you."

"All on me. I'm already prepped for you."

Testing that out, I sink two fingers inside him. His slick hole sucks me deep, and I buzz at the thought of taking him here. "You planned for this?"

"Well, yes. For days now. I was hoping to do this after the game while people were clearing out because Roe needs to be back before the break ends, but you looked like you were going to lose your head back there. So, plan B and quickie it is."

"Lane … I …" I can't believe he'd do this for me.

"You can tell me how awesome I am later. I need you to fuck me and fuck me fast."

I pull my fingers out of him and replace them with my cock, both of us letting out a loud breath of relief. But it's not enough.

His ass holds me tight, and when I move even the tiniest bit, ripples of pleasure shoot down my spine.

"Look out there. At all the people in the stands," he says breathlessly. "None of them can see through the glass, but imagine if they could. They could see your long, muscular frame thrusting inside me while I'm bent over and taking everything you're giving."

I pull out to the tip, only to push deep inside him again.

"Maybe the DJ left the mic on, and they can hear the sounds in here. All the moans you give when you're close. The slapping of our bodies meeting over and over again. The sound of sex filling the arena."

Holy shit. I've never been this close to the edge so soon, but I think that's Lane's intention. We need to be as fast as we can, and his words keep driving me closer and closer.

Even though I no longer have that need to fuck publicly for the attention, the fantasy of it is still hot. If I'd known I could get this type of rush from safe public sex, I wouldn't have needed Lane to babysit me at all.

But then, we never would have happened, so I wouldn't change a thing. Because even though what's going on between us doesn't have an official definition, there's no denying that Lane has changed my life for the better.

He didn't want to change who I was. He could tell from the beginning that my front was all an act. He just wanted to rein in that fake behavior and have me be myself. He has given me what I want while managing to keep my private life private. And after years of having my sex life splashed all over the tabloids, I didn't think it was possible to be a private person.

I have to laugh at myself because I am literally dicking out my PR manager in front of seventeen thousand unknowing people. So much for being a private person. But the point is, Lane doesn't force me to be anyone I'm not. He's shown me that my old motto of *any attention is better than no attention at all* isn't healthy and that I don't need to do that. Because he gives me what I want. What I need. And I don't have to do anything for his affection.

He gives it freely. He gives his support. And right now, he's giving all of him to me.

I slam inside him, over and over again, loving the heat surrounding my cock and only wanting more. At the same time, I want to slow down and savor this, but I know I can't.

The DJ could be back at any moment. The rest of the game will start.

"Oskar, I'm close."

I take my gaze off the crowd and see Lane jerking himself off hard and fast while I pound his ass.

"Where are you going to come?" I ask.

"Where do you want it? You want me to hold out until you've come and then get on your knees for me?"

"Mm, I was more thinking I want you to come in your underwear so that for the rest of the night, all that discomfort you feel will be because of me. Every time you squirm, it will be because I made you come."

"Fuck!" he hisses and then tenses. His ass tightens around my cock, triggering my own orgasm, and I grunt my release as it fills the condom.

My hips begin to move slower, my thrusts becoming infrequent and more gentle until I finally slump against his back, but he doesn't let me fully recover.

He elbows me to move, and as soon as I'm free of him, he bends to pull his pants back up and hold his jacket over his front. Which he'll have to do for the rest of the night with his underwear full of cum.

I'm slower to pull my pants up, and then I realize ... "Shit. Where do I get rid of the condom?"

As I ask, the sound of the door opening has me scrambling to get my dick away.

Roe enters and pulls back at us standing in his office space. "Uh ..."

Lane backhands my chest. "See, Voyjik? It's the same view as the corporate box. One level doesn't make a difference." He shakes his head. "Hockey players. Can't tell them anything once they get an idea in their thick heads."

Roe nods. "Right. Uh ... sure."

"Sorry to interrupt. You better get back to it." Lane's overly bubbly tone doesn't match his usual demeanor, so

I don't know if Roe is confused because we're in here at all or because Lane is being nice.

We get back into the hall, and as if holding our breaths together, we both burst into laughter as soon as we're in the clear.

"That was too close," Lane says.

"Even for me."

Lane steps closer to me, almost chest to chest, and then he reaches up and pats my cheek. "But was it worth it?"

How do I tell him that what he just gave me is worth *everything*?

"More than worth it. It was ... indescribable."

He steps back and gestures toward my crotch. "You better go deal with that."

"And you better not deal with yours."

Lane smiles up at me. "Wouldn't dream of it."

Chapter Twenty-Nine

Lane

After the game—another devastating loss—Oskar can barely look at his team and heads straight home rather than out to drown his sorrows. But instead of us splitting off into separate bedrooms like usual, he wordlessly takes my hand and leads me into his room.

Which is how my obnoxiously loud ringtone wakes us both the next morning. Oskar groans and lifts his head to pull out his pillow and smother his face with it, but then he remembers his injury and throws it across the room. I force myself up, blinking sleep from my eyes as I reach for my phone and swipe to answer.

" 'ello?"

"Lane, Mick here."

That wakes me up properly. "Hey, what do you need?" I'm tallying all the ways one of the players could have gotten up to shit after their loss last night before he even answers.

"A meeting. This morning would be preferable."

"Who is it?" Oskar's raspy voice asks.

My gaze flicks over to where he's resurfaced, and I make a slashing noise at my throat.

"Better bring Voyjik too," he says, and then the line goes dead.

Motherfucker. I stare at the phone in my hand, knowing that whatever he has to say won't be good, and if he wants Oskar there ...

He *knows*. A month ago and it could have been fifty-fifty between that and Oskar doing something Oskar-like, but he's been behaving himself. He's been with me all night.

Somehow, Mick has figured it out.

The only question left is how I'm going to play this. We've been careful even when we've been riskier than is sensible, so there's no possible way someone could have seen us. I checked that there were no cameras in the DJ booth, and no matter what I said to Oskar, the mic definitely wasn't on while we were in there.

So ... *how*? And if there's no proof, do I deny it to try to keep my job? Walk away from Oskar in just over a week and pretend like none of this ever happened? Going back to work means moving back into my place and then sneaking around. That's if Oskar wants something with me at all. And after all that, I still might end up fired.

So my choices are to end it ... or pick him. Give everything up for a man whose feelings are totally unknown. The truth is, Oskar is a complete gamble. He's too much like my exes. I could walk out of this meeting with no job and no Oskar.

"Hey ..." His warm hand rests on my shoulder, and I pull in a long breath. "What's going on?"

"Mick wants a meeting with us. *Both* of us."

"But I haven't done anything."

I turn to give him a look. "I think we both know what this is."

"No way." Oskar sits up, shaking his head. "There's no way we could have been caught."

"I'm open to suggestions, but I think we probably need to be prepared for that conversation."

"Prepared how?"

"*If* that's what it's about, do we confirm or deny?"

"Deny, of course." He scowls. "You'll be fired."

"Like I said, I went into this knowing the risks."

He swallows and looks away, and then he reaches for my hand. His is warm and large in mine. Comforting. "We deny it unless they have black-and-white photographic evidence. Which they won't because we've been careful. You're the best at what you do, and the team needs you. I don't want you to lose it all for me."

I give him a dry look. "Yes, unscrupulous PR managers are hard to come by."

"I can't believe I'm the one wanting to actually be serious here. If you're fired ..."

I won't be picked up by another team. He doesn't say it, but he doesn't need to. Sleeping with one of the players when I'm the one responsible for their reputations won't look good on my resume.

"We'll see what happens. It might not even be about that." I climb out to find some clothes when Oskar walks over and takes my shirt from my hands and lays it over the side of the bed.

"This is the plan. We deny until we can't any longer. Then if it comes to it, I'll say I pressured you into it."

I recoil. "Not a chance."

"It's the only way for you to get out of it."

"Yeah, and possibly get you arrested."

"Not if you're unwilling to press charges."

I step closer and cup his face, careful of his healing scar. "I will never, ever say it. And if you try to, I'll tell them everything."

"So stubborn." He scowls and steps away from me. "My reputation will barely take a hit from this. Maybe I'll be traded, who knows? But you'll lose everything you've worked for. They'll think you fucking preyed on me or something."

"I won't tell them that you forced me."

"Okay, maybe not that. But if we have to admit it, and *only* if we have to admit it ... we'll end it."

My heart beats faster. "What?"

"Yeah." He's nodding to himself. "If denying it doesn't work, then we'll cut all ties and keep the whole thing quiet so long as you're allowed to keep your job."

"That's what you want?"

"If it keeps you out of trouble, then yes."

I study his face for a moment. The clenched jaw, pleading eyes. He's completely serious about this.

I shove the invading emotions down. "We'll hope it doesn't come to that."

We're mostly quiet as we drive to the San Jose facilities, and Oskar's hand doesn't leave my thigh once. I'm grateful for the connection, but I'm determined for us to get out of this intact. As nervous as I am, it helps to go back over every time we've been together in my head because the more I do, the more I'm sure they've got jack shit when it comes to us.

I pull into a parking space and give Oskar's hand a squeeze before he can withdraw it. "We're okay," I say. "They've got nothing, and as soon as we're done here, we're going to fuck the afternoon and all this stress away."

He finally grins over at me. "You know me far too well. I think you're my soul mate."

I bark a laugh, ignoring the longing swoop in my gut at what was obviously a joke, and jump out of the car, trying to stamp down the nerves. This is just another meeting, probably about Oskar's career with nothing at all to do with us. It could be a trade for all I know; even though the likelihood of Mick being the one to deliver the news is low, it could happen. Maybe.

Positive vibes only.

I school my face into its politely detached, professional mask and hold the door open for Oskar to pass. Then we take the elevator up to Mick's floor, and I force down a deep breath before knocking.

"Come in."

Oskar flicks his messy hair back and nods at me that he's ready.

We've got this.

My footsteps falter slightly when I walk in and see Keerson sitting on Mick's side of the table. He throws me a confused sort of half smile, like he doesn't know what he's doing here any more than we do.

"Thank you for coming on short notice," Mick says, standing and offering his hand. "I'm sure you had better things to do with your day."

"Better than meeting with the man who pays my salary?" Oskar asks. "No such thing."

Mick chuckles and gestures for us to have a seat, and his relaxed demeanor gives me hope. Until he claps his hands over his gut and leans back into his chair, the way I've seen him do a handful of times. "Look, we're here to clear up a little confusion, and I've asked Keerson to be here for the discussion on the off chance we need the PR department involved."

"Excuse me for interrupting," I say. "But aren't I capable of representing my own department?"

"That remains to be seen. Last night Roe, our game DJ, reported that the two of you had been in the DJ booth during intermission and you were acting strangely. He was concerned that equipment may have been stolen or tampered with. As he didn't want to be made liable should that be the case, he asked security to review the footage."

My gut sinks through my ass. There were no cameras in that booth. *Fuck, was there?* Is it possible I missed something? If I did, that's going to make our plan of denying things a whole lot harder. I guess there's no more hoping the conversation was going to go any other way.

Mick turns his monitor so we can see the screen, and it doesn't escape my notice that this is similar to the first conversation I had with Oskar before everything got started. He was a whole lot more cocky then than he is now. Now, his hands are clasped between his knees, trying to look casual, but the tension in his fists says otherwise.

I want to reach for his hand so badly, but that would only make the situation worse.

"I'm hoping we can clarify what's happening here." Mick hits Play right as Oskar and I step out of the DJ booth into the hall and burst into laughter. I almost sigh in relief. There's no evidence there. Or, at least, that's what I think before the me on the screen steps forward, presses close to Oskar, and touches his face.

There's nothing friendly about the exchange. There's nothing friendly about our expressions. We're looking at each other like ... fuck, how hadn't I noticed that Oskar looks at me like that? Viewing this from the outside makes me uncomfortably aware of how unsubtle we really have been.

Mick hits Pause as we disappear down the hall, and then he sits back again, hands rested over his stomach.

No one talks, and I know with every disappearing second that I'm quickly losing credibility for whatever I can come up with.

"I thought it would distract him," I say before I've even worked out where I'm going with this. "He was getting too worked up during the game, so I thought taking him somewhere away from the team's sponsors was a good idea."

"Which explains what you were doing *in there* but doesn't tell me what ... *this* was."

And considering I spin stories into a positive light for a living, it really shouldn't be this hard to respond.

"I said my face hurt, so he was checking it," Oskar blurts. "From the laughing. The laughing, uh, hurt it ..."

I want to groan, but I guess that's what we're rolling with. "I was checking his wound."

"I didn't realize you were a doctor."

"No, but I've seen Oskar every day since he got injured, so I'd notice if there were any changes."

Keerson's eyebrows scrunch as his gaze flicks from the screen to me and then onto Oskar. "His injury isn't even on that side."

That little ... I bite off my need to tell him to keep his stupid mouth closed.

"Well, he's not going to touch *that*, is he?" Oskar throws back, eyeing Keerson like he's shit under his skate.

"But why did he need to touch you at all?"

"I was reassuring him," I say, an edge to my voice, telling him to drop it. "If you haven't noticed, the team has been choking."

Keerson still looks conflicted though. He sends a concerned look my way and mouths, *What are you doing*?

I turn my attention back to Mick. "What exactly did you think was happening here?"

"Exactly what it looks like."

"Which is?"

"You and Voyjik have been close the last few months. Then with his injury, you refused to leave his side, held hands in that hospital room, I'm told, took a trip together to Vermont—"

"That was for a charity event, which I had cleared before we left. Just say what you mean."

"Well, you can't claim that my reasons for looking at this and speculating that you're in some kind of relationship are unfounded."

"We *are* in a relationship. That of PR manager and player."

"Come on," Keerson scoffs. "Since when has Voyjik cared about that?"

"Keerson—"

"No, I'm sorry, Lane, but we all know exactly what this looks like. I knew he was playing you. I told you to be careful." Keerson turns to Mick. "You can't keep letting Voyjik off the hook because he's a good player. He's never cared about the team, and this proves it."

"Fuck you. Of course I care about the team," Oskar throws back *so* professionally.

"Things are getting heated." I send a sharp look Oskar's way. "Oskar hasn't done anything—"

"Bullshit." Keerson turns back to me, eyes pleading. "Don't go down for him. You're the best PR manager we've had, and I knew he'd try something like this. I knew it had to be *something* for Voyjik to do a complete one-eighty. At what point is enough enough?" He glares at Mick. "He's clearly coerced Lane into this—"

"If we go by footage alone, I'd say it looks like the complete opposite. Lane's the one who swiped into that booth, and he's also the one who approached Voyjik in the hall."

I try not to react as I realize it looks exactly like that.

"There have been sexual harassment claims all over the NHL, and the last thing this team needs is that kind of scandal," Mick continues calmly. "How am I to know everything that happened was consensual?"

"Of course it was consensual," Oskar snaps. "Lane could never force me to do anything I didn't want to."

Oh, holy shit.

"Oskar …"

"No." He glares at me. "You won't let them say anything negative about me. They're not doing the same to you."

"So it's true?" Mick says.

"See?" Keerson stands, pointing right at Oskar. "He had one more chance, and he's blown it."

Mick doesn't immediately answer, and I know exactly what he's thinking. Ever since Oskar's been off the ice, they haven't won a game. Oskar truly does hold this team together. Before Mick can say anything, I play into those fears.

"There's no way you can fire him," I say. "I don't care what you do to me, but you know that you're fucked without him. Do you really want that kind of publicity? Heading into the construction of a new facility, and all anyone is going to be able to talk about is San Jose choking before playoffs and starting next season on a losing streak."

"Anything can be spun positively," Keerson says, trying to reason with me. And I get it. Oskar has been nothing more than a pain in his ass the entire time he's worked for this department. He made a fool of him when Keerson was his minder and didn't care how Keerson's career was affected by Oskar constantly giving him the slip. "But no one in this room can tell me Voyjik deserves to be on this team over every other hockey player who's busting their ass to make it to the NHL."

Oskar goes to respond, but I cut him off.

"And that's where you're wrong. Oskar has always given one hundred percent when it comes to hockey, and the last few months, he's worked his ass off to do exactly what we asked of him and cleaned up his image. Plus, with the injury and his stats, he's San Jose's golden boy. Do you really want to fire someone on the IR list? Anything can be spun positively when all parties are quiet, but if it got out that ..." I whistle. "Oskar refused to get the plastic surgery he was being pressured to get and ended up fired ..." I shrug and sit back in my seat.

"I don't like your tone, Lane," Mick says.

"No tone from me. All I'm saying is that if Oskar's fired, I can't control him anymore. Who knows what he'd do?"

As Oskar clues in to what I'm implying, the knowing look he sends me is evil as he links his hands behind his head. "I always have had trouble keeping things private."

"There's no need anyway because I have no plans to fire him." Mick huffs.

"*What?*" Keerson cries. "Does he have to murder someone to face any consequences at all?"

"There'll be consequences." Mick turns to me, face drawn. "You know I can't allow for this kind of thing to go on."

"I do," I croak.

Then Mick does the worst thing imaginable. He stares at me with defeated sympathy. "If anyone found out, there'd be all kinds of speculation ranging from consent to the ethics—"

"I understand."

Keerson's mouth drops. "You're firing *Lane*? Is this a joke? He's the best there is."

I want to point out that sleeping with a player probably doesn't support that theory.

"No way," Oskar says before Mick can say anything. "Let me make this simple. You fire him, I walk."

"Your contract—"

"Fuck the contract. What are you going to do? Make me pay the money back? Not like I spend any of it anyway. You going to tattle on me to the press? It's just same shit, different day. No one will care." Oskar laughs bitterly. "I think my *stellar* reputation can take the hit."

"What are you doing?" I hiss at him.

He waves my concern away and glares at Mick. "Call my bluff. I dare you."

Mick holds up his hand. "Can everyone take a breath? I never mentioned firing him."

He didn't?

He heaves a deep breath and looks over at me. "It's up to you, but my hands really are tied here. You can stay with the team *if* this whole thing ends right this second and not a word of it gets out. If you can't agree to that, then I'll be forced to let you go."

"Fine. Agreed. It's over." Oskar lifts his hands like it's a done deal. "Can we go home now?"

Mick ignores him. "Lane?"

And I know this is what Oskar thought we agreed to earlier. I know this is an easy out. Walk away with my career and reputation intact.

But is any of it worth it without him?

I already know the answer to that question.

It was back in his room when Oskar said for us to end this so I could keep my career that solidified my decision. He meant every word—but it was the words he didn't say that spoke louder. When I asked him if it's what he wanted, his response?

If it keeps you out of trouble, then yes.

Because he doesn't want to end this. What he wants is what's best for *me*.

Oskar put *me* first.

So I'm sure as hell going to do the same with him. Because maybe what's best for me ... is him.

I stand and hold out my hand to Mick. "Thank you for meeting with us. Please take this as the start of my two weeks' notice, but I'll have my official resignation to you by this afternoon. It's been a real honor to work here."

Then I turn on my heel and leave before anyone can stop me.

Chapter Thirty

Oskar

I storm after Lane. "What the fuck was that?"

He's as calm as ever, even though he just quit his job. Because of me. Pretending he didn't hear me, he keeps moving through the offices toward the exit, but I grip his arm to stop him.

He pulls out of my hold. "Not here, Oskar."

"I think here is perfect. Because as soon as you realize I'm not worth losing your livelihood for, you're going to want to march back in there and get your job back."

Lane's lips quirk on one side. "Never going to happen." He heads toward the parking lot, and I have no choice but to follow him.

"You're making a mistake."

That makes him stop. He slowly turns, and his gaze narrows. "Am I? Why is sticking up for you a mistake?"

"Because ..." My words get stuck in my throat.

Lane steps closer, standing chest to chest with me and way too close to be professional. He really doesn't care about saving his own skin, does he?

Well, he should because ... "I'm not worth it."

"Don't you think that's my decision to make?"

"No. Because I know myself better than you know me. Therefore, I can make the judgment call that I am not good enough for you."

"It's a good thing *I'm* the perceptive one, because you've never known who you are. If I say you're worth more to me than my job, I mean it."

A rush of *something* passes through me so quickly my knees go weak. "You'll regret throwing away everything you've worked for because of me."

One of the administration assistants walks by and gives us a weird look, but Lane's stoic glare makes her move on quickly.

"Not here," Lane says again, turning on his heel.

I reluctantly follow him to his car across the street, but I'm determined to not let him out of this parking garage until he gets his job back. "I'm not going with you." I fold my arms.

"No?" He smirks as he leans against the hood of his car.

"How the fuck have our roles reversed? Since when are you impulsive and I'm rational? Go back in there and beg."

Lane licks his lips. "I'd rather take you home and beg you to cheer me up with your cock."

I groan and almost give in immediately. "Lane. I can't ... You can't ..." I run a hand through my hair.

"I can't what?"

"Only a dumbass would choose me like you did back there because eventually I'm going to screw up again, and you would have lost it all for nothing."

Lane pushes off the side of the car and steps toward me. His whiskey-colored eyes are calculating as he closes the gap, and I hold my breath because I'm terrified he sees right through me.

"Aside from the fact that you are *not* nothing, I only did what you did in there. When it was me on the line, you were willing to end things to save my ass."

"How do you know I didn't end things because I just don't give a fuck about you?" The crack in my voice is anything but convincing, and he knows it.

"Is that the reason why you did it? Because you don't give a shit what happens to me?" There's a tone of amusement, but it's laced with a tiny bit of doubt.

Here's where I need to do the Oskar thing and push him away. I could tell him that he means nothing, that the last few months were just more ways to mess with him, the team, and my life that I was so determined to tear down before Lane came into it.

I could walk away and not give a damn about what he'll do now.

But ... I can't.

For my whole life, I've been immune to feelings. Real feelings. But it's obvious that I care about Lane—more than I've cared about anyone else before.

When I still haven't answered Lane's question, he presses himself against me.

"You might think that this is me choosing you with some naïve hope that you could choose me back, but you're wrong." With him against me, all I want to do is wrap my arms around him and never let go, but I force myself to stay still. "You chose me first," Lane says. "I know you're a professional D-man, but you don't have to defend yourself against everything. Let me in."

"I can't let you go down for me."

We're so close, his pink lips mere inches away from mine, his throat working as he swallows hard, and I want to kiss him and strangle him at the same damn time.

"What about letting me go down *on* you?"

Yep. Really not liking the role reversal here.

"Come on. I'm going to take you home, where I will spend all day convincing you that I'm completely on board with my decision."

"How do you know you're not going to regret it tomorrow?"

Lane lifts his lips, locking them with mine for a soft kiss that only lasts a couple of seconds. "Because I don't have any regrets when it comes to you."

For some unknown, fucked-up reason, my eyes sting, and my nose tingles. I'm helpless against this man, and I'm realizing all too late that he has a hold over me. A hold I don't want to break. One I can't walk away from.

This time, I'm the one to close the gap and bring our mouths together. It's the most gentle we've been with each other, and it feels like more than kissing.

It's giving in.

It's taking down that wall between us and admitting that we're more than a PR manager trying to wrangle his player.

It's giving up pretenses.

It's taking off masks.

It's opening up the possibility for more.

And while my body and my heart are on board, it's my brain that's screaming at me I'm making a mistake. Yet, the rest of me won't let myself stop.

I pull back from Lane's lips but stay close and breathe him in. "Why are you doing this to me?"

"*To* you?" he asks. "What am I doing *to* you?"

My voice is shaky as I admit something I have never admitted before because it's never happened. "You're making me fall for you."

I try to kiss him again so he can't say anything back that I don't want to hear, but he pulls away quickly and steps back. Just when I'm about to tell him I didn't mean it because I'm scared I've admitted too much, Lane smiles.

"Then I'm definitely not going back in there to beg for my job. Get in the car, Oskar, before I push you against it and fuck you for all the cameras to see. I know you'd love for that to happen, but if what you said is true, no one gets to see you like that anymore. Only me."

The possessiveness in his tone sends shivers down my spine, and it's like a zap of electricity to my balls. It turns me on like crazy, possibly even more than the idea of CCTV capturing Lane bending me over the hood of his car and taking my ass right here.

Lane gets into the driver's side, but before I take the passenger seat, I have to readjust myself.

Lane's looking damn proud of himself when I finally climb in the car. He's already got his seat belt on, but the car isn't running. "I expected you to put up a fight and ask me to dick you out right here."

"It was tempting," I admit. "But if we're doing this—if you're giving up your job to actually pursue this for real—then rules are rules. No one gets to see me having sex anymore."

Lane's eyes narrow. "Who are you, and where is the real Oskar?"

"Turns out he might have a bigger kink than public sex and the thrill of possibly being caught."

"What's that?"

"Regular, boring sex with his ... boyfriend? Is that what's happening here?"

"I'm probably too old to be throwing around the boyfriend word, but if you're asking if this is a relationship now, all I really have to say is I think we've been in one for a while and just didn't acknowledge it."

That's probably true. "And hey, I haven't fucked it up yet. Does that mean there's hope?"

Lane leans across the center console. "I'm not hoping." The disappointing sting about his lack of trust in me only hurts for a second because then he says, "I have *faith*."

I don't know if that makes him stupid or the perfect man for me.

Either way, I fall for him a little more.

Chapter Thirty-One

Lane

My phone is already being flooded with messages by the time we get back to Oskar's, and I have no desire to deal with any of it. In truth, I'm worried. Worried that I haven't learned a single lesson from my past relationships and am going to end up emotionally fucked-up again, but ... I'll never regret the decision I made.

I trust Oskar. I think I love him. And if we have that chance to build something together, then I'm going to try. It's not fair to Oskar that I put my past issues on him, and I've done everything in my power to make sure that the comparisons don't interfere with what we have. So while I'm worried, I'm not worried about *him*. Because he's done something those other men never did: he fought for me.

Even when I asked him not to.

"So, what'll it be, Mr. Pierce?" Oskar asks, his rough voice dropping until he sounds like pure sex.

"First, you're going to text Damon."

Oskar's face screws up. "You need to work on your dirty talk."

I laugh and grab his phone, handing it over. "We don't know what the team will say about this, but there'll be questions when it gets out. You need to give him the heads-up that we're together and I'm no longer your PR manager."

"Fine." He lets out a dramatic sigh and types a message. "You can't help managing me, can you?"

"You know how I like to be in control."

He hums and tosses his phone on the nightstand. "*Now* we're getting to the sexy talk. What do you want to do with me? Spank me? Eat me out? Choke me on your cock?"

"All excellent ideas." I step in close and brush a soft kiss over his lips. "But just this once, I don't want to play games. I want to enjoy you and show you what you mean to me."

"Awww ..." Oskar actually fucking pouts. "Stop being cute. I'll get used to it way too quickly."

I shove him back onto the bed and crawl up over the top of him. "Get used to it." I brush a kiss along his jaw. "Because I'm not going anywhere."

He leans up to press his lips to mine. The kiss is slower than usual between us but every bit as claiming. Strong lips, tongues sweeping deep, my hands traveling south to close over his delicious hockey ass as I pull him up against me. There are too many clothes between us, and even though I'm not in a hurry, don't want to rush this, I need to feel him.

The warm press of skin against mine, his hairy thighs, that gorgeous ink ... I want it all.

We keep kissing as I lazily rut against him and strip us out of our clothes. Every inch of skin that's revealed to me is a temptation for my lips, and when it's time to remove his pants, I can't stop myself. My lips trail along the side of his scar, over his jaw, down the column of his neck. I press a kiss to his round shoulder before licking his nipple into my mouth and giving it a sharp bite. He hisses, but I immediately let go to drag my tongue over his delicious abs all the way down to that *la petite mort* tattoo.

"I'm going to make you *la petite mort* so hard your vision will black out."

His smile is crooked. "That's not how that phrase works, but challenge accepted."

"Time for the fun zone," I say, then kneel up and slide his pants off, revealing that tattoo as well. Oskar is incredible. Perfection. Every part of him, from his messy tattoos to his gorgeous muscles to the scar that makes him even sexier than ever—because I *know* it makes him happy. A shiver ripples through me, and I grip his thighs, grounding myself against the balloon of happiness building in my chest. Then I flip him over and slap his ass cheek hard.

Oskar gasps as a bright red hand mark blooms against his skin, and the sight is so sexy, I do it again, then lean down and bite the spot.

His back muscles pull tight at the pain, but when he lets out a shaky breath, it's followed by, "Your mouth needs to be a little to the left."

I lick a stripe against his skin. "Here?"

"More."

I hum and do it again. "*Here?*"

"Fuck." He tilts his hips, arching his back as his body begs me for what he wants. "You know where, asshole."

I chuckle, then pull his cheeks apart and give him what he wants. Oskar's moan is sinful, and despite my self-control being pathetic when it comes to him, I somehow manage to stop myself from shoving him down and driving my cock into him. It's close though, and the more I use my mouth, the more shameless the sounds he's making become. I've teased him about it a hundred times, but I'll never get tired of how vocal he is.

"You know what you're missing," I say, tilting my head to sink my teeth into his hard muscle again. "A tattoo. Right here. That says Property of Lane Pierce." I lick the bite mark, only half-serious. It's too early to talk about shit like that, but *damn* that would turn me on. My name on his skin. That mark of forever that would be more than a dumb set of rings.

"Matching ones."

"What?" I ask, not sure that I've heard him right.

"I want Property of Oskar Voyjik on yours. I want to see that virgin skin fucked up with my name."

I shudder, hands closing over his ribs as I press a kiss between his shoulder blades. There's every chance he's going to be my undoing, but if that's the case, I gladly sacrifice my sanity to him. "It would be fitting," I tell him. "You've already fucked up my heart."

"Lane ..." He rolls over, pulling me down against him and kissing me again. Then he lets out a long whine when his hips make contact with my pants. "How do you still have clothes on? New rule. No clothes in my bed. Ever. Actually, let's go back to my original rule. This house will be a clothes-free zone, always."

"And when we have guests?"

"They'll be jealous as hell when they see the D I get to come home to every day."

I turn my smile into his hair. "I think you mean *man* you get to come home to."

"I said what I said. Now"—he flips me onto my back—"time to put the rule into effect." He wrestles down my pants and briefs while I lie back and watch him. His muscles bunch under his tattoos, his fuck-me hair falls over his forehead, and his grin when he sits back on his heels and runs his eyes over me is completely filthy. The whole image makes my heart stutter.

"I bet I can fuck you before you fuck me," he says.

"Wha—"

Oskar lunges for his nightstand, but I grab him around the waist and haul him back, wrestling him onto the bed. It takes real effort to keep him pinned.

"What happened to me showing you how much I care about you?"

He leans up to peck the tip of my nose. "You are. If you really, really care about me, you'll get your dick inside of me first."

Oh, it's on.

I have a split second to decide whether to play along before Oskar bucks me off and goes for the drawer again. I throw my weight on him, holding him down while I try to reach the supplies, but Oskar knocks me off him. He scrambles forward, I pull him back, and I swear to fucking hell I'm holding back a goddamn laugh.

I make it to the side of the bed and reach for the handle, but before I can take hold, Oskar drops onto my shoulders and forces the breath from my lungs.

"Little shit—"

He cackles as he jumps off the bed and yanks the drawer open, pulling out the supplies, but I stand and reach the lube first.

Oskar swipes for me, but I back away and cross the room.

We're both panting as we straighten, him with the condoms and me with the lube, out of each other's reach.

Oskar's eyes flick to the bottle and back to me again. "Sharing's caring."

"What do you propose?"

"We take what we need and then trade."

My eyes narrow. "You just want me to get myself ready so you can win."

He shrugs. "I'm going to win anyway, so if you want me to go in dry, you do you."

The thought of him entering me makes my cock twitch. "How much will your hockey ego be bruised when you lose?"

He tears open a condom packet. "See, that's the thing about playing with me—there *is* no losing."

And hasn't he got that right? "Fine." I make quick work of lubing up and shoving two fingers in. I get myself stretched enough that nothing is going to tear while he rolls a condom on, but that's about as easy as I'm going to make it. We inch forward to make the trade, and as my grasp closes over the condom packets, I yank them away and toss the lube to the other side of the room.

Oskar swears and darts after it as I hurry to get my own condom on, and then I watch as he snaps open the lube and presses his fingers to his hole.

My cock is *throbbing* as I approach him, stare dragging over that gorgeous fucking body. "You have until the count of three," I warn.

"Shit."

"One …" I stalk closer. "Two …" I step behind him, sheathed cock resting against his ass cheek—

"Three!" Oskar shoves me into the wall, trying to pin me and turn me at the same time. Neither of us holds back as we wrestle against each other, and somehow, I manage to get him over to the bed. His back hits the mattress first, but he rolls out of the way before I can climb on him, and then it's an all-out showdown.

His nails dig into my back, and I respond with a warning bite of my own. I get a knee to the kidney and an elbow to the eye, and other than being careful of his face, I'm just as rough with him. Between scratches and pulled hair, body jabs and twisted nipples, somehow, I find Oskar under me on the bed. My full weight is pressed into his shoulders, and I don't hesitate.

I grab my cock, line up, and press forward.

"Oh, *shit*," Oskar gasps, but nothing about the sound hints at disappointment.

The second I breach him, he stops struggling, whole body turning to liquid under my hands, and I take my time pressing in, cautious because he didn't have a lot of prep time.

My arms snake around his body to hold him close, and when Oskar turns his head to the side, I kiss his cheek under his scar.

"You okay?" I check.

He's still breathing heavily. "Perfect." He tilts his hips to take me deeper. "Unbelievably perfect."

"I was just thinking the same about you."

He smiles softly, eyes drifting closed as my hips meet his ass, and I take a second to memorize this moment. I don't think I've ever seen Oskar look so carefree.

I hug him to me as I start out with smooth, slow strokes. Every thrust is a tease, fast enough to feel good but nowhere near enough to get off. I want to rock inside him all day, to slowly and surely bring him to the edge over and over until he's sobbing and cursing my name in equal measure. I want to take my time, to prove to Oskar that he's worth every second, and mostly, I want to block out the rest of the fucked-up world and give all my attention to the amazing man under me.

The one that the world tried to tear down.
The one who built up all those defenses.
The one who let them all down for me.

My moan is long and low as I suck on his neck, rolling my hips with more purpose, driving as deep into him as I can. His ass is perfect, a tight vise around my cock that makes it feel like it belongs. Like there's nowhere else for it.

My property to use and own and treasure.

Just like mine is for him.

"You're the greatest thing that ever happened to me," I rasp. "You make me take risks and have fun. You challenge me constantly."

He grunts, one hand burrowing beneath his chest to close around mine. "You take me out of my comfort zone, but I always feel safe. We're good for each other."

"Perfectly matched."

He shoves back onto me. "I'm so glad I won."

"Remind me, who's inside who right now? That wasn't the aim of the game."

"It was the aim of *my* game."

I huff. "Of course it was."

"I'm going to need you to fuck me now," he begs.

"Gladly." I plant my knees into the mattress and pull his hips up with me. He scrambles to get his arms under him. "But, Oskar ..." I press my lips to his ear. "No coming until I say."

"*Urgh*, I hate you."

I laugh. "We'll revisit that once this is over."

My hands close over his hips as I straighten, and after two agonizingly slow thrusts, I let loose. The slap of skin on skin is obscene, especially when mixed with Oskar's gasps of pleasure. My balls hit his with every thrust, my fingers digging into his sides, and Oskar pushes back to meet me every time, never the passive participant. It turns me on so much to see how good I make him feel, to know how desperate he is for more.

My muscles tense as I give him the pounding of a lifetime, loving the sight of my cock disappearing between his cheeks. A bead of sweat rolls down the middle of my back, but I'm determined to keep going. My orgasm is getting close, rolling toward me and building by the second.

I swear his ass must be goddamn magic because I'm close way too soon every time. I wish I could stay in this moment, hovering right on the edge, my brain fuzzing over and tunnel-visioning until nothing else but me and Oskar and this incredible feeling between us remains.

"I'm so fucking close," I warn him.

"Shit." His hand flies between his legs, and I release his hip to slap his ass hard.

"Remember what I said."

"I do. It's why I'm holding on to my balls for dear life." His voice has turned to a whine, and every gasp sounds needier than the one before it. "Please come," he begs. "Please, please, please …"

His rough voice sounds wrecked. It makes my balls ache with need, makes my ass tense, and shock waves tremble down my spine.

"Lane … please … I want to be good for you."

It's those words that do it.

I slam home, brain cutting out as I finally find my release. My cock jerks with every pulse of come, and when the high starts to calm, I notice Oskar's arm working under him.

"Not yet you don't," I growl.

I pull out of him, flip him onto his back, and then straddle his waist.

"Oh, shit yes." His hands find my thighs as I hold his cock and lower myself onto it, taking every inch. It's tight and uncomfortable, but the lust-drunk expressions playing over his face make it all worth it.

"Sharing's caring, right?" I ask, leaning down to kiss him. "I take care of my man."

Then I ride him like my life fucking depends on it. I'm already exhausted, my legs are cramping, but I push through because I promised to show Oskar how I feel about him, and this ... right here ... this is me giving him everything. Proving that I'll never stop until he's happy. That I'll put myself through hell for him, and I won't even care.

We lock eyes, and he looks desperate and wrecked. "Oskar ... come."

"Yesss ..." He bucks up into me, uncontrolled and eager, and only a few seconds later, his cry fills the room. Fingers bite into my skin, and his abs flex as he comes, and the entire time I'm watching him, my heart feels that bit fuller.

When he's finished, I climb off and stretch out beside him. He rolls into my arms, and we spend the next few minutes in blissful silence, trailing light touches over each other's bodies.

"Should we make a wager on how many times Damon's tried to call?" he finally asks.

"Eh. Whatever the number is, it's going to be a few more because I'm not ready to deal with that yet."

He hums, pressing his face to my neck. "Agreed. We at least need to get rid of the condoms first."

"Good plan." I chuckle and squeeze him to me tighter. "You know, that was a good start to our relationship."

Oskar pulls back slightly, propping his head on his hand. "How so?"

"Well, we compromised. We challenged each other, and I made sure to give you everything. I promise that will never change."

His eyes practically shine. "I like that. But you forgot one more thing."

I give him a quizzical look as he leans in and brushes a kiss over my lips.

"No matter what … you will always come first."

Chapter Thirty-Two

Oskar

I smack Lane's bare ass as I get out of bed. "Ugh. My unemployed boyfriend is so lazy. Shouldn't you have been up before me to make my breakfast and kiss my cheek as you send me on my way to work?"

Lane rolls onto his back, and the glare he sends me almost has me running out the door. "This isn't the fifties, and I ain't your housewife."

I wince. "Too soon to joke about the job thing?"

"Considering the phone call I got last night? Yes."

Yeah, that was pretty bad. Seeing as Keerson had been doing Lane's job the whole time Lane's been with me, management decided Lane's services were no longer needed to fulfill his two weeks. He still gets paid for them because they're playing nice, but the dismissal was a kick in the guts for him.

Then Coach had the audacity to call me to come in today. He wants the team doctor to assess my readiness to go back on the ice earlier than originally planned because my stitches are out with my gash mostly healed, and we are dying out there. They *need* me.

But the vindictive side of me hopes I'm not cleared to play.

I'm anticipating a trade next season with everything I've put the team through this year, and it would be welcomed. The thing is, I can see Mick's side of it all. Lane and I being together will be scandalous because of nasty shit that has happened in the past with other teams and allegations made. I'm surprised I haven't been let out of my contract as well, but that's what pisses me off. They're only keeping me because they can't go to the playoffs without me, and they view Lane as expendable.

We both fucked up, but he's wearing the consequences.

Lane sits up and pulls the sheet over his lap but keeps his head low.

I hate seeing him so dejected. "Fuck San Jose."

"You don't mean that. They've been a good team to you."

I check the time on my phone. I really need to go, but this is more important.

Shit. Something more important than hockey? Lane really has done the impossible.

I take a seat next to him on the mattress, but that might be a bad idea because he smells like expensive cologne and cheap sex. My perfect guy. It's taking all of my willpower not to distract him away from his misery with more naked fun. But then I really will be late, and I'm in enough trouble as it is. Even if I'm as pissed at team management as they are with me.

I grip Lane's hand. "You'll find something else. At least they didn't fire you?"

His brown eyes meet mine. "You think that's going to stop the gossip? Everyone will know why I had to leave San Jose."

"Will it be so terrible if you tell them you left for me? So we could date and be together ethically?"

"Everyone will still talk."

I nudge him. "Everyone always talks. Look at all the gossip about me out there that's not true."

"Most of it is true," he mutters.

"But thanks to you, they don't know that. What's true and what's not? Oh no, no one knows what to believe anymore."

"Lucky I was good at my job, then, huh?"

"Exactly. I have no doubt you'll bounce back. Another team will take you, and then you can tell them to give me a contract where we have to stay together." I think about that. "That's actually not a bad idea, you know."

"What?"

"Trying to get contracts with another team. Surely, if we are employed together with our relationship being out in the open, it takes away the ickiness of how we got together, doesn't it?"

He hums. "Mm. Maybe."

I wish there was a way I could fix this for him. "Ooh, I know. I could hire you to be my own personal carer. Who takes care of allllll of me."

Rightfully so, he side-eyes me. "That sounds a lot like prostitution or sexual harassment from an employer, and we're trying to avoid our relationship being labeled as problematic."

"Well, I'm open to suggestions here."

When he looks at me again, the sorrow in his eyes is evident. "I might have to get a job outside of hockey."

I gasp. "You mean ... you might have to switch to ..." I pretend to gag. "Football? How would you even survive?"

Yay, I finally get a smile.

"I'd find a way to manage. Football players wear tighter pants. I can focus on that."

I scowl, which makes him smile even wider.

I squeeze his leg. "I have to get to the arena. Are you going to be okay?"

"I'm fine. I promise."

"Do me a favor?"

"If it's cook dinner in an apron and heels, I'm going to have to go with no."

"Damn. It wasn't, but now it is. That visual ..." My mouth hangs open, and I try not to drool.

He shoves me.

"Okay, no. It was to take today easy and don't stress over finding a new job. Relax for once."

Lane frowns. "How does one do that exactly?"

"Watch trashy reality TV?"

"Do I look like the type of person who watches that?"

"It could be cathartic for you."

"How so?"

"How else does anyone feel better about the shit in their lives than seeing trash humans do trash things? No matter how down you are, at least you're not them."

He slumps. "I hate that you actually make sense."

"Try it. For me."

"I will. And don't let them tell you you're ready to go back on the ice. You're still not completely healed." His fingers brush over my cheek, just under my scar.

"I'll see what they have to say first."

"I hate to say it, but at this point, I don't think they've got your best interests in mind. Only the playoffs. Your eye is more important than the stupid playoffs."

"You bite your tongue. The playoffs are in the top three things in life."

"What are the other two?"

"Sex."

Lane glowers at me. "Should've guessed that one. And?"

I lean over and kiss his cheek. "You."

"I come before the playoffs though, right?"

I hesitate until real doubt begins to cross his face, and then I can't hold it back. "Abso-fucking-lutely."

"The majority of your wound is healing well," the team doctor says.

"So you're clearing me to play?"

He hesitates. "I'm not going to lie. The area closest to your eye is still healing. I can butterfly tape it, but if you take a hard hit, there's no way it'll hold."

"So you're *not* clearing me to play."

Dr. Denali, or Dr. D as we all call him, stands over me, his lips pursed. "Look, I'm going to level with you. Team management wants me to clear you, but I'm torn. Professionally speaking, you could get back out there with little risk, but there *is* a risk. The wrong hit, a stick getting under your visor, an elbow to the face during a fight ... anything could make it worse. You're on the border. I could let you play, or I could keep you on the IR list for another week to be sure, but by then—"

"The season will be over, and our chance at playoffs could be done if the team doesn't pull their heads out of their asses and get a win."

"Exactly."

I so desperately want to get back out there, but at the same time, I'm a stubborn son of a bitch, and my loyalty to this team is practically nonexistent, even though Lane and I were the ones in the wrong initially. Yes, we crossed lines and put this club's reputation in jeopardy, but now they're dismissing Lane after all that he's done for the team while also asking me to risk my career so we can *maybe* make the playoffs.

"If I'm not ready, I'm not ready. Team management will just have to deal with that."

Dr. D nods. "Then it's my stern professional opinion that getting back out on the ice at this point will risk your eye too much for me to sign off on it."

"Thanks, Dr. D. I'll let you deal with management over your decision."

"Wow, Voyjik. You're so generous," he deadpans.

"Aren't I? Everyone is lucky to have me in their life."

"Everyone or just Lane?"

My amusement dies. "I'm guessing word has gotten out, then."

"Oh yeah. Big-time. Everyone has heard about how Lane has been asked not to come back to work. Permanently."

But ... "Lane quit."

"Officially, but everyone knows he's already gone. What, he didn't have to give notice?"

I try not to get angry. Management is doing what it can to save face. Still, when I head for the locker room to let the guys know I haven't been cleared and tell them to kick ass, it's obvious how far the chatter has spread.

All talk dies as I walk into the locker room.

My neck burns, and I pull at the collar of my San Jose T-shirt. I'm used to being the topic of discussion. I used to welcome it and crave it because I've always had that need for attention—good or bad. But this ... I've finally found my boundaries.

And Lane is it. He means too much to me to play us down, and if I get into it here and now, I'm going to say some shit that will definitely get me fired.

Instead of addressing the elephant in the room, I make my way over to Aleks because out of everyone, he might be the only one who understands.

But when his first words out of his mouth are "You couldn't help yourself, could you?" I can't tell if he's pissed or resigned to the fact I'm that much of a screwup.

The normal defenses of "It wasn't my fault" or a half-hearted "Oops" don't pass my lips.

"Yeah, we both know we fucked up, but it also wasn't supposed to get as far as it did." I glance around the locker room, and the others are doing that thing where they're pretending they're not listening but probably are.

"Now we're stuck with Keerson, who doesn't know hockey from his ass. It's like he gets joy from sending the worst player of the game to the press conferences when they're at their lowest. Like he feels we need to explain ourselves for why we individually did so terribly to the media. At least Lane cared about *us* and the team equally."

I screw up my nose. "Yeah, I saw that interview of yours. Brutal, man."

"Please tell me you're coming back today?"

Okay then. If he is angry about the Lane situation, at least he's not too angry.

I shake my head. "Nah. Doc says it's too risky."

"Fuck," he snaps. "This team needs new talent. One guy being put on the IR list shouldn't affect the scores this much."

"Aww. It's cute you think it's all me, but even I'm not that conceited. It's not my absence that is making the team suck. It's a losing streak. All teams have them. Look at Vegas this season."

Aleks winces.

"Exactly. They're not even in with a shot of the playoffs. But we still are. The team only needs to win the next game, and our season isn't done."

"Sure. I'll get right on that. As well as the game after that, and the one after that …"

I grip his shoulder. "I should get out of here before all the questions start. Have a good practice."

"Really?" Aleks asks. "That's all you're going to give me? I have been so restrained here. I need details. Preferably all the dirty ones. But, like, big-picture stuff too."

I laugh.

"Let's just say Lane and I are in a relationship that neither of us saw coming, and not everyone is happy about it." I lower my voice. "Mick told him to end it or lose his job. So Lane quit."

Aleks looks shocked. "Well, shit. That's …"

I wait for him to say something like that's the stupidest thing Lane's ever done, and I'd have to agree with him because the idea of a future with me still seems so out of the realm of possibilities. I'm not convinced I won't fuck things up between us. But we chose each other, and I want to see it through to the end. Whatever that end may be.

In a dumpster fire of broken hearts? Possibly.

With matching rings and tuxes and spouting I love yous in front of everyone we know? Not likely.

Happiness? This is the one I'm rooting for. The one I want to strive for.

Even if I'm scared as all hell of screwing it all up.

"That's what?" I ask Aleks. "Dumb? I know."

"I was going to say it's romantic, so no wonder I'm divorced."

"Those things kind of contradict themselves."

"Nah, I was thinking about Rebecca and how she hated that I was away so much. Giving it all up didn't even occur to me to be an option."

"The right person wouldn't want you to give up your job for them."

"Lane did though."

I huff. "Oh, I fought him on it. I even tried to break up with him."

Aleks smiles. "And he quit anyway. Rebecca did break up with me, and I let her walk."

"See? Wrong person for you, then. You'll find the right one."

"Eventually. I have a lot of manwhoring to do first."

"Well, with me being taken now, I pass the San Jose slutbag crown to you." I mime taking a crown off my head and placing it on his.

"It's an honor." He puts his hand over his heart and says, "I solemnly swear to share my dick with every man, woman, enby, and any other gender who wants it."

"Ah. The Hippocratic oath of manwhores."

Coach walks in at that moment and locks glaring eyes with me.

"Oh shit, you're in trouble," Aleks says.

"Yep."

"Shouldn't you be at home resting seeing as you're too injured to play?" Coach barks.

I mock salute him. "On my way now." I turn to Aleks. "Good luck for the game tomorrow. We need the win."

His eyes don't fill me with confidence, but there's nothing I can personally do now.

I'm going to go home to my man and worship his body again.

And again, and again, and again.

Chapter Thirty-Three

Lane

As soon as Oskar leaves, I deflate. I'm trying to keep reasonably upbeat about this whole thing whenever he's around, but I'd be lying if I said I wasn't freaking out.

No other team has reached out to me, and I'm hesitant to be the one to make the first move as I don't know how far the news of us has spread. What we did may not have been technically against any rules or laws, but it also wasn't ethical either. I know Oskar is worried that I'm going to wake up one day and resent him for everything that has happened, but I went into this knowing what I was doing. Every single choice has been my own, and now I'm facing the consequences of those choices.

Maybe when I was younger, I would've tried to blame someone else, but I'm old enough now to understand that that's how the world works.

Two hours after Oskar leaves, there's a knock at the door. As far as I know, he wasn't expecting any visitors, and it's way too early for him to be back yet. Plus, he wouldn't knock on his own door.

I'm still in the sweats I haphazardly pulled on when I finally climbed out of bed this morning, but hey, it's better than being naked. I mute the TV and find the last person I'd expect on Oskar's front porch.

"Damon." I hesitate, half-concerned he's going to kick my ass. "You sure do like to fly out here rather than use the phone. Should I be concerned you and Oskar are having a scandalous affair?"

The bastard actually rolls his eyes at me. "The two of you have already filled that space on my bingo card. Can I come in?"

"Sure." I step aside. "But Oskar isn't here. He's gone to the rink for a checkup with the team doctor. Actually, that's probably something you should be there for." Concern hits my gut as I follow Damon into the house. "We think they're going to clear him to play the next game when he's not ready."

"One of the good parts of being an agent is learning to tell when you need to fight for your clients and when they can do it themselves." He drops his laptop bag on the couch and takes a seat. "Since when have you ever known Oskar to do something he doesn't want to?"

"I dunno, he was pretty reluctant when I organized that positive PR stuff for him."

"My point remains. If he didn't want to do it, he wouldn't have done it."

I think back to how easily he took to it, and my heart warms. "You're right."

"Besides, it'd be a ballsy team doctor to clear a patient they weren't confident about and risk losing their license to practice."

I flop back onto the couch I was sitting on earlier. "It's not like it doesn't happen."

"Yes, but in those cases, they're not dealing with a fiery, loudmouthed hockey player who can't keep a single thing quiet and already has a chip on his shoulder over the team who let his boyfriend go." He gives me a shrewd look, and I relent.

"So I should stop worrying. Got it."

"I'd say you have bigger things to be worried about, don't you?"

My reputation? My job? How I'm going to make a living? "Nothing's more important than Oskar."

Damon's bright green gaze assesses me, and I sigh.

"If you're here to lecture me, you might as well get it over with. I have a full day of television calling my name. Oskar will be very annoyed if you get between me and his idea of therapy." I gesture toward where the reality show I'm not even sure I understand is playing silently.

Damon casts a pitiful look toward the TV and back to me again. "So this is how you want to be spending your days?"

"It was a toss-up between this and an apron and heels. I'm comfortable with my choice."

"You know, there will come a day when both you and Oskar don't feel the need to fill me in on every little thing going on in your lives."

"Maybe. But we're not there yet."

"It'll be going in the contract," he says.

I tilt my head. "Doesn't Oskar already have a contract?"

"I wasn't talking about his."

It takes me a moment to puzzle that out, and while I'm a smart guy and have an inkling of what he's getting at, I'm not going to get too excited. "Last I checked, househusbands don't need an agent."

"I'm not taking on clients."

"Then ..." I swallow back my nerves. "What's this conversation about? An NDA? That ship has sailed."

"My PR team could use more people like you."

I swear my eyebrows try to jump from my face. "You like your staff sleeping with clients?"

"Fuck no, and you can be assured there'll be a clause in yours to specifically say that."

"You don't need a clause when I have Oskar." My amusement fades slightly as what he's said starts to sink in. "You're serious?"

"I am."

"But ... at the risk of totally messing this up, why? My reputation in the business is a mess, and what I did was highly unethical. It's not like any of that was a secret to me when we started this relationship."

Damon spreads his hands like I've made his point for him. "You've never lied to me. When all of this got started, you didn't worry about your own job security. You were worried about making sure I had a plan for Oskar if it came out. I could have used that against you. I could have painted the picture that you were taking advantage of my client, but you weren't worried about any of that."

"You've never struck me as someone who'd do something underhanded."

"Because I'm not. But that wasn't the only time you put Oskar's career first. You love your job, and yet you gave me the heads-up about San Jose possibly terminating his contract, which allowed me time to stockpile a mountainload of arguments to prevent that from happening, and then you walked away from all of it. For him."

"And while I love that you have this high of an opinion of me, I didn't walk away because I was responsible for him. I walked away because I couldn't end it."

"Oskar's never had anyone fight for him like that."

"I'd fight for him like that every day if he let me."

Damon watches me for a moment. "I've looked into your career. Your record is spotless. Every team you manage is low on scandals. What happened with Oskar was an anomaly after years of ethical, diligent hard work. San Jose is already falling apart without you, and while they might be comfortable forcing a man to choose between the career he loves or the man he loves, I will never do that."

And even though Oskar and I have never used that word, I don't argue because I'm pretty certain it's true. Which causes another problem, because while having Damon walk in and offer me a position solves all of my current problems, it also creates a big one of its own. "You're based in New York."

Damon pulls out his phone and does something before nodding at mine. "I've emailed my proposal through to you. My company is expanding quickly, and while my PR manager position is already filled, I have something that might interest you more."

More than a position I've held for almost the last decade? I hurry to open my emails and find the contract attached.

Public Relations Liaison – Remote
"What …"
"My players are all across the country, so it doesn't make sense for my team to all be based out of one city. I already have a liaison who covers the East Coast, and I'm open to more. You'll primarily work out of your home with the expectation that once an LA office is opened, you'll visit, possibly head a team, and when I need someone to clean up a mess, you'll travel to whatever location I need you in."

"That's … incredible."

"Off the record, where Oskar is concerned, there's already been talk. Nothing official because of the trade cutoff date, but I have a source who is like the TMZ of hockey. He knows everything first, and he's ninety percent sure San Jose is going to trade him come next season. I know your home is here, but—"

"I'll move with him."

"That's what I thought you'd say." He gives me a smug look. "If you're my employee, relocation costs would be covered. I have good health benefits and a competitive salary. Take a few days to—"

"I'll take it."

He blinks at me. "You haven't even read over the contract."

"I assume you'll have to update it anyway. Since apparently I'm getting a clause about not sharing my sex life."

"Are you going to at least check the salary?"

"Nope. In the spirit of keeping the honesty going, you could be undercutting me like an asshole, and I wouldn't have a choice. I'm at your mercy."

"Good thing I'm not an asshole, then."

"And *that's* why I don't need to check it."

There's a clatter as the front door opens and Oskar yells out, "Lane, you better be naked!"

Damon groans.

"I was interrupted," I shout back.

Oskar rounds the corner, and when his eyes land on Damon and then flick to me, he throws up his hands like a busted perp. "I didn't do it!"

I jump up before he gets a chance to realize that not everything is about him and haul him against me. Then I give him the longest, happiest, filthiest kiss I can manage. I'd thought I was happy before, but this? Nothing can beat this. I get Oskar, and I get to work in a field I love, that I'm good at, and I don't have to sneak around or make sacrifices to do that.

A throat clears behind us. "I've just thought of another clause to add."

I smile against Oskar's mouth and reluctantly pull back. "Add whatever shit you need to. I'll sign it."

"Sign what?" Oskar's attention ping-pongs between us.

Damon picks up his bag and moves to leave. "I'll let you two talk. Maddy came with me for once, and he's waiting for me back at the hotel."

Oskar barely says goodbye before he's on me. "What do we need to talk about?"

"You're going to have to table your dreams of a fifties househusband. I have a job."

"With *Damon*? But you're not an agent."

"And while I love the confidence you have in me to be able to do anything, King Sports has a PR department too."

Oskar's face falls. "In New York." I can tell he's trying to hold back his rejection, but I don't leave him questioning for long.

"I'll be working remotely, which means ..."

"You can stay here?"

"Anywhere." This time I kiss him. "Wherever you go, I go. I'll follow you across the whole of the country if I need to."

He tilts his head. "What if I'm traded to Canada?"

I cringe. "My love has *some* limits."

I'm expecting Oskar to throw out a retort or thump me in the shoulder or *something*, but all he does is stare at me.

"You okay?"

"*Love?*"

Ah ... fuck. I clear my throat, somehow more nervous than I was being called in for the meeting with Mick. My career was something special, but what we have is *everything*. "My answer to that question depends on your answer to mine."

"No one's ever loved me before," he says, sounding stunned.

"Your parents?"

"That's the most basic expectation for a parent. You ... you don't have to, you know?"

I chuckle and run my fingers through his messy hair. "I think at this point, I'm helpless against it."

"Good." He clings to me desperately. "Because if you love me, you can't leave me. That's how this works."

"That's exactly how this works."

His face explodes with the most heart-stopping smile I've ever seen. And if that's what Oskar looks like truly happy, the world better watch out. "If I say I love you too, does that mean we can get matching tattoos now?"

"Is your love dependent on that?"

"Well, no pressure, but ..."

"I'm *really* feeling the love."

"There's just *so* much of me to go around. I need to be careful about locking all this down. Think of all the men in the world who haven't had a turn."

I slap his ass, and he yelps.

"I'm *joking*."

"Yeah? Prove it."

"Fine, you want proof that I love you? How about that I love everything about you? I love that you're bossy and fuck me like you mean it. I love that you see more of me than anyone, and not because I couldn't keep it hidden from you, but because you *wanted* to see. You looked for good where no one believed it existed—even me. You're smart, and fun, and go against all common sense to make sure I'm happy. I think you're an idiot for settling down with someone as reckless as me, but I'm never letting you go. Not now that I know what real love feels like. Not when I know what it's like to be someone's first choice. And because you've shown me how amazing those things are, I'll spend every day doing the same for you. How's that for proof, huh?"

I pretend to think for a moment, but I can't keep it up for long. The happiness I'm fighting escapes, and fuck him for thinking he's too reckless for me. "Oskar …"

He swallows and meets my eyes.

"You say you're too reckless for me, but I say you're selling yourself short. Your attitude, your love, your humor, your defensiveness, your vulnerability. It's all *too much*. And I would never settle for anything less than what you give me."

He huffs a laugh that I'm not so sure isn't holding back the type of emotion he never lets out. "Fuck. I thought I had you beat there, and you had to go and one-up me."

"And I promise you I always will."

He kisses me, and I hug him, but there's one more thing I need to make sure he knows.

"What you said … about no one loving you who didn't have to."

"Yeah?"

"You're wrong."

He snorts. "I'm never wrong."

"Oh, yeah? I bet you have a whole *collective* of friends who beg to differ."

He thinks about it a moment but then nods. "Damn it, I think you're right again."

Epilogue

Oskar

Off-Season

"Are you ready?" I side-eye Aleks in the private elevator taking us to the Sky Room in the middle of New York City.

"I still can't believe your PR department is *letting* you do this," Lane says beside me.

"Technically, they don't know, but I figure so long as it was on the down low ..." Aleks runs a hand through his hair. "Shit, is this the wrong thing to do?"

"I'm keeping my mouth shut," Lane says. "It's not my job anymore."

I backhand Aleks's chest. "You should change agents. If you hire Damon for your next contract, you'll get Lane thrown in, and then he could give his opinion on this."

"Or he could offer it to me for free because he's a nice and decent human being?"

I can't deny he is that, but ... "If you think he's nice and decent, you should see what he does to me when I've been naughty."

Lane tugs on my hand and talks over me. "Ignore him. If you want my professional opinion, coming to this event tonight is foolish, but not as foolish as, say—"

"Having a threesome with two guys in an alley," I supply helpfully.

"Are you going to always bring that up?" Lane grumbles.

"I have fond memories of it."

Lane glares at me, and I wrap my arms around him.

"Because it brought me you. Duh."

He melts into my arms, but then I look over at Aleks with a subtle shake of my head and mouth, "So hot."

"The elevator is reflective, asshole." Lane looks up at me. "The love you have for me was so worth the cost of my career. Honestly. It hurts how much you love me."

I lean in and say, "I can show you later how much I love you."

"Eww, loved-up people," Aleks says. "I'm finally free of monogamy. I'm going to spend the next few years spreading my seed far and wide. But, you know, metaphorically. I don't actually want babies. Or STDs."

I nod. "They're not fun. Either of them."

Aleks narrows his gaze at me. "It was chlamydia, wasn't it?"

"The clap, actually. Hooray for azithromycin."

"And this is why I checked his health records before ditching condoms," Lane says.

"That sounds an awful lot like slut shaming, sir, and I will not stand for it."

"Can I point out you were the one who brought up the threesome in the alley comment? I watched that CCTV footage about a billion times. No condoms anywhere."

I pretend to be pissed, but he has a point. Before he came along, I did share the love and wasn't always responsible. I was on PrEP, but that only goes so far. I was completely shameless and didn't care about the consequences to my body or my life in general because I thought I was invincible.

While growing up sucks, I can say I have more self-worth than I ever have before, and it's not because of falling in love with Lane. A man didn't rescue me. He showed me what I could be. *Who* I could be.

But there will always be a bit of old me deep down. "I bet you jerked off to that footage a million times."

Aleks steps forward and repeatedly hits the button for our floor. "This has got to be the slowest elevator in history."

"Quick, he needs to make his escape from all this monogamy!" And fuck, those words are weird coming out of my mouth. Of all people.

Lane knocks his head against mine. "Ten bucks says Aleks falls for the first person he dates."

"Not going to happen," Aleks sings.

"It's so going to happen," I say.

The doors finally open, and we step out into a function room that has a terrace with an amazing view of the city skyline.

Hockey players are scattered throughout the entire venue. Everyone from the New York team is here, as well as some old dudes from Boston. Damon is with his partner at the bar, and there's a group of giant Viking-looking Norse gods out on the terrace.

I spot the other guys from the Queer Collective in one corner, but before we can make a move over to them, Lennon, Ollie Stromberg's partner, approaches and gives me a hug.

"Thanks for coming."

"That's what he—"

Lane pinches me. "Don't."

Yes, sir.

"We wouldn't have missed Ollie's retirement party for the world," I say instead.

"New blood," a booming voice sounds from behind Lennon.

We look up to see Ezra approaching us with Anton and a few other Collective guys trailing him.

"Yep. New blood." I shove Aleks forward.

"No, I meant this one." Ezra pulls Ayri Quinn from Buffalo next to him.

At that same moment, Westly Dalton appears with his partner, Jasper, and his younger brother, Asher.

"Do I really have to join this stupid thing?" Asher Dalton asks with a scowl on his face.

"Little Dalton!" Ezra yells and then tries to hug him.

Asher steps back. "What is our one rule?"

Ezra cocks his head. "Uh, not to touch you?"

"That's right. This whole thing"—he waves his hand over his body—"is off-limits to Ezra Palaszczuk."

"Even on the ice?" Ezra asks.

"Even then."

"I don't think you know how hockey works," Ezra says.

Anton possessively puts his hand behind Ezra's back. "Okay, what story am I missing?"

West grins. "Do you really need us to draw you a picture?"

Anton turns to Ezra. "You had sex with West's little brother, didn't you?"

"It was years ago. Just one of many who didn't come close to you."

West and Asher turn to each other and in unison and very sarcastically say, "Ouch." Then they burst out laughing.

Two bros sharing a dude? Hey, I'd be down for it, especially the Dalton brothers.

"Asher Dalton?" Ayri holds out his hand. "Heard you're joining Buffalo. Will be good to have another queer guy on the team."

They shake hands, and then Asher says to his brother with awe in his voice, "Ayri Quinn knows my name."

A guy hovering behind Asher steps forward. "You know who else knows your name? Your boyfriend."

Asher wraps his arm around the guy's shoulders. "Ayri, this is my ball and chain, Kole."

Kole smacks Asher's chest.

"Oh, and I love him very, very much."

Kole sighs.

"Wait, so we're inducting three guys into the Queer Collective tonight?" I ask.

"And saying goodbye to one," Anton says.

Ezra shakes his head. "We never say goodbye. Collective for life."

Asher looks at West. "I used to think you were so cool, man. This feels very Babysitter Club."

"I knew I caught you reading Hazel's collection of those books," West says. "You said she left them in your room."

"Look at that, time for a drink." Asher takes his boyfriend's hand and drags him toward the bar.

"I'll come with," Ayri says.

And in true Collective tradition, we call out, "Macallan!"

"One for all of us," Ezra adds. "It's tradition."

"You're starting to get your wish, Ez," I say. "We're taking over the league. Three newbies at once?"

"It's a shame those two play for Buffalo. We need one for each team, damn it, yet somehow we've ended up with two in Boston, two in Vegas, two in Buffalo, and you two in San Jose."

Aleks and I look at each other, thinking of the news we shared before we got here.

My gaze moves to Lane, and he nods for me to tell them. These are my friends, and Lane was right when he said they also love me unconditionally. And it's not like this will be shocking to them anyway.

"That's not actually accurate," I say. "Neither of us will be playing for San Jose next season."

Everyone's mouth drops. Eyes widen. Someone even squeaks, but I don't know where it comes from.

"I didn't renew my contract," Aleks says. "The team not making the playoffs when we practically had it in the bag was bad enough, but I also didn't like how they handled the Oskar and Lane situation. Management made the wrong choice there. Plus, they were lowballing me. And with Oskar being traded—"

"What?" everyone cuts in. It's like the Collective share one brain.

"Oh, yeah. That's my fun news. There had been rumors, and basically, Damon went to them and said I'd go quietly if they make a deal with a team on the West Coast because that's where Lane will be."

"Where did you get?" Ezra asks.

"Anaheim."

Ez turns to Aleks. "Where are you going? If you say Anaheim too, I'll kick your ass. We all need to be on board with this world domination thing."

"You're safe. I signed with Seattle."

It sucks that Aleks is going to be that far away when we just became close, but that's the game.

"Yes," Ezra says excitedly. "It's happening."

"You know," I point out, "you could take one for the Collective and sign with a different team than the one your boyfriend is on."

Ezra frowns. "Why would I do that when I can ask you all to inconvenience your lives? That's much easier for me. Duh."

I snort.

Ayri, Asher, and Kole come back with Ollie, Soren, Foster, Foster's partner, Tripp, and Dex. Damn, we really are starting to take over. There are two trays full of drinks, and we all take one.

"We all here?" Ezra asks.

"We are, but we need to keep the next part on the DL because this one isn't officially out yet." I point to Aleks.

Aleks shrugs. "Your boyfriend ain't my PR rep anymore. I'm coming out, bitches."

Fingers crossed that doesn't backfire with his new team.

"In that case." Ezra holds up his glass of Macallan. "Cheero to being queero."

"Yeah, that's me out," Asher says until his boyfriend nudges him. "Fine. Cheero to no labels though."

"This toast gets longer and longer every year," Ezra mutters.

"And also, here's to Strömberg." Anton lifts his glass. "For bowing out gracefully after the crap year he had."

Ollie laughs. "Excuse me, but did anyone here make the playoffs this year?"

We glance around and realize none of our teams did.

"Well, shit. We need to fix that next season," Ezra says. "Anton and I have already done our part by winning a

Stanley Cup. And even though they weren't together at the time, Tripp and Dex have a win too. Who's next to bring the Cup home for the Collective?"

Anton leans in. "Can't we just win again?"

Ezra lowers his voice, but we can still hear him. "Shh. We have to give these losers some kind of hope."

"Just for that," I cut in, "I say we all fight to knock Boston out of the running for the playoffs next year."

"Now that, I'll cheers to," Asher says.

"Can we toast now?" Ezra asks. "Jesus Christ. You try to have a moment with your friends, and they ruin it by having more fun than you."

I lift my glass. "Cheers."

There's a chorus of cheers, and we all drink down the smooth whiskey. Flashes go off, and if Aleks had any doubts about coming out, it's too late now. I look around at my friends, at the whole ridiculous lot of us flying in to show Ollie our support, and I know, without a doubt, they'd do exactly the same for me.

We're a messed-up—and thanks to Ezra, kinda incestuous—family, and I'm lucky to have them in my life.

"As my retirement gift," Ollie says, "I want us all to hang out tonight. After all this mess of the media, my team, and my intrusive as fuck family out there"—he thumbs behind him to where the Norse gods are—"I want to hang with my people. It's so rare we all get to be in the one room."

Ezra lifts his glass. "Keep these coming, and you'll never get rid of us."

Lane leans in and whispers in my ear, "I don't know if I'll make it all night without giving you an orgasm."

I'm about to tell everyone that we're out, but then my boyfriend shocks the hell out of me.

"I might have to drag you into a bathroom stall and fuck your brains out while we're here, then."

My gaze flies to his. "Really?"

"Like Aleks said. I'm not your PR rep anymore."

"Well, technically, you work for my agent, so—"

"Do you not want to have mostly public sex with me? Keep talking and make me second-guess myself."

I groan. "You broke me. Old me wouldn't have even cared about that technicality. I'd already be naked and bent over in a disgusting bathroom. You've ruined me."

"Ruined you … made you less selfish. Same thing, right?"

I kiss his cheek. "You've ruined me in the best possible way."

Read on for a preview of
Foolish Puckboy...

ALEKS

The word "divorce" is supposed to elicit an eruption of all-out screaming and anger. So when Rebecca first mentioned it with a defeated sigh, I was shocked. Not because I didn't expect it but in the way the words were delivered. They might have been whispered, but they held finality, and with one simple sentence, my marriage was over.

I had the opportunity to pack up and leave San Jose, so I jumped at it, signed with Seattle, and made the move north.

It was the right decision. It's a clean break. New city. New team. New me.

Then why does sitting on the balcony of my new place, drinking scotch, looking out at the water, feel like the same ol' shit?

Coming out as pansexual was supposed to open me up to more possibilities than ever before, but my old PR manager was right. The announcement happening fresh off my divorce has made the public think that I'm actually gay and what Rebecca and I had for all those years was a ruse. Or that I got so over being with a woman I wanted to try dick. It's one stereotype after the other. Lane did warn me, so I only have myself to blame. No, I have society to blame as a whole. I'm only thankful this PR nightmare happened during the off-season, but because of the backlash, I haven't tried to date anyone. Of any gender. Technically, I've gone on PR dates with some models—female, of course—a Canadian actress who films her TV show in Vancouver, and a couple of women my new PR team set me up with, but none of them have been real. They've been photo ops.

When Rebecca and I split up, I was excited to get back out there. Now, I'm too self-conscious to date anyone for real.

I foolishly thought I'd be the next Ezra Palaszczuk or Oskar Voyjik, the two biggest slutbags of the league. Oskar even gave me the imaginary crown when he fell in love with our PR manager.

It's not sitting so pretty on my head right now.

When my doorbell rings, I freeze because the only person who knows my new address is— Fuck. I'm gonna kill him.

I stand and make my way to the side of my balcony and look down to the right near my front door.

I'm doubly gonna kill him.

Oskar Voyjik didn't only show up unannounced, but he brought nearly the whole Queer Collective with him. Almost every queer man in the NHL is at my doorstep, trying to be quiet and snickering to themselves like a bunch of dumbasses.

"No one's home," I call out, and all seven of them look up at me.

"Don't make us drag you out of there," Ezra yells.

Maybe the company will do me good. Real company. Not PR fakeness. I've been whining about things being too much of the same, and if there's anything I can count on these guys for, it's disrupting the normalcy.

I head inside and down the glass stairs of my fancy-ass new house to let them in.

Oskar smiles at me when I open the door. "Hey, fuckface. Miss me yet?"

"Like a hole in the head." I step aside. "Come on in."

"I dunno," Oskar muses. "The hole in Lane's head comes in very useful."

I pretend to groan at his comment. Not gonna lie though, I will miss being on the same team as Oskar. Even though he only recently found out about my sexuality, being on the same team as another queer player was comforting. As far as I'm aware, I'm the only queer dude with Seattle. Definitely the only out one.

The guys file in, Oskar, Ezra, Ezra's boyfriend and teammate Anton, Tripp and his husband Dex from the Vegas team, and trailing behind them are Ayri Quinn and Asher Dalton from Buffalo—the two other newest recruits to the Collective alongside me. Ayri's been playing for a few seasons already, but Asher's a rookie this upcoming season.

I nod at them. "Asher. Ayri."

Asher wears a stoic scowl, and I can't tell if it's just his face or if he's mad at something.

"Call me Quinn," Ayri says.

Asher adds, "He hates being called Ayri because his name rhymes with fairy."

"And thanks for bringing that up," Quinn says.

"I'm an orphan. You should revel in your childhood trauma like meeeee."

Okay, I really don't know how to take Asher.

"Uh, come on in."

They've been here two seconds, and the other guys have all made themselves at home. Ezra and Anton are on the couch play fighting ... or what might be considered foreplay for them, I'm not sure. Dex and Oskar are on the lower balcony, checking the place out, and Tripp is opening all my kitchen cupboards, looking for something.

"What are you after?" I ask.

"Blender. We bought stuff for margaritas."

"I don't have a blender yet."

"You don't own a blender?"

"When you get a divorce, everything has to be divided."

"She got the *blender*? Dude, how do you expect to make all those shakes the team dieticians always put us on?"

"I was going to buy a new one. Preseason doesn't start for two more weeks."

"Okay, we need to go shopping," Tripp says. "What else don't you have? Plates? Cutlery? Anything?"

"Uhhh ... Yeah, I need all of that too. Rebecca basically got everything. It was easier that way."

Tripp moves to the living room, where the others are. "Everyone back into the rental cars. We have to go shopping."

The room fills with complaints. All except one voice.

Ezra stands. "Yes. This is perfect." He turns to me. "We need to find the nearest thrift store."

"Uh, I can afford new stuff."

"Not for that. After we get the things you need, we're going to pick out attire for the party we're throwing here."

I'm suspicious. "Why does that sound tame and wholesome coming from you?"

Ezra grins. "Because the catch is you'll be blindfolded when you pick your clothes."

"And there it is."

They might be over-the-top, and I'm dreading what we're all going to look like by the end of the night, but hey, this is better than wallowing over my lack of dating life.

—

"I'll go first," Ezra says. "Anton, blindfold me."

"Things Ezra says during sex," Tripp mutters.

Ezra flips him the bird.

I lean in closer to Oskar. "Not that I'm complaining too much, but why the visit?"

"Seeing as you blew us all off for the group vacay at the start of the break to date all those beautiful women, we thought we'd come rescue you from that hell."

I snort. "It really is terrible dating models."

He doesn't need to know it's true. They were all lovely women, but it was all so fake.

"Quinn's single." He nods toward where he and Asher are standing off to the side, murmuring to each other like we are.

"I'll pass. Hockey players are way too much work."

"Truth," Oskar says. "But I'm warning you now, Ez is going to try to push you two together. Quinn brought Asher as a buffer so he wouldn't be forced upon you."

I laugh. "Thanks for the warning."

I glance at Quinn's profile, his messy hair with golden highlights, his flawless skin that makes him look like he's younger than he is, and I have to admit he is an attractive man ... if, you know, it wasn't for the god-awful mustache he's growing for whatever reason. Maybe he hates being pretty.

Either way, I'm not lying to Oskar when I say hockey players aren't my type. We're selfish, we're never home, and our schedules are so messed up we'd never see each other during the season unless our teams were playing against one another.

I'm shutting that down early. Too complicated.

I want something easy but sizzling.

I've done comfortable. I want ... *zing*. And the thought of Quinn doesn't give me zing.

Ezra, now blindfolded, gets spun three times and then led to a rack of clothing. Women's clothing. Fucking great. I'm not opposed to bending gender norms or people expressing themselves through the art of fashion. But when it comes to me, I like my jeans and T-shirts. They don't even need to be designer. I hate wearing suits, and the only reason I do it is because the NHL makes me.

Actually, the NHL makes me do a lot of things I'd rather not do, but at least the sacrifices on my diet and my body don't have to be done while wearing a suit. Or a dress.

"We're all going to end up wearing dresses, aren't we?" I ask Oskar.

"Now, it's up to me when I say stop," Ezra says.

Anton guides him up and down the rows of clothing until he eventually says, "Stop."

When he pulls out the garment, it's a one-piece romper with reaaaaally short shorts.

None of us want to do this—okay, Dex, the big puppy dog, does, and he jumps in to go next—but the rest of us are over it before we even pick our outfits. Even so, we're good sports about it because it is only a bit of fun, and it's not like we're going anywhere but back to my house to wear it. That, and by the time we're forced to wear whatever, we'll hopefully be drunk off our tits.

Dex, either cheating and trying to go for a tux in the formal wear section or actually wanting to wear that much tulle, stops on a wedding dress.

How fitting for him.

Ezra cheats when it's Anton's turn because he keeps walking the poor guy around the same clothing rack six times until Anton picks one of the many bikinis in the line.

Asher, led by Quinn because he said he'd rather take a bath in acid than let Ezra touch him—apparently, they have history—manages to score a giant trench coat. Sure, it's a ladies' one, but I would kill to land on something not so embarrassing like that. But then Ez throws in a fedora for free to "match the look," and I realize this isn't a game of chance. It's a game of making fools of ourselves.

Ah, hockey players. We're so evolved.

Quinn lands on an old-school tux, pale blue with ruffled sleeves, and a shirt. Oskar gets a leopard-print skintight dress, and Tripp gets a plain black skirt. Ezra says he'll allow Tripp to keep the shirt he has on with it. Which is a team T-shirt.

That only leaves me left. I rub my chin. "Seeing as Quinn was the only one lucky enough to get a suit, what are the chances of me getting something masculine?"

"Just for that," Ezra says, "zero. Kilts are masculine and technically skirts. Clothing is clothing. None of it should be feminine or masculine."

"See, I would totally agree with you. Actually, I do agree with that statement. Wear what the fuck you want. But don't for one second think I believe you're doing this for the nonbinary agenda. You're doing it to make us uncomfortable."

Ezra puts his hand on his heart. "You think so little of me?"

Everyone else answers "Yes" for me.

I step forward. "Okay, let me have it, then. If I can't laugh at myself, I can't exactly laugh at anyone else, can I? Hit me with your best shot."

And they do. After Ezra leads me in what feels like one huge circle, bumping me into nearly everything, I finally get over it when I stub my toe on God knows what. "Ouch, motherfucker, stop."

"Also what Ezra says during sex," Dex calls out. Way too loudly. In the middle of the store.

"Ooh, good news for me," I say. "Surely, they'll kick us out."

"Nope. All good." Ezra removes my blindfold.

Of course I land on ... *that*. It's one of those 1920s dresses with tassels and layers and sparkly beads.

"It's a slapper dress," Dex says excitedly.

We all glance around at each other, trying to silently decide who's gonna tell him.

"It's flapper," Tripp says. "Good try though."

"Nah, slapper sounds right," Asher says. "Because you get to slap the person wearing it."

I turn to Quinn. "Is he always so violent?"

"He's a teddy bear underneath it all," Ezra says. "I saw it. Once. Of course, the next morning, he turned into an actual bear. Grizzly kind, not the sexy kind."

"What is our second rule?" Asher asks Ezra.

"Uh, don't mention that night ever again?"

"So why you doing it?"

I glance at Anton on reflex to see if he's as disturbed as the rest of us by this conversation, but he's just smirking at his boyfriend in a dangerous way.

"Because I like to remind you of back in the day when we both made poor choices," Ezra says. "Now we're all mature and smart and—"

"Making half of us wear dresses ... or a bikini," I add.

"That's not immature. That's fun," Ezra says.

"Sure. Fun. I can't wait to see what else you think is ... fun."

"Patience, oh horny one. Let's go!" As we move to the front of the store to pay, Ezra finds a headpiece with a giant feather on it. "Ooh, perfect!"

Tripp nudges me. "Don't worry. With all your new kitchen tools, I'm going to make lethal margaritas."

"That'll help." But I can see it now. Tonight is going to be messy.